STEP INTO THE WORLD OF DINOSAURS IN NINE GREAT SCIENCE FICTION STORIES

In "Day of the Hunters," Isaac Asimov asks the question: why did the dinosaurs die out? And with an unusual twist, he explores what might have happened to those powerful rulers of the earth. Were they the cause of their own demise . . . and will man be any different?

In "Our Lady of the Sauropods" by Robert Silverberg, a malicious plot leaves a female scientist stranded on a world inhabited solely by dinosaurs—a world from which there's no escape. And there she makes a discovery that will change the course of history.

In Poul Anderson's "Wildcat," an oil prospecting colony has been established—one hundred million years in the past. Thrown into an alien environment threatened by dinosaur attacks, the colony discovers that their purpose is greater than just the search for oil.

These are just a taste of three of the utterly fantastic and unusual stories that make up this collection. So step into the world of dinosaurs and read . . .

THE SCIENCE FICTIONAL DINOSAUR

EDITED BY ROBERT SILVERBERG,
CHARLES G. WAUGH, AND MARTIN HARRY GREENBERG

AN AVON 🔥 FLARE BOOK

AVON BOOKS
A division of
The Hearst Corporation
959 Eighth Avenue
New York, New York 10019

Copyright © 1982 by Robert Silverberg, Martin Harry Greenberg and Charles G. Waugh
Published by arrangement with the authors
Library of Congress Catalog Card Number 81-66467
ISBN: 0-380-77974-9

Library of Congress Cataloging in Publication Data
Main entry under title:

The Science fictional dinosaur.
    (An Avon/Flare book)
    Contents: Wings of a bat / by Pauline Ashwell—The ever-branching tree / by Harry Harrison—When time was new / by Robert F. Young—[etc.]
    1. Science fiction. 2. Dinosaurs—Juvenile fiction. 3. Children's stories. [1. Science fiction. 2. Dinosaurs—Fiction. 3. Short stories] I. Silverberg, Robert. II. Greenberg, Martin Harry. III. Waugh, Charles.
PZ5.S416.   [Fic]   81-66467
ISBN 0-380-77974-9   AACR2

First Flare Printing, February, 1982

FLARE trademark application is pending before the U. S. Patent and Trademark Office.

Printed in the U. S. A.

WFH 10 9 8 7 6 5 4 3 2 1

Dedicated to Jenny-Lynn Waugh

ACKNOWLEDGMENTS

We would like to acknowledge Edward and Peggy Wood and Frank D. McSherry, Jr., for their assistance in locating stories.

"The Wings of a Bat" by Paul Ash. Copyright © 1966 by Condé Nast Publications, Inc. Every effort has been made to contact the author, who is urged to contact Avon Books so that payment now in escrow can be received.

"The Ever-Branching Tree" by Harry Harrison. Copyright © 1970 by Avon Books. Reprinted by permission of the author.

"When Time Was New" by Robert F. Young. Copyright © 1964 by Galaxy Publishing Corporation. Reprinted by permission of the author.

"Poor Little Warrior!" by Brian W. Aldiss. Copyright © 1958 by Fantasy House, Inc. From *The Magazine of Fantasy and Science Fiction*. Reprinted by permission of the author.

"Day of the Hunters" by Isaac Asimov. Copyright © 1950 by Columbia Publications, Inc. Reprinted by permission of the author.

"Hermes to the Ages" by Frederick D. Gottfried. Copyright © 1980 by Condé Nast Publications, Inc.

"A Statue for Father" by Isaac Asimov. Copyright © 1958 by Renown Publications, Inc. Reprinted by permission of the author.

"Wildcat" by Poul Anderson. Copyright © 1958 by Fantasy House, Inc. From *The Magazine of Fantasy and Science Fiction*. Reprinted by permission of the author and the

CONTENTS

INTRODUCTION

Once upon a time the storytellers loved to tingle the imaginations of their listeners with gaudy tales of dragons and monsters. Homer enlivened *The Odyssey* with such creatures as Scylla and Charybdis, the unknown Mesopotamian author of the Gilgamesh mythos had a keen eye for the bizarre creature or two, and doubtless around the Cro-Magnon campfires the same sort of contemplation of the horrendous was popular nighttime fare.

Times change, and although the dragons of fantasy have not lost their appeal, the skill of the paleontologist has given us a tribe of authentic dragons with which we can titillate our fancies. The first dinosaur bones were excavated in medieval times and were thought to be relics of ancient dragons drowned by Noah's flood. But in the nineteenth century, that great epoch of fossil-hunting, it became clear that the huge remains were vestiges of giant reptilian creatures that once had dominated the earth, unimaginable millions of years ago. Ingeniously reassembled, placed on display in every great city of the western world, these vast and astonishing beings quickly came to exert a powerful effect over the imagination, so that every small child grew familiar with them and could rattle off their names—*Brontosaurus*, (now called *Apatosaurus*), *Tyrannosaurus*, *Stegosaurus*, *Triceratops*, and so on.

It was inevitable that modern-day myth-makers would seize on the dinosaurs as central images for stories of science fiction. From the late nineteenth century on, paleontological fantasy became an important segment of science fiction, exemplified by such early works as Sir Arthur Conan Doyle's *The Lost World* (1912), Jules Verne's *A Journey to the Center of the Earth* (1864), and John Jacob Astor's *A Journey in Other Worlds* (1894). Such motion pictures as *King Kong* and *One Million B.C.* helped make the dinosaurs part of popular mythology in the 1930s. And, of course, the rise of science fiction as widely distributed reading matter in our own day has greatly multiplied the use of dinosaurs and other prehistoric creatures in imaginative literature.

The early writers were content merely to describe the terrifying beasts and turn them loose to wreak havoc; contemporary writers prefer, instead, to explore the nature of the dinosaurs in the light of genuine scientific knowledge and to attempt to understand something of the world in which they lived. The ongoing advances in dinosaur research—for example, the recent theory that unlike other reptiles they may have been warm-blooded creatures—have played important parts in the work of the modern science-fiction writers.

One of the great mysteries about the dinosaurs involves their sudden disappearance. Speculations as to the reasons for their extinction play an important part in several of these stories. What could have destroyed such powerful beasts in such a short period of time? Could it have been (1) a rapid ice age advance that lowered the temperature over the Earth, killing them; (2) the development of small animals which ate the eggs of the dinosaurs; and (3) great volcanic activity spewing huge amounts of ash into the atmosphere, suffocating the creatures? Currently, the most plausible theory is that a large asteroid smashed into the north Atlantic ocean, pierced the Earth's crust, and formed Iceland as well as producing a covering of dust in the atmosphere that dramatically reduced sunlight and temperatures thus causing the death of much vegetation, which in turn caused the death of the dinosaurs.

We have collected here a group of science-fiction stories about dinosaurs that will, we hope, fulfill two main goals. The first is to convey through the medium of fiction such knowledge of the giant reptiles as science has by now uncovered; the other is to provide, much as the author of *The Odyssey* did, that peculiarly delightful thrill that comes from the contemplation of the strange, the marvelous, the utterly fantastic.

THE WINGS OF A BAT

Paul Ash

Set sometime during the Cretaceous Era, this story by Paul Ash suggests that mining may be an important reason for exploring the past. It also provides excellent speculation about the behaviors of pterosaurs (or flying reptiles), based upon current animal research. The intelligence Fiona demonstrates may seem surprising to those who know that many dinosaurs, such as the Stegosaurus, with a walnut-sized brain, were not very smart, but present beliefs are that Pteranodons possessed an "intelligence" far above that associated with any living reptile. Since the publication of "The Wings of a Bat," however, scientists have discovered the remains of a pterosaur (Quetzalcoatlus) with a fifty-foot wing span, which would make it twice as big as the Pteranodon. And the present belief about Pteranodons is that they were probably warm-blooded and protected by a thick coat of white fur which also served to reduce heat absorption while flying.

I do *not* like pterodactyls. No doubt they have their good points; the evening flight over Lake Possible lends a picturesque touch to the Cretaceous sunset, and breast of young *Pteranodon*, suitably marinated, makes a passable roast. But as a result of personal and unfortunate experience I have taken a dislike to them, and nobody can claim they haven't heard me mention the fact—nobody, that is, at Indication One. And this means the whole—human—population of the world at the present date.

I am employed by the Mining and Processing Branch of Cretaceous Minerals, Inc. as a doctor—my contract says so. Of course, with a total planetary population of twenty-eight,

13

there is not a great amount of doctoring to be done. I understand that the original staff list of Indication One did not call for a doctor; the Board intended to have all members of the team take a hypnocourse in nursing so that, if necessary, they could take care of each other. Yaro Land, the mining boss, knocked that idea on the head. He said he wasn't going to have his staff tinkering with each other, and that if anyone got injured or sick in the absence of proper medical attention, he would Displace them right back to 2071.

The Board amended its calculations and advertised for: Doctor, qualified; no dependents; willing to travel; Midget Preferred.

Time Displacement is expensive even now—or perhaps I should say, even *then*—even, that is, in the year when I was recruited, fifty-three years after I was born and somewhere between 100 and 110 million years after the date at which I am writing this.

When Dr. Winton Boatrace first displaced a milligram of matter it went back twenty-four hours, and the experiment cost him 272 Credits for power alone. C.M. Inc.'s engineers can do better than that, but even so, the power to displace the average staff member costs about Cr.500,000, give or take Cr.100,000—or thereabouts. It's not the date that counts— Displacement is a threshold effect and it takes no more *power* to get to the Middle Cretaceous than to the middle of last week—it's the weight. I suppose someone in Personnel did read my diploma and references, but their most important checking was done with a pair of scales. I weighed forty-one kilograms, and got the job. Except for Henry, I'm the smallest man here.

Yaro Land is the biggest—five-foot-seven, and stocky. I imagine the Board couldn't get first-class knowledge of sea-mining, combined with all-round engineering experience, plus administrative ability—and the sheer guts to make the first displacement of all, not knowing whether he might find himself in the ocean or right in front of a Tyrannosaur—in a smaller package.

As a matter of fact, the details of my qualifications weren't that important. Diploma or no, there are not so many things I could do that anyone else on the team couldn't do almost as well. They've all been trained in the first-aid treatment of injuries, from a sprained pinkie to a fractured skull. The deep freeze contains a billion units of Unimycin, the latest, safest, most powerful antibiotic on the market, in self-injecting ampoules. And if anyone needs major back surgery or really elaborate nursing he'll *still* have to go back to 2071—or, to be quite accurate, 2071 plus however much time he spent at Indication One. But, if anyone gets moderately sick—the kind of condition that cures itself in a week or two, provided someone feeds the patient nourishing meals and keeps him from getting out of bed—I'm at hand.

No doubt any member of the team could do that, too. The weak point in the Board's original plan was that it provided no spare wheels at all—for nursing, or anything else. Even the most skilled specialist sometimes needs a third hand, or an eye on dials somewhere at the back of his head. So it's also in my contract that I lend a hand—or eye, or foot—as and when required. I don't mind, even though I'm seldom trusted with anything that could not be done just as well by one of these dexterous little egg-eating dinosaurs, if you caught it and trained it young. I still have a good deal of free time; among other things I edit and print our weekly newspaper— with a great deal of interference from the subscribers and contributors. Within reason, I'll do anything that's asked . . . bring in the tapes from the meteorology station, watch dials on the mineralometer, cook supper. But I will *not* act as veterinary surgeon to stray items of the Cretaceous fauna. It isn't reasonable, it isn't in my contract, and one must draw the line somewhere.

I hold surgery every morning; that is, I sit in my office, and anyone who feels like it drops in for a chat. Mostly they come to complain about the cuts in their last literary effort. If anyone has any symptoms they care to discuss I'm there to listen and help. That Unimycin has been burning a hole in the deep freeze for over a year.

When Henry came in I was polishing up my editorial for the next issue, and I took the opportunity to read him part of it. He seemed restless, but I paid no attention; he usually is. Too much thyroid, I suspect. Also, we have different ideas on literary style. It was Henry who got the name of the paper, *Weekly Bulletin of the Indication One Branch of Cretaceous Minerals, Inc.*—which at least had the merit of accuracy—

shortened to *The Chalk Age Gazette*. The switch, admittedly, was carried by the unanimous vote of the subscribers and contributors—the Editor abstaining—but it was Henry's idea.

Halfway through my third paragraph he interrupted.

"Doc, it's *suffering!* Please!"

"Henry," I said, "I am accustomed to criticism. Lack of appreciation I have grown to expect. But downright abuse, combined with atrocious grammar—"

He pointed a quivering finger at my blotter.

"But it's *sick!*"

I began to suspect that I had here the first case of delusional insanity in the Middle Cretaceous—which would, of course, be the earliest on record. I looked at the blotter. On it—put there by Henry, presumably, while I thought he was listening—was a lumpish something which seemed to be wrapped in large, withered leaves. I took it to be crude tobacco—the plant grows like a weed in this climate, but nobody has managed a satisfactory cure—and poked it experimentally with the tip of my pen.

Henry groaned—loudly. I looked up in astonishment, whereupon the pen jerked violently against my hand and was twitched away.

I looked down. The lump on my blotter had expanded to twice its previous size, revealing that the "leaves" were broad leathery wrinkled wings. A bloodshot little eye had opened in the middle. It had produced from somewhere a sharp, swordlike beak about seven inches long, and with this, and a set of bony fingers, like a spider's legs, it was trying to dismember the pen.

I said: "Get that creature out of here!"

"But, Doc," protested Henry, "she's *sick!* and she's only a baby!"

I valued that pen. Pouncing, I attempted to get it back. The "baby's" grip tightened; pen, pterosaur and blotter slid toward me as a unit. The head drew back, preparing for a thrust. I reversed direction hastily and shoved the whole outfit to the other side of the desk.

"Henry, I will *not* have pterodactyls in my office! Take it away!"

I maintain that my attitude was not unreasonable, nor even unkind. I knew no more about the treatment of sick pterodactyls than Henry did—if anything, less. And, as I said, I dislike them. I had a very nasty experience once with a pterodactyl, and, if Henry doesn't know that, he ought to; he's heard the story often enough.

It happened when I was out on Lake Possible, fishing in a glass-fiber dinghy—about six weeks after my Displacement—at the end of a beautiful day.

That lake! C.M. Inc.'s engineers claim that they understand Dr. Boatrace's Theorems of Temporal Displacement—if "understand" is the word, when you have to plod through three brand-new systems of calculus before you can even begin—but they don't pretend to know how he made his map of Indication One.

So far as I can see, getting a fix on a section of past time is like casting a line over weeks: you can be pretty sure the hook will catch *somewhere*, but how far away depends not only on the length of your line but also on the current, the distribution of weeds, and how hard and fast you reel in. Boatrace's "hook" was the gadget he called his Minimal Temporal Trace; I gather he was pretty sure he could Displace it to somewhere in the Middle or Upper Cretaceous, and so he did, but there's still a slight uncertainty about the exact date—a factor of ten million years or so.

Once the Trace was fixed he could Displace other items to the same point—like sliding a ring along your snagged line. I understand that—I think. What I don't see, and neither does anyone else, is how the Trace—a bit of metal and crystal no bigger than the top of my thumb—could send back and tell him what kind of place it had landed in.

Well, there it is. I'm told he used to Displace one, and shut himself up for several hours, then come out and Displace another. One day, he came out with a penciled map that looked as though Baby had got hold of the telephone pad, and told them he'd found what he wanted and they could dust off the big machine—the one built to Displace a man.

Yaro, who's not afraid to use a dirty word when there's no other that fits, told me once he reckoned the old man was using some form of Psi technique. Boatrace knew what he wanted—the ideal setup for sea-mining, a medium-sized island with strong deep-water currents close by—and he just went on casting until the "feel" of the line told him that this time he was into a fish instead of a snag.

Another thing I'll never understand is why Yaro was willing
to make that first Displacement, with only Boatrace's map as
evidence that he'd find solid ground at the Exit Point. It's just
a faint wavering oval, about twice as long as it is wide, with a
scribble underneath that reads—I'm told—"*First Indication
of Desires* . . ." Not even his daughter can decipher the final
word. There's just one feature marked: a clear, hard-edged
circle, near one end, about half the width of the oval. It looks
as though he put a semicredit on the paper and ran the pencil
around it. By some freak the label he wrote on is quite
legible, even to me: "*Aq.p . . .? Lake, possibly??*"

As a drawing of a natural feature, it's about as convincing
as a monocle on an amoeba. Well, I'm a respectable matter-
fearing materialist, but if Boatrace was really using
Psi . . . No. As a member in good standing of the WMA I
prefer to assume he was using something else, (The principle
of hyperdimensic transductility, perhaps, or a couple of
patent double million magnifying gas microscopes of extra
power.) But Lake Possible is a flooded caldera: seen from
above—from the island's central peak, for instance—it forms
an unbelievably perfect ring.

Seen from dinghy level, that afternoon, it looked like the
best fishing water I'd ever seen. Great clumsy twelve-inch
insects, something like dragonflies, were blundering into the
wavelets, and big fat red-lipped fishes—a kind of coelacanth
—were popping up to take them all around the boat. The only
trouble was that they didn't see the desirability of any lure in
my book.

I didn't really care; it was such a perfect day. The air was
warm, but crisp, not steamy; there was just enough wind to
dry the sweat on my face. However, our cook-housekeeper
wanted to try her hand at fish chowder and I'd promised to
bring in the raw materials. So an hour before sunset I decided
to try trolling from a moving boat. I fixed a couple of rods,
one with a minnow, one with a spoon, and hoisted the sail.

Close-hauled, the boat moved through the water at just the
proper speed. I sat back, with half an eye on the rods and
another half on the sail, leaving myself free to enjoy the
general peacefulness of the scene. Then, after about ten
minutes, I glanced over my shoulder, and the Devil was after
me.

Well, what would *you* have thought? Bat wings, twenty feet

across—rolling eyeballs, China white and black—a scarlet devil's grin and a horn on its head.

I let out a yell, and ducked. The sail flapped, once; I automatically tightened the sheet and the rough feel of it brought me back to my senses—or I thought it did. The actual effect was to make me assume I'd had a brief hallucination; I simply could not have seen what I thought I had.

I screwed up my courage to look back—and there it was, huge, hideous and three-dimensional as I remembered it. Like the boat, it was headed into the wind. There was a single row of bony struts along the front of each wing, and the great leathery membrane was ballooning like a spinnaker behind. It wasn't Old Nick, of course. However, I did not feel that much better when I realized that I was being followed by a *Pteranodon.*

I'd seen them often enough at a distance, planing slowly around the circle of the cliffs; or out at sea, skimming along with those incredible beaks half-opened, just above the surface of the waves. That had not prepared me for the sheer *monstrosity* of the creature riding the wind behind me, twenty feet away. It looked big enough to carry me off and feed me to its young.

The beak was foreshortened, of course, since I was seeing it head-on; it was also half agape, so that I saw the bright-red lining of the mouth. The "horn" was that great sloping bony crest that continues the line of the beak back over the shoulders, which was foreshortened, too, when I first caught sight of it.

I couldn't cram on more sail—I had only a little balanced lug—but I could get the wind behind me by heading in to the nearer shore. However, if I did that straightaway I would wind up at the base of a two-hundred-foot cliff. I would have to hold on for a quarter of a mile, then run for Landing Gap.

May I never have such a sail again. I tried to keep my mind on flag, sheet and tiller, but I couldn't refrain, any more than Lot's wife could, from looking back. Once when I glanced over my shoulder I found that frightful thing wagging its head at me—left, right, left, right—showing off the two-foot length of beak and the bright blue streaks on the side of the crest.

When I headed in to the Gap I hoped the wind would bother it, blowing directly from behind it, but it wheeled along with the boat and just flattened out a little, holding station without so much as a flap. Aerodynamically, those things aren't primitive; they're the culmination of seventy million years of evolution. The air is their home. I was in such a lather that I didn't think at all about shedding way from the boat. I left the sail full until I heard the keel grate on the shingle. I had just enough sense, then, to let the sheet go, but it was too late. The mast was just a little pole of green wood—there had been no time to season it; even Yaro had been less than a year at Indication One—and it snapped clean in two. Down came the sail on top of me as I sprawled on the bottom of the boat, and by the time I mustered up enough spunk to crawl out from under, the *Pteranodon* had gone.

That's why I don't like pterodactyls—pterosaurs—*Pteranodons*—in the Cretaceous all three words come to the same thing. If the little fluttering *Pterodactylus* were still around, or even the hen-sized *Rhamphorhynchus*, I might be able to regard them as fellow-creatures, but they both died out at the end of the Jurassic. The creature Henry had dumped on my desk was another *Pteranodon*. It was a very young one, admittedly, about the size of a pigeon apart from those shrouding wings, and with only a faint ridge to mark the incipient crest. Nevertheless its beak was quite large enough to do damage.

"Doc, she's *sick*," Henry told me in accents of maudlin reproach. "I found her on the roof this morning . . . she must have lost her mammy during the night. Did you, Fiona?" He spread his hands in a protective gesture over the leathery bundle, removing them just in time to avoid a fast jab.

Pteranodons are viviparous, bearing one young at a time. After birth the infant clings head-down to the lower part of the mother's belly, held in place partly by her feet, partly by its own and by the four unmodified "fingers" projecting from the second joint of the wing. I had no idea how big they were when they first ventured on independent flight.

I looked up at Henry in an incredulous double-take.

"*What* did you call her?" Hastily I recollected myself. "Never mind. Get her *out* of here."

Henry is not quite twenty, and it has never seriously occurred to him that anybody might disagree with him, fundamentally, over anything that really *mattered* . . . such as the right-to-life—and hence to medical assistance—of a sick infant reptile of repulsive appearance and dubious disposition. He thought I was simply acting crusty and middle-aged for the fun of being a "character," and hadn't time to humor me.

"I think the trouble is exhaustion," he said earnestly. "It's been blowing half a gale for three days, so probably her mother couldn't get fish for her. Are you hungry, Fiona?"

"Henry!" Yaro loomed in the doorway, monumentally disapproving. "We wait for you!"

"BettertryheronfishDoctthere'ssomeinthiscanI'llbebackas soonaspossiblebegoodnowFiona," said Henry on his way to the door, and was gone.

I had drawn the line at acting as vet, but Henry's assumption that all good men come to the aid of the party was a powerful eraser. Besides, it's very difficult deliberately to let an animal starve. I couldn't even make believe that I was too busy. Yaro's team were busy assembling and testing a cadmium extraction unit, which is not a job for unskilled labor, and the other specialists were immersed in their various routines. Even Elsa was doing the week's baking—not quite like Mother's, but you'd never think the base was carbohydrate extracted from pulped water-weed—and the kitchen was out of bounds until she finished.

Fiona had found my "IN" tray and was squatting in it, tented in her wings. The pen lay on the desk, slobbered but undamaged. I rolled it cautiously towards me with a ruler and she opened her mouth—the lining was shell-pink, not the adult scarlet—and hissed faintly, but seemed to lack energy for anything else. I got out a pair of heavy gauntlets, made from the belly-leather of a sea-crocodile, and a pair of long bone forceps and opened Henry's can. It contained pieces of steamed fish left from dinner the night before.

How do you persuade a pterodactyl to open its jaws? I hesitated to use force—the bones looked fragile. I tried tapping the tip of her beak with a morsel of fish, held in the forceps. She retreated promptly to the farthest confines of the "IN" tray and pulled her wings over her head. I spread several choice fragments on a small dish and put them in front of her. Fiona inspected them with a red-rimmed eye, then, deciding they were harmless, paid no further heed to them.

I tried hissing, while waving the forceps under her beak; I even picked up bits of fish in my gloved fingers and thrust them upon her. No good. She hid inside her capacious wings and this time showed no sign of coming out. I removed some bits of fish from my chair and sat down to think things out.

Fish-eating birds, I seemed to remember, did not simply drop bits of fish for their offspring to pick up; they stuck food right down their throat. Which meant that the beak had to be open. Vague recollections of high-school biology indicated that the opening of the beak was often a reflex response to the sight of the mother—or father—bearing supplies. No, not even that. A dummy with just a few parental features would often set off the response.

Wildly I thought about draping myself in a tarpaulin to suggest wings. But in all probability the essential feature was the beak, from which, after all, the food would come. I considered ways and means of constructing one before I remembered that there were a couple of *Pteranodon* heads, dried and mounted, on the common-room wall. We did not hunt for amusement, but we had tested the edibility and other useful characteristics of every species on the island, and somebody with baronial instincts had imposed this form of decoration. Elsa was always wanting to get rid of the trophies, but so far as I remembered they were still in place.

They were. I unhooked the larger one and brought it back to the office. It had been varnished, and kept its color quite well; even the eye, thanks to the bony ring in the sclerotic, was still quite lifelike. I got a bit of fish ready, worked my hand into the skull, and hissed to attract attention.

Fiona drew back the edge of her wing and peered at me suspiciously from one half-open eye. Then her wings shut down as abruptly as an umbrella, and she was shuffling towards the head, beak gaping and neck outstretched. I pushed the bit of fish to the back of her throat.

Fiona closed her beak thoughtfully, and I whipped the head out of sight. The underside of her baggy throat heaved once, twice, and I thought she was swallowing. Then she stretched forward, shook her head up and down a few times, and opened her beak. The bit of fish fell out.

I rushed off to the kitchen and begged a raw fish from Elsa. This time I thought I'd got it; for about ten minutes Fiona gaped obediently at the dried head and then I thrust the fish into her beak. I saw it go down, until there was a distinct bulge under her sternum and she was weighed down in front.

Apparently she would have gone on feeding forever, but I called a halt at that point, not knowing how to cope with indigestion in a pterodactyl. I left her, as I thought, digesting. About an hour later I heard a faint rhythmic gasping, and looking up from the proofs I was correcting. I saw Fiona, beak downwards, regurgitating the lot.

The fragments were unchanged; no sign of digestion. Perhaps parent *Pteranodons* pre-digested food for their young. By this time my blood was up; I didn't intend to let this infuriating creature die if I could help it. I've had less prepossessing patients in my time. I had no pepsin in stock, but Elsa had brought some pawpaw seeds with her, and while the resulting trees had not yet borne ripe fruit there were plenty of leaves. I knew these could be used as tenderizers; they might do the trick. I sneaked into the kitchen garden and removed a few, wrapped the remainder of the fish in them, and left them for an hour in the sun.

Henry came in as I was shoveling the messy, part-digested result into Fiona's beak, and was, I am glad to say, impressed. He removed Fiona, the "IN" tray, the forceps, and what was left of the fish, and I cleaned up the office and myself and went to lunch.

I felt distinctly pleased with myself, which was tempting Fate, of course, and I should have known better. The staff abounded in amateur naturalists, many of them with strongly developed maternal—or paternal—instincts. I had a pretty picture of myself advising and directing them in the care and feeding of the young *Pteranodon*. What I had forgotten, of course, was that, however pleased they might be to baby-sit with Fiona, their professional schedules would make it impossible for them to do so during working hours.

There was great competition to take care of her once work was over; but *Pteranodon*, like most reptiles, is a strictly diurnal creature. Half an hour after sunset, which in those latitudes occurred every day at 18:15 hours, Fiona was asleep. At least I didn't have to get up and feed her at dawn. Half the camp took turns at keeping her overnight, until nearly every cabin had acquired a faint lingering stink of predigested fish. Henry, with one person chosen by rota for the privilege, looked after her during the luncheon break. But from 8:00 till 12:30, 14:00 till 17:30 hours, she was mine, all mine.

You may wonder why, feeling as I did, I allowed myself to get stuck with the brute. The explanation, though complicated, can be given in one word: Morale. It's a tricky thing in any community. When twenty-nine people make up the total population of the world and will for the next nine years, it's the most important thing of all. It was outrageous of Henry to foist his beastly protégée on me, but then Henry, as I have mentioned, was quite incapable of seeing the matter in that light. A Henry who knew and accepted the fact that some men just don't care to act as foster-fathers to the strayed young of other classes of vertebrates would be someone quite different from the Henry I knew. And sudden personality changes are upsetting in a small community. Or, to put it another way, we all had to depend on each other for things far outside the services we had contracted to supply, and anything that upset that dependence—reasonable or not—was dangerous and bad. Or, to put it in the simplest way possible, I simply hadn't the moral courage to refuse.

Fiona ate voraciously and grew at an inordinate rate—she must have put on about two ounces a day. At the end of two weeks she weighed four pounds, with a wing-span of more than eight feet, and I began to think, hopefully, that any day now she would start flying and be able to fend for herself. My hopes took a severe setback when someone pointed out that, for all we knew to the contrary, she had no inborn instincts in that direction and would have to be *taught* to fly. Several people tried it; they took her out into the clearing around the cabins, perched her on rocks, trees, or roofs, withdrew to a distance, waved pieces of fish, and called her to come. Fiona, after gaping hopefully for some minutes—she had now learned to open her beak at the sight of a human being— usually turned her back on them and signified disapproval in a vulgar but unmistakable manner. To some extent I sympathized. After all, none of her would-be-instructors was able to fly.

Quite by accident, this time, I solved the problem myself. A small outdoor shelter had been constructed for Fiona alongside my office. Three weeks after her arrival I had given her the second feed of the day and returned to the office to read some manuscripts. It was becoming increasingly difficult to get people to write anything except Nature notes, a development which had started with Fiona's arrival. I had just unearthed a perfunctory review on the latest batch of books—C.M. Inc. sent us a dozen, on micro-microfilm, once a month—when I heard an irritable hiss, and there was Fiona shuffling through the door.

She made straight for the desk, gave an inefficient-looking hop and caught the raised edge at the back with the fingers of one wing. With a prodigious effort she got a grip with the other "hand," and there she hung, feet scuffling at the smooth surface, waving her beak angrily at me over the top until I came out of my stupefaction and got to my feet. This seemed to stimulate her. She brought up one hind foot, took a grip on the raised edge, and heaved up and forward. A moment's confused and indescribable activity and she landed with a flop on my pile of manuscripts.

Half of them shot off the desk, but she caught the top one in her foot and began methodically ripping it to pieces. I seized a towel which was hanging over the back of my chair—I needed a shower every time I fed her—and flapped it angrily.

"Go away, Fiona! Shoo—!"

Fiona unfolded her wings and flapped vigorously back, sending the remainder of the papers flying.

Idiotically, I flapped again. Fiona drew herself up, raised her wings as high as she could, ran at me over the blotter—and took off.

I, of course, knew that she *ought* to be able to fly, but I doubt whether she had ever suspected the fact. Anyway, there was no room to do it in the office. She sailed straight into the wall and was knocked out.

For the rest of the morning she was punch-drunk, but I had discovered how to teach her to fly. She simply needed a stimulus: the sight of something that flapped. In Nature, no doubt, it would have been a parent's wings, unfolding and limbering up, but the towel was a sufficient substitute. In a couple of days Fiona was flying from the top of the computer building right across the clearing—a distance of a hundred yards. In a week she had discovered how to use a thermal and would spiral effortlessly in the updraft over the sun-warmed rooms—and come down only to be fed.

That was the snag. Fiona had no idea of fishing for her own food. Taken to the lake, she would fly there for a while, but

every time she got hungry she wheeled and planed unerringly
for home. We tried throwing fish to her, to teach her to feed
on the wing. If it fell on the ground, she landed and picked it
up. If it fell in the water she squawked angrily, landed, and
opened her beak to show us where it ought to have gone.

"The trouble is," Henry informed me accusingly, "Fiona
doesn't know she's a *Pteranodon*. She probably thinks she's a
human being," He reflected. "Or perhaps sne thinks *Pteranodons* look like you."

It seemed improbable to me, but various works on animal
behavior seemed to agree with him. A bird—and pterodactyls
are more similar to birds than to any other Tertiary group—
reared in captivity tends to direct many of its instinctive
activities towards people, rather than its own species. Konrad
Lorenz was fed on caterpillars by a pet raven; and there are
numerous sad cases of geese and peacocks and other large
birds which fell in love with their keepers and tried to lure
them onto the nest. Henry and I were almost equally
disquieted by what we read; Henry on behalf of Fiona's
psyche and future sex life, I because I was beginning to doubt
whether I would ever be free again.

In the end, by simply throwing her fish into a small
pool—dead at first, later on alive—I taught Fiona to take
food from water. It was not at all the same thing as fishing on
the wing, but it was the best I could do. Then Henry and I
took her out on Lake Possible one evening, in the dinghy, and
marooned her on a rock.

We rigged the sail to cover the boat, and, when she was not
looking, crawled underneath it and hid. Presently we heard
indignant hissings and the gulping squawk that indicated she
wanted to be fed. Then there was a scrabbling on the side of
the boat, and a weight descended on the canvas covering my
back.

I kept as still as I could while Fiona shuffled around on my
shoulderblades and finally came to rest on the back of my
head. I wanted nothing to distract her at the critical moment,
which must—I thought, resolutely stifling discomfort as sharp
claws probed the crevice between my ear and my skull—come
soon. Ten minutes later we heard a series of rustling flaps: the
Pteranodons on their homeward flight dipping down to
inspect Fiona, and rising again as they made for the caves and
ledges of the cliffs. I began to think that we were on a fruitless

errand; then I felt Fiona's grip tighten on my occipital bones
and heard her wings flap, once. Then nothing for a moment;
until there was one last swooping rush above me—a belated
member of the flock—and my face was pushed down onto the
thwart as Fiona took off.

We waited until full dark, not to risk distracting her, then
rowed to shore and plodded home. Henry seemed rather
dispirited and I felt that a show of pleasure would be out of
place. As we parted on the way to our respective cabins he
looked back over his shoulder.

"Cheer up, Doc," he said. "At least we know that *she*
knows the way home."

I gave him a cold look—wasted, of course, in the darkness
—and went off to shower and change. I slept badly that
night—waking three or four times from a doze, in the belief
that I had heard the click of claws on the fiber-glass roof. In
the morning I opened the door cautiously, half expecting
twenty pounds of young *Pteranodon* to come plummeting
down with an urgent squawk, demanding to be fed. But no.
Fiona's favorite roosts and perches were still clearly marked,
both to the eye and the olfactory sense, but they were all
vacant. Fiona, it appeared, had left us for good.

The details of the mining operations are not, for the most
part, relevant to this story, and some of them—for instance,
the reason why it's economically practical to carry out the
process in the Cretaceous, although sea-mining in the
Twenty-first Century pays no Displacement costs—form part
of a very big industrial secret. So I'll just say that the
extraction units consist of gently tapering tunnels about fifty
feet long, constructed of hoops and slats, and lined with
plastic-coated cloth. They're not heavy—in fact, they are
amazingly fragile for the work they have to do—but they're
unwieldy. When a whole battery of tunnels is complete, they
are lashed side by side into rafts, towed out to sea, stacked
one raft on top of another, and sunk in water deep enough to
put them safely below the turbulence zone. The units float at
first, but after an hour's soaking they lose buoyancy. That's
the moment when you maneuver the next raft over the top
and get them bolted together; then the next, and so on. The
timing's tricky, and the whole operation calls for a flat
calm—twelve hours of it.

The first battery—thirty-five units—was ready for assembly just about two years after I arrived at Indication One. Yaro was closer to jitters than I'd ever have thought he could be. Those units represented two years of hard work for all concerned—even me. The assembly and sinking *had* to go right. This was the test. Of course, since all the basic manufactures—aluminum, fiber glass, cloth, plastic—had been set up, it would only take three months to produce the next battery. If anything went wrong with this one, morale would take a terrible beating and the whole project would be set back far more than three months. Besides, he needed to make tests, check that the thing really did work as it should—it would take most of a year to be certain of that.

We waited out three days of light winds and loppetty little waves—some people wanted to take a chance on them, but Yaro was taking no risks with this first batch of babies—and then on the fourth morning I woke to a flat, oppressive stillness and thought: *This is it.*

Everyone else thought so, too; breakfast arrived half an hour early and found everyone present, except for half a dozen who'd grabbed themselves sandwiches and gone to start the units on their way to the beach. At least, I hadn't noticed that anyone else was missing, until Yaro wanted to ask Linda McDonough a question and then found that she wasn't there.

Linda is our astronomer; she also took a six-month cram course in meteorology before being Displaced. If you wonder why a mining company needs an astronomer—enough to pay Cr.500,000 just for her fare—I have to say that that's part of the industrial secret aforesaid. The reasons why we need a meteorologist are obvious; we needed her particularly that morning and she was missing.

One of the girls went to her cabin, and came back in a hurry for me. I went—in fact, I ran; not that Linda sounded dangerously sick, but it was the first call for my professional services in over a month.

I found Linda half-dressed and very cross with herself for oversleeping; she was also feverish, puffy, and covered with an irritating rash.

She admitted having been slightly off-color for several days. It was plainly an allergy of some sort. I was planning scratch tests, and had just realized the interesting possibilities—she hadn't been affected by any of the common allergens in the Twenty-first Century, such as eggs, or shellfish, or pollen, but proteins, as well as physical structure, can undergo a lot of evolution in a hundred million years—when Linda gave me details. For the last few days, since she'd done all the calculations she could on the data available and further observation had been impossible owing to overcast, she'd been helping to apply plastic to the filter-cloths for the extraction units. She began to feel seedy the following day.

That left nothing to investigate, except which of the plastics caused the trouble. There are several in use here, all with molecules so complex they're halfway to being alive; the whole extraction process depends on their peculiar properties. I had to admit, though, that the question was of purely academic interest. Standard anti-allergen treatment would clear up the trouble and she'd have to stay away from the filters, whichever plastic she was allergic to. Linda said that she wasn't going to be scratched to bits simply in the name of medical science—a deplorable attitude and an extreme overstatement—and we were still arguing when Yaro arrived, wanting to know whether the calm would last out the day, or not.

Linda tottered over to her desk and found the latest computer-digest of the meteorology data. Her eyes were watering and she obviously found it hard to concentrate. After several minutes she announced that there had been a slight, steady drop in the barometer readings for two days, which probably meant a blow coming up; it might be today or it might be tomorrow but without last night's data tapes she couldn't be sure.

I thought Yaro was about to explode. It was very unlike him—or very unlike anything I knew of him so far—but the situation was clearly getting on nerves he had never realized he possessed.

"I'll go and get the new tapes," promised Linda feverishly, reaching for her clothes. "I'll be able to tell you in an hour or so."

"You're not going anywhere," I told her. "*I'll* fetch the tapes. I've done it before."

"But if I go I can get a direct reading on the barometer and call Yaro on the radio and—"

"Young lady," I said, "that meteorology diploma has gone to your head. I was reading barometers before you were born."

"*Why* I permitted that station to be set up on a hill top two miles away . . ." came in a threatening background rumble. I knew that the site had been chosen, with his approval, for several excellent reasons, and that Linda had suggested asking for a few duplicate instruments to be kept in the settlement—but that, on grounds of Displacement costs, Yaro had turned her down.

Plodding up the way to the Peak, with the two-way radio strapped to my back, I found myself thinking: *The calm before the storm.* In our weather-controlled society the cliché has lost all contact with its real meaning. I simply didn't know whether it applied to this situation, or not. There had been quite a number of gales in the two years I had spent at Indication One; I seemed to remember that there *had* been an interval of calm before most of them, but how long it lasted, and whether calm was *always* followed by a storm, I simply could not decide. There seemed, now, an ominous heaviness in the air. I was not sure that I had noticed it before Linda had mentioned the drop in barometric pressure.

Yaro's dilemma was plain. If he called off the assembly of the battery today and there was no storm—or if it held off for twelve hours—he would have wasted the best opportunity he was likely to have for at least a week, and probably more. It would give his reputation a heavy knock, which was important; faith in Yaro's judgment was a very vital factor in general morale. In some ways it might be worse than losing part of the battery in an unexpected storm that could be written off as bad luck. Holding things up unnecessarily might be considered old-maidish.

I came out on the first ridge, high enough to see over the rise on the other side of the settlement, and caught a glimpse of the sea. It was so smooth it didn't even sparkle, though that might have been partly due to the haze of overcast. There were no distinct clouds; I found I didn't care for the look of the sky.

A long train of light, big-wheeled carts was assembling at the edge of the settlements. There were caves—pumice—in the hillside, and we used them for storage and for working on rainy days—mostly we worked out of doors. At the moment those precious extractor units could be wheeled back under cover in ten minutes or less, but once they'd been taken down to the beach it would need an hour. If they'd been unloaded from the carriers—

I dropped that line of thought and pressed on. The path led through a strand of cycads in a sheltered dip, then out onto bare rock, where it was marked only by cairns. One of the things one misses in this era is grass, also heather, gorse, bracken—cover-plants in general. I had been walking rapidly for twenty minutes, most of it uphill, and was sweating freely, but I was pleased to note that my respiration was steady and undistressed. Two years ago I'd have been panting after half as much exercise.

The Met station was on top of a bluff; the shortest way up to it involved leaving the path and climbing twenty feet of rock-face. It was easy enough in daylight, broken into convenient ledges. I knew that Linda used the path only after sunset or when her hands were full.

I had just got up onto the first ledge and was reaching for a handhold when two things happened simultaneously. The radio receiver gave a loud click, indicating that someone had turned on a transmitter, and a huge triangular shadow slid suddenly down the rocks and away over my head.

For a moment I simply froze; then I got a grip on a knob of rock and turned my head very carefully to look behind me.

Yaro's voice said sharply, "Doctor, have you read the barometer?"

His voice seemed to come from my shoulderblades, which was one minor element in my confusion—I kept wanting to get around and see where it was coming from. However, my attention had already been split three ways. Part for his question—by no means the biggest part. Another—even smaller—for an unexpected glimpse of the sea, with a dull steely shine to it now and a dark purple line on the horizon that had not been there before. But the largest—paralyzingly large—fragment was taken up with the full-grown *Pteranodon* that was just wheeling to pass over me again.

"Doctor, answer, please. What is the pressure?"

I said, "I can't—" Then, at the top of my voice, *"Go away!"*

The *Pteranodon* was circling in a tighter curve than I would have believed possible for those twenty-foot wings. It was going to brush right over my scalp if it didn't hit me in the face. I flattened against the rocks. There was a thump above me and the brief rattle of a pebble dislodged. I squeezed a glance past the rock-face an inch from my eyeballs, and saw the *Pteranodon* sitting on the ledge above me, huddled in its wings.

"Doctor, what is wrong? Did you fall just then? Are you hurt?"

I managed a rather croaky *"No."* Then, coming to my senses with a rush: "I haven't got to the Met station yet. I just started the final climb, but there's a *Pteranodon* in the way!"

"A what?"

"It's sitting on a ledge above me. Maybe it's got a nest here or something. I'll go around by the path; I'll be there in ten minutes. Don't worry, I'll get that reading." An idea which had been nagging away at the back of my brain suddenly surged to the front. "Yaro! Don't let the carriers move any farther! There's a storm coming up over the sea—I *saw* it!"

Yaro said sharply, "I am looking at the sea. I see nothing."

"I'm higher up than you; I can see farther. Over the horizon, a dark line. I think it's getting closer. Put those units under cover. If it comes up fast you won't—"

"Calm yourself; they have not started the journey. This storm, how sure are you that it approaches us?"

That was a nasty one. The situation did not exactly make for accurate judgment, even if I'd had any experience on which to base one. That dark line might not be a storm at all. It was not as though I spent much of my time gazing out to sea; for all I knew the horizon might have a thick purple border every second day.

I didn't want to be responsible for holding up the job, possibly for nothing. The answer, of course, was to get those barometric records as quickly as I could. I looked up at the *Pteranodon* and yelled, *"Shoo!"*

By way of answer the creature unfolded its wings halfway and leaned forward over the ledge, and I stepped backwards into the air and dropped four feet onto a rock.

It was a flat rock, and by some miracle I didn't tumble backwards and break the radio; I managed a flop forwards and landed on all fours. I scrambled away crab-fashion, got to my feet, and ran. Fifty yards around the base of the bluff would bring me to a relatively gentle slope, and another hundred yards up that was the Met station. The first stretch was flat, in the sense that it wasn't rising, but it was far from smooth. I was panting hard, now, and my legs were only half under control, but I had almost reached the beginning of the slope when there was a *swoosh!* A vast canopy of wings slid over me, dipped into a curtain, and then suddenly shut down into a shape no bigger than a two-year-old.

It had a beak, though. I stopped, and backed away. I was vaguely conscious of Yaro shouting to somebody—not me—he was calling someone to take over the radio. I sidled slowly along a wall of rock, keeping an eye on the enemy, remembering that presently I would come to a sort of niche or alcove about six feet wide. If I wasn't careful I could get backed into it and trapped—

"Hey! Doc!" It was Henry, sounding excited. "What's wrong? Yaro said you were having trouble with a *Pteranodon.* Is it Fiona?"

As though stimulated by the sound of his voice, the creature half unfolded itself, then shut down tight and waddled a few steps after me.

"*Now* look what you've done," I muttered crossly. "Don't *shout.*"

Henry obediently lowered his voice, "What's happening? What's she doing? *Is* it Fiona, Doc?"

With difficulty I kept my voice down to an infuriated whisper. "How would I know?"

It was nine months since I'd last seen Fiona. It was almost as long since I'd even thought of her. This creature was about twice as large as she'd been when I'd loosed her. Would Fiona be full grown now? I hadn't the slightest idea. Nor did I find it even faintly reassuring that this creature *might* be my former acquaintance. Even when we were closest she had no inhibitions about taking a peck at me.

The *Pteranodon*—Fiona or not—repeated its performance, opening, shutting, and coming a few steps closer. I backed, and found the rock curving away into the alcove. I hastily abandoned my hold on it and took two steps rapidly backward, intending to get past the gap and have my back to solid stone once more.

With an angry-sounding squawk, the *Pteranodon* jumped. I did a complicated and ungainly dance-step that took me backward and sideways—into the alcove. Then my foot slipped and I landed with a bone-shaking thump on hard dampish mud.

The reptile took a little run at me, folding its wings the while. I flopped wildly away from it on elbows and bottom until I hit my head on a rock. I was at the back of the alcove. Being unable to retreat farther, I sat up—there was just room to do so without braining myself on the overhang—and shrank into the smallest possible space: knees up, head down, arms folded over it to protect my eyes. There was a rustle and a hiss like a gas-leak, but no savage thrust. Instead, after a minute or so, I felt a sharp but not unfriendly nudge; I became conscious of a strong dry musky odor; and peeking cautiously under my folded arms I found the *Pteranodon* sitting quietly beside me.

Henry was uttering questions and exhortations in a steady whispered string.

"Shut up!" I breathed back. "No, I'm not hurt. I'm in a sort of shallow cave. The brute's right here alongside—if I try to escape it'll probably attack."

"Doc, listen, this is important. It *must* be Fiona. It's like we said, she thinks she's human, or maybe she thinks you're a *Pteranodon*. What was she doing before? How did she get you into the cave?"

"For God's sake!" I whispered fiercely. "Forget your blasted Nature Notes! I can't get to the Met station. Tell Yaro I'm dead *certain* there's a storm coming and I'll take the responsibility if I'm wrong. . . . No, don't say that, just tell him I'm *sure*."

I felt my voice weaken on the last word. I still wasn't sure—and there was no way for me to take the responsibility for the decision. The team would still blame Yaro for trusting me if I turned out to be wrong.

Henry was still whispering. "Doc, did she keep opening and shutting her wings? Shutting them *right* down, as though she wanted to take up as little space as possible? And did she chase you into the cave? Did she—"

"Yes!" I screamed—so far as one can scream in a whisper. "Yes, she did! And now that you've proved how much you know about *Pteranodons*, will you get your alleged mind off your hobby and onto your job? Will you tell Yaro—"

"Doc, it's all *right*. Yaro decided five minutes ago to put

everything under cover; it's being done right now. The cabins
were battened down before he called you, just in case. You
don't have to worry. We can see the storm from here, now;
the sky's changing. There's a sort of dark edge sliding up it.
It'll be overhead in two minutes. But listen, that opening and
shutting the wings—that's the Wind Dance. I mean that's
what the old *Pteranodons* do to warn the young ones there's a
blow coming and to get under cover. George and I saw them
at it three or four times, and there was *always* a high wind
afterward. Maybe they see it coming from high up, like you
did. Fiona was trying to warn you, that's all."

I was just preparing a comment when I heard the storm
break.

It hit the settlement thirty seconds before reaching the
Peak, so that I heard the rising howl twice over—once on the
radio, once, incomparably louder, right overhead. Fiona also
heard the transmitted sound of it and huddled even tighter
into her wings. I saw the nictitating membrane slide over her
eyeball—and then the wind came.

It whipped past the cave mouth with a noise like torn silk,
carrying a mass of leaves and twigs ripped from the cycads
a quarter of a mile away. It must have torn the trees bare
in its first rush. One moment the air outside seemed solid
with flying greenery, the next it had gone past, still in
one mass—except for a small part that eddied into the
cave and whirled around us before it was snatched out
again.

The cave was about six feet deep; it kept us out of the path
of the storm, but the stray tendrils that reached in the mouth
of it were enough to pluck violently at my hair and clothes—
and Fiona's wings. I saw her quiver at the first tug of it, and
put an arm across in front of her. Henry was yelling something about adaptive behavior, the one really dangerous
enemy of *Pteranodons* being a really strong wind. I heard the
words *ritual behavior* and *adaptation* emerging above the
transmitted noise—Henry was indoors, of course. They were
vaguely familiar to me from the reams of notes which he and
several others, apparently mistaking the *Gazette* for *The
Journal of Animal Behavior* and undeterred by previous
rejections, were always sending in. Then, incredibly, the
noise began to increase, to a level where not even Henry

could compete. Battered by sheer volume of sound even more than the the searching fingers of the wind, I crouched dazedly at the back of the cave. I was vaguely aware of pressure as Fiona shoved in behind me—having done her bit by getting me under cover, she was now capitalizing on it. Then I ceased, really, to be aware of anything outside the small tight-packed huddle of my own body.

After the wind, rain. How long either of them lasted I had no idea. Suddenly the howling died, and a moment later the floor of the cave was swamped; its mouth was curtained with a waterfall, and my already deafened ears were assaulted by the drumming of water on naked rock. That didn't stop all at once; the rain eased off slowly, so that I was barely conscious that the noise decreased.

Then something moved beside me. Fiona pushed out from behind my back and waddled, squelching, to the cave mouth. She sat there for a minute or two, folding and unfolding her wings in an irritable manner. Then she waddled outside. Six feet away was a boulder; she scrambled up onto it, stretched to her full height, and began limbering up—shaking, flapping, jumping up and down.

I watched, without really taking it in. I hadn't moved; I didn't think I *could* move; I was stiff, soaked, and too numb to be really aware of it. Then I noticed Yaro. He was talking to me, from a little way off—quietly, insistently. I realized suddenly that he'd been talking for quite a while, but I hadn't paid attention to him.

I said, "Sorry, Yaro. What did you say?"

That at least was the idea. It was kind of creaky and not, I gather, very audible, but it was speech of sorts.

There was a wild shout: "He answered!" It didn't sound like Yaro at all. I mean, it was his voice, all right; but completely out of character: positively excited.

I said, "Sorry; must have dropped off."

"Dropped off!" He sounded rather wild and positively hilarious. I began to feel something must be *really* out of key. "Caught out of doors in a hurricane, he drops off! Doc, you found some shelter? You are not hurt?"

Now that he mentioned it, I wasn't sure. I tried to unfold myself and investigate, but my hands were locked around my knees and I seemed to have lost the combination; also, I had stiffened in one piece. I couldn't figure out how to get undone. Then I realized that the view had altered outside. Something was missing.

"She's gone," I said. "Fiona. She's gone."

I managed to start moving after a while. I didn't get very far, though. They came to fetch me as fast as they could— nearly every man in the team. There were all sorts of new gulleys in the way; a couple of temporary rivers several feet deep; tree trunks and boulders scattered in all directions. I could have walked, though; there was no need to carry me. But they did, taking turns until I came out of my daze sufficiently to rebel. I got back to the settlement walking on my own feet.

The damage was surprisingly small. Linda says we caught just the fringe of a hurricane, or maybe a typhoon—the Met station was blown right off the bluff, so she didn't get the records to see how it developed. The units, and all the more important machinery, had been moved into the caves and the entrance blocked. Only one cabin blew away. They're domes of fiber glass, securely anchored six feet down—nothing for the wind to catch hold of, providing the windows and doors were properly closed. It was three weeks before the extraction units could be assembled, but when the weather finally quieted it was done without a single hitch.

There's been a lot of nonsense about the whole affair. Maybe Fiona saved my life; I don't know. I imagine one glance at the barometer would have been enough for me; I'd have run for shelter, and I might have reached it—there are lots of caves. But it's certainly nonsense to say that her warning saved the whole of Indication One. Yaro had given the orders to batten down before he knew anything about the Wind Dance; in fact, I heard Henry and George explaining it to him next day, with pantomime—very odd they looked. And, if she'd only let me get to the Met station, the figures would have warned him a lot more convincingly than anything else could.

But there it is—nearly everyone is firmly convinced that Henry's stray baby grew up to save the settlement, and, of course, me. It creates a sort of moral climate which is irresistible. I no longer dare to turn down contributions on natural history, and the name of the paper has been changed to *The Chalk Age Gazette and Pterodactyl-Watchers' Guide*.

THE EVER-BRANCHING TREE

Harry Harrison

The upper Cretaceous Period of the Mesozoic Era was the golden age of dinosaurs. It was the prime of many species: Scolosaurus (spiked-tailed ankylosaurs), Pteranodons, Tyrannosaurus, and Triceratops—while some members of the sauropods or "brontosaurs," such as the Alamosaurus and Hypselosaurus, still survived. So it seems fitting that Harry Harrison has his teacher make a stop there as part of a student field trip designed to investigate the evolution of life.

In stating that all dinosaurs were cold-blooded, however, the teacher appears to err, for recent evidence suggests that Pteranodons, Struthiomimi (ostrichlike dinosaurs), and several other genera may have been warm-blooded.*

The children had spread up and down the beach, and some of them had even ventured into the surf where the tall green waves crashed down upon them. Glaring from a deep blue sky, the sun burned on the yellow sand. A wave broke into foam, surging far up the shore with a soundless rush. The sharp clap-clap of Teacher's hands could easily be heard in the sunlit silence.

"Playtime is over—put your clothes back on, Grosbit-9, all of them—and the class is about to begin."

They straggled toward Teacher as slowly as they could. The bathers emerged dry from the ocean, while not a grain of sand adhered to skin or garment of the others. They gathered

---

*For a good discussion of this, see Adrian J. Desmond, *The Hot-Blooded Dinosaurs: A Revolution in Palaeontology* (New York: The Dial Press, 1976).

about Teacher, their chatter gradually dying away, and he pointed dramatically at a tiny creature writhing across the sand.

"Uhggh, a worm!" Mandi-2 said and shivered deliciously, shaking her red curls.

"A worm, correct. A first worm, an early worm, a proto-worm. An important worm. Although it is not on the direct evolutionary track that we are studying we must pause to give it notice. A little more attention, Ched-3, your eyes are closing. For here, for the first time, we see segmentation, as important a step in the development of life as was the development of multicellular forms. See, look carefully, at those series of rings about the creature's body. It looks as though it were made of little rings of tissue fused together—and it is."

They bent close, a circle of lowered heads above the brown worm that writhed a track across the sand. It moved slowly toward Grosbit-9 who raised his foot and stamped down hard on the creature. The other students tittered. The worm crawled out through the side of his shoe and kept on.

"Grosbit-9, you have the wrong attitude," Teacher said sternly. "Much energy is being expended to send this class back through time, to view the wonders of evolution at work. We cannot feel or touch or hear or change the past, but we can move through it and see it about us. So we stand in awe of the power that permits us to do this, to visit our Earth as it was millions of years ago, to view the ocean from which all life sprung, to see one of the first life forms on the ever-branching tree of evolution. And what is your response to this awe-inspiring experience? You *stamp* on the annelid! For shame, Grosbit-9, for shame."

Far from feeling shameful, Grosbit-9 chewed a hangnail on his thumb and looked about out of the corners of his eyes, the trace of a smirk upon his lips. Teacher wondered, not for the first time, how a 9 had gotten into this class. A father with important contacts, no doubt, high placed friends.

"Perhaps I had better recap for those of you who are paying less than full attention." He stared hard at Grosbit-9 as he said this, with no apparent effect. "Evolution is how we reached the high estate we now inhabit. Evolution is the forward march of life, from the one-celled creatures to multi-celled, thinking man. What will come after us we do not know, what came before us we are now seeing. Yesterday we watched the lightning strike the primordial chemical soup of the seas and saw the more complex chemicals being made that developed into the first life forms. We saw this single-celled life triumph over time and eternity by first developing the ability to divide into two cells, then to develop into composite, many-celled life forms. What do you remember about yesterday?"

"The melted lava poured into the ocean!"

"The land rose from the sea!"

"The lightning hit the water!"

"The squirmy things were so ugghhy!"

Teacher nodded and smiled and ignored the last comment. He had no idea why Mandi-2 was registered in this science course and had a strong feeling she would not stay long.

"Very good. So now we reach the annelids, like our worm here. Segmented, with each segment almost living a life of its own. Here are the first blood vessels to carry food to all the tissues most efficiently. Here is the first hemoglobin to carry oxygen to all the cells. Here is the first heart, a little pump to force the blood through those tubes. But one thing is missing yet. Do you know what it is?"

Their faces were empty of answers, their eyes wide with expectation.

"Think about it. What would have happened if Grosbit-9 had really stepped on this worm?"

"It would have squashed," Agon-1 answered with eight-year-old practicality. Mandi-2 shivered.

"Correct. It would have been killed. It is soft, without a shell or a skeleton. Which brings us to the next branch on the evolutionary tree."

Teacher pressed the activating button on the control unit at his waist, and the programmed computer seized them and hurled them through time to their next appointment. There was a swift, all-encompassing grayness, with no feeling of motion at all, which vanished suddenly to be replaced by a green dimness. Twenty feet above their heads the sun sparkled on the surface of the ocean while all about them silent fish moved in swift patterns. A great monster, all plates and shining teeth hurtled at and through them and Mandi-2 gave a little squeal of surprise.

"Your attention down here, if you please. The fish will

come later. First we must study these, the first echinoderms. Phill-4, will you point out an echinoderm and tell us what the term means."

"Echinoderm," the boy said, keying his memory. The training techniques that all the children learned in their first years of schooling brought the words to his lips. Like the others he had a perfect memory. "Is Greek for spiny skin. That must be one there, the big hairy starfish."

"Correct. An important evolutionary step. Before this, animals were either unprotected, like our annelid worm, or had skeletons outside like snails or lobsters or insects. This is very limiting and inefficient. But an internal skeleton can give flexible support and is light in weight. An important evolutionary step has been made. We are almost there, children, almost there! This simple internal skeleton evolved into a more practical notochord, a single bone the length of the body protecting a main nerve fiber. And the Chordata, the creatures with this notochord, were only a single evolutionary step away from this—all *this!*"

Teacher threw his arms wide just as the sea about them burst into darting life. A school of silvery, yard-long fishes flashed around and through the students, while sharp-toothed shark-like predators struck through their midst. Teacher's speech had been nicely timed to end at this precise and dramatic moment. Some of the smaller children shied away from the flurry of life and death while Grosbit-9 swung his fist at one of the giants as it glided by.

"We have arrived," Teacher said, vibrantly, carried away by his own enthusiasm. "The Chordata give way to the Vertebrata, life as we know it. A strong, flexible internal skeleton that shields the soft inner organs and supports at the same time. Soft cartilage in these sharks—the same sort of tissue that stiffens your ears—changes to hard bone in these fishes. Mankind, so to speak, is just around the corner! What is it, Ched-3?" He was aware of a tugging on his toga.

"I have to go to the . . ."

"Well press the return button on your belt and don't be too long about it."

Ched-3 pressed the button and vanished, whisked back to their classroom with its superior functional plumbing. Teacher smacked his lips annoyedly while the teeming life whirled and dived about them. Children could be difficult at times.

"How did these animals know to get a notochord and bones?" Agon-1 asked. "How did they know the right way to go to end up with the Vertebrata—and us?"

Teacher almost patted him on the head, but smiled instead.

"A good question, a very good question. Someone has been listening and thinking. The answer is they didn't know, it wasn't planned. The ever-branching tree of evolution has no goals. Its changes are random, mutations caused by alterations in the germ plasm caused by natural radiation. The successful changes live, the unsuccessful ones die. The notochord creatures could move about easier, were more successful than the other creatures. They lived to evolve further. Which brings us to a new word I want you to remember. The word is 'ecology' and we are talking about ecological niches. Ecology is the whole world, everything in it, how all the plants and animals live together and how they relate one to the other. An ecological niche is where a creature lives in this world, the special place where it can thrive and survive and reproduce. All creatures that find an ecological niche that they can survive in are successful."

"The survival of the fittest?" Agon-1 asked.

"You have been reading some of the old books. That is what evolution was once called, but it was called wrong. *All* living organisms are fit, because they are alive. One can be no more fit than the other. Can we say that we, mankind, are more fit than an oyster?"

"Yes," Phill-4 said, with absolute surety, his attention on Ched-3 who had just returned, apparently emerging from the side of one of the sharks.

"Really? Come over here, Ched-3, and try to pay attention. We live and the oysters live. But what would happen if the world were to suddenly be covered by shallow water?"

"How could that happen?"

"The how is not important," Teacher snapped, then took a deep breath. "Let us just say it happened. What would happen to all the people?"

"They would all drown!" Mandi-2 said, unhappily.

"Correct. Our ecological niche would be gone. The oysters would thrive and cover the world. If we survive we are all equally fit in the eyes of nature. Now let us see how our animals with skeletons are faring in a new niche. Dry land."

A press, a motionless movement, and they were on a muddy shore by a brackish swamp. Teacher pointed to the trace of a feathery fin cutting through the floating algae.

"The subclass Crossopterygii, which means fringed fins. Sturdy little fish who have managed to survive in this stagnant water by adopting their swim bladders to breathe air directly and to get their oxygen in this manner. Many fish have these bladders that enable them to hover at any given depth, but now they have been adapted to a different use. Watch!"

The water became shallower until the fish's back was above the water, then its bulging eyes. Staring about, round and wide, as though terrified by his new environment. The sturdy fins, reinforced by bone, thrashed at the mud, driving it forward, further and further from its home, the sea. Then it was out of the water, struggling across the drying mud. A dragonfly hovered low, landed—and was engulfed by the fish's open mouth.

"The land is being conquered," Teacher said, pointing to the humped back of the fish now vanishing among the reeds. "First by plants, then insects—and now the animals. In a few million years, still over 225 million years before our own time, we have this . . ."

Through time again, rushing away on the cue word, to another swampy scene, a feathery marsh of ferns as big as trees and a hot sun burning through low-lying clouds.

And life. Roaring, thrashing, eating, killing life. The time researchers must have searched diligently for this place, this instant in the history of the world. No words were needed to describe or explain.

The age of reptiles. Small ones scampered by quickly to avoid the carnage falling on them. *Scolosaurus*, armored and knobbed like a tiny tank, pushed through the reeds, his spiked tail dragging a rut in the mud. Great *Brontosaurus* stood high against the sky, his tiny, foolish head, with its teacup of brains, waving at the end of his lengthy neck, turned back to see what was bothering him as some message crept through his indifferent nervous system. His back humped up, a mountain of gristle and bone and flesh and hooked to it was the demon form of *Tyrannosaurus*. His tiny forepaws scratched feebly against the other's leathery skin while his yards-long razor-toothed jaws tore at the heaving wall of flesh. *Brontosaurus*, still not sure what was happening, dredged up a quarter ton of mud and water and plants and chewed it, wondering, while high above, heaving and flapping its leathery wings, *Pteranodon* wheeled by, long jaws agape.

"That one's hurting the other one," Mandi-2 said. "Can't you make them stop?"

"We are only observers, child. What you see happened so very long ago and is unalterable in any way."

"Kill!" Grosbit-9 muttered, his attention captured for the very first time. They all watched, mouths dropping open at the silent fury.

"These are reptiles, the first successful animals to conquer the land. Before them were the Amphibia, like our modern frogs, tied unbreakably to the water where their eggs are laid and the young grow up. But the reptiles lay eggs that can hatch on land. The link with the sea has been cut. Land has been conquered at last. They lack but a single characteristic that will permit them to survive in all the parts of the globe. You have all been preparing for this trip. Can anyone tell me what is still missing?"

The answer was only silence. *Brontosaurus* fell and large pieces of flesh were torn from his body. *Pteranodon* flapped away. A rain squall blotted out the sun.

"I am talking about temperature. These reptiles get a good deal of their body heat from the sun. They must live in a warm environment because as their surroundings get cooler their bodies get cooler . . ."

"Warm-blooded!" Agon-1 said with shrill excitement.

"Correct. Someone, at least, has been doing the required studying. I see you sticking your tongue out, Ched-3. How would you like it if you couldn't draw it back and it stayed that way? Controlled body temperature, the last major branch on the ever-branching tree. The first class of what might be called centrally heated animals is the Mammalia. The mammals. If we all go a little bit deeper into this forest you will see what I mean. Don't straggle, keep up there. In this clearing, everyone. On this side. Watch those shrubs there. Any moment now . . ."

Expectantly they waited. The leaves stirred, and they leaned forward. A piglike snout pushed out, sniffing the air, and two suspicious, slightly crossed eyes looked about the clearing. Satisfied that there was no danger for the moment, the creature came into sight.

"Coot! Is that ever ugly," Phill-4 said.

"Beauty is in the eye of the beholder, young man. I'll ask you to hold your tongue. This is a perfect example of the subclass Prototheria, the first beasts, *Tritylodon* itself. For many years a source of controversy as to whether it was mammal or reptile. The smooth skin and shiny plates of a reptile—but notice the tufts of hair between the plates. Reptiles do not have hair. And it lays eggs, as reptiles do. But it, she, this fine creature here also suckles her young as do the mammals. Look with awe at this bridge between the old class of reptiles and emerging class of mammals."

"Oh, how *cute!*" Mandi-2 squealed as four tiny pink duplicates of the mother staggered out of the shrubbery after her. *Tritylodon* dropped heavily onto her side and the young began to nurse.

"That is another thing that the mammals brought into the world," Teacher said as the students looked on with rapt fascination. "Mother love. Reptile offspring, either born live or when they emerge from the egg, are left to fend for themselves. But warm-blooded mammals must be warmed, protected, fed while they develop. They need mothering and, as you see, they receive it in sufficiency."

Some sound must have troubled the *Tritylodon* because she looked around, then sprang to her feet and trundled off into the underbrush, her young falling and stumbling after her. No sooner was the clearing empty than the hulking form of *Triceratops* pushed by, the great horns and bony frill held high. Thirty feet of lumbering flesh, its tail tip twitching as it dragged behind.

"The great lizards are still here, but doomed soon to final destruction. The mammals will survive and multiply and cover the earth. We will later discuss the many paths traveled by the mammals, but today we are going to leap ahead millions of years to the order Primates which may look familiar to you."

A taller, deeper, more tangled jungle replaced the one they had been visiting, a fruit filled, flower filled, life filled maze. Multicolored birds shot by, insects hung in clouds, and brown forms moved along the branches.

"Monkeys," Grosbit-9 said and looked around for something to throw at them.

"Primates. A relatively primitive group that took to these trees some fifty million years in our past. See how they are adapting to the arboreal life? They must see clearly in front of them and gauge distances correctly, so their eyes are now on the front of their heads, and they have developed binocular vision. To hold securely to the branches their nails have shortened and become flat, their thumbs opposed to strengthen their grip. These primates will continue to develop until the wonderful, important day when they descend from the trees and venture from the shelter of the all-protecting forest.

"Africa," Teacher said as the time machine once more moved them across the centuries. "It could be today, so little have things changed in the relatively short time since these higher primates ventured forth."

"I don't see anything," Ched-3 said, looking about at the sun scorched grass of the veldt, at the verdant jungle pressing up next to it.

"Patience. The scene begins. Watch the herd of deer that is coming towards us. The landscape has changed, become drier, the seas of grass are pushing back the jungle. There is still food to be had in the jungle, fruit and nuts there for the taking, but the competition is becoming somewhat fierce. Many different primates now fill that ecological niche and it is running over. Is there a niche vacant? Certainly not out here on the veldt? Here are the fleet-footed grass eaters; look how they run; their survival depends upon their speed. For they have their enemies, the carnivores, the meat-eaters who live on their flesh."

Dust rose, and the deer bounded towards them, through them, around them. Wide eyes, hammering hooves, sun glinting from their horns, and then they were gone. And the lions followed. They had a buck, cut off from the rest of the herd by the lionesses, surrounded, clawed at and wounded. Then a talon-tipped paw hamstrung the beast and it fell, quickly dead as its throat was chewed out and the hot red blood sank into the dust. The pride of lions ate. The children watched, struck silent, and Mandi-2 sniffled and rubbed at her nose.

"The lions eat a bit, but they are already gorged from

another kill. The sun is reaching the zenith and they are hot, sleepy. They will find shade and go to sleep, and the corpse will remain for the scavengers to dispose of, the carrion-eaters."

Even as Teacher spoke the first vulture was dropping down out of the sky, folding its dusty wings and waddling towards the kill. Two more descended, tearing at the flesh and squabbling and screaming soundlessly at one another.

Then from the jungle's edge there emerged first one, then two more apes. They blinked in the sunlight, looking around fearfully, then ran towards the newly killed deer, using their knuckles on the ground to help them as they ran. The blood-drenched vultures looked at them apprehensively, then flapped into the air as one of the apes hurled a stone at them. Then it was the apes' turn. They too tore at the flesh.

"Look and admire, children. The tailless ape emerges from the forest. These are your remote ancestors."

"Not mine!"

"They're *awful*."

"I think I am going to be sick."

"Children—stop, think! With your minds not your viscera just for once. These ape-men or man-apes have occupied a new cultural niche. They are already adapting to it. They are almost hairless so that they can sweat and not overheat when other animals must seek shelter. They are tool using. They hurl rocks to chase away the vultures. And, see, that one there—he has a sharp bit of splintered rock that he is using to cut off the meat. They stand erect on their legs to free their hands for the tasks of feeding and survival. Man is emerging, and you are privileged to behold his first tremulous steps away from the jungle. Fix this scene in your memory; it is a glorious one. And you will remember it better, Mandi-2, if you watch with your eyes open."

The older classes were usually much more enthusiastic. Only Agon-1 seemed to be watching with any degree of interest. Other than Grosbit-9 who was watching with too much interest indeed. Well, they said one good student in a class made it worthwhile, made one feel as though something were being accomplished.

"That is the end of today's lesson, but I'll tell you something about tomorrow's class." Africa vanished and some cold and rainswept northern land appeared. High mountains loomed through the mist in the background, and a thin trickle of smoke rose from a low sod house half buried in the ground. "We will see how man emerged from his primate background, grew sure and grew strong. How these early people moved from the family group to the simple Neolithic community. How they used tools and bent nature to their will. We are going to find out who lives in that house and what he does there. It is a lesson that I know you are all looking forward to."

There seemed very little actual evidence to back this assumption, and Teacher stabbed the button, and the class was over. Their familiar classroom appeared around them, and the dismissal bell was jingling its sweet music. Shouting loudly, without a backward look, they ran from the room, and Teacher, suddenly tired, unclipped the controls from his waist and locked them into his desk. It had been a very long day. He turned out the lights and left.

At the street entrance he was just behind a young matron, most attractive and pink in miniaturized mini, hair a flaming red. Mandi-2's mother, he realized, he should have known by the hair, as she reached down to take an even tinier, pinker hand. They went out before him.

"And what did you learn in school today, darling," the mother asked. And, although he did not approve of eavesdropping, Teacher could not help but hear the question. Yes, what did you learn? It would be nice to know.

Mandi-2 skipped down the steps, bouncing with happiness to be free again.

"Oh, nothing much," she said, and they vanished around the corner.

"Without knowing he did it, Teacher sighed a great weary sigh and turned in the other direction and went home.

WHEN TIME WAS NEW

Robert F. Young

When a fossilized body is found, Howard Carpenter is ordered to take his triceratank back to the upper Cretaceous Period to investigate. He runs into Pteranodon, *a type of "brontosaur" (probably* Alamosaurus *or* Hypselosaurus), Anatosaurus *(a duck-billed dinosaur),* Struthiomimus, Archaeopteryx *(a feathered, bird dinosaur), ornithopods (bird-footed dinosaurs),* Tyrannosaurus, *and two children who claim to be kidnap victims from Mars. After a series of adventures, the body is identified, the children are saved, and as is commonly the case in the works of Robert F. Young, the story ultimately turns out to have been a romance.*

I

The young *Alamosaurus* standing beneath the ginkgo tree didn't surprise Carpenter, but the two kids sitting in the branches did. He had expected to meet up with this variety of brontosaur sooner or later, but he hadn't expected to meet up with a boy and a girl. What in the name of all that was Mesozoic were they doing in the upper Cretaceous Period!

Maybe, he reflected, leaning forward in the driver's seat of his battery-powered triceratank, they were tied in in some way with the anachronistic fossil he had come back to the Age of Dinosaurs to investigate. Certainly the fact that Miss Sands, his chief assistant who had cased the place-time on the timescope, had said nothing about a couple of kids, meant nothing. Timescopes registered only the general lay of the

51

land. They seldom showed anything smaller than a medium-sized mountain.

The bronto nudged the trunk of the ginkgo with a hip as high as a hill. The tree gave such a convulsive shudder that the two children nearly fell off the branch they were sitting on and came tumbling down upon the huge monster's back. Their faces were as white as the line of cliffs that showed distantly beyond the scatterings of dogwoods and magnolias and live oaks, and the stands of willows and laurels and fan palms that patterned the prehistoric plain.

Carpenter braced himself in the driver's seat. "Come on, Sam," he said, addressing the triceratank by nickname, "let's go get it!"

Since leaving the entry area several hours ago, he had been moving along in low gear in order not to miss any potential clues that might point the way to the anachronistic fossil's place of origin—a locale which, as was usually the case with unidentifiable anachronisms, the paleontological society that employed him had been able to pinpoint much more accurately in time than in space. Now, he threw Sam into second and focused the three horn-howitzers jutting from the reptivehicle's facial regions on the sacral ganglion of the offending sauropod. *Plugg! Plugg! Plugg!* went the three stun-charges as they struck home, and down went the *a posteriori* section of the bronto. The anterior section apprised by the pea-sized brain that something had gone haywire, twisted far enough around for one of the little eyes in the snake-like head to take in the approaching triceratank, whereupon the stubby forelegs immediately began the herculean task of dragging the ten-ton, humpbacked body out of the theater of operations.

Carpenter grinned. "Take it easy, old mountainsides," he said. "You'll be on all four feet again in less time than it takes to say *'Tyrannosaurus rex.'*"

After bringing Sam to a halt a dozen yards from the base of the ginkgo, he looked up at the two terrified children through the one-way transparency of the reptivehicle's skull-nacelle. If anything, their faces were even whiter than they had been before. Small wonder. Sam looked more like a triceratops than most real triceratops did. Raising the nacelle, Carpenter recoiled a little from the sudden contrast between the humid heat of the midsummer's day and Sam's air-conditioned interior. He stood up in the driver's compartment and showed himself. "Come on down you two," he called. "Nobody's going to eat you."

Two pairs of the widest and bluest eyes that he had ever seen came to rest upon his face. In neither pair, however, was there the faintest gleam of understanding. "I said come on down," he repeated. "There's nothing to be afraid of."

The boy turned to the girl, and the two of them began jabbering back and forth in a sing-song tongue that resembled Chinese, but only as the mist resembles the rain. It had no more in common with modern American than its speakers had with their surroundings. Clearly they hadn't understood a word he had said. But, equally as clearly, they must have found reassurance in his plain and honest face, or perhaps in the gentle tone of his voice. After talking the matter over for a few moments, they left their aerie and shinned down the trunk, the boy going first and helping the girl over the rough spots. He was about nine; she was about eleven.

Carpenter stepped out of the compartment, vaulted down from Sam's steel snout and went over to where they were standing. By this time, the bronto had recovered the use of its hind legs and was high-tailing—or rather, high-stepping—it over the plain. The boy was wearing a loose, apricot-colored blouse which was considerably stained and disheveled from his recent arboreal activities, a pair of apricot-colored slacks which were similarly stained and disheveled and which terminated at his thin calves and a pair of open-toe sandals. The girl's outfit was identical, save that it was azure in hue and somewhat less stained and disheveled. She was about an inch taller than the boy, but no less thin. Both of them had delicate features, and hair the color of buttercups, and both of them wore expressions so solemn as to be almost ludicrous. It was virtually a sure bet that they were brother and sister.

Gazing earnestly up into Carpenter's gray eyes, the girl gave voice a series of sing-song phrases, each of them, judging from the nuances of pronunciation, representative of a different language.

When she finished, Carpenter shook his head. "I just don't dig you, pumpkin," he said. Then, just to make sure, he repeated the remark in Anglo Saxon, Aeolic Greek, lower Cro-Magnonese, upper-Acheulian, Middle English, Iro-

quoian and Hyannis-Portese smatterings of which tongues
and dialects he had picked up during his various sojourns in
the past. No dice. Every word he spoke was just plain Greek
to the girl and the boy.

Suddenly the girl's eyes sparkled with excitement, and,
plunging her hand into a plastic reticule that hung from the
belt that supported her slacks, she withdrew what appeared
to be three pairs of earrings. She handed one pair to
Carpenter, one to the boy, and kept one for herself; then she
and the boy proceeded to affix the objects to their ear lobes,
motioning to Carpenter to do the same. Complying, he
discovered that the tiny disks which he had taken for pen-
dants were in reality tiny diaphragms of some kind. Once the
minute clamps were tightened into place, they fitted just
within the ear openings. The girl regarded his handiwork
critically for a moment, then, standing on tiptoe, reached up
and adjusted each disk with deft fingers. Satisfied, she
stepped back. "Now," she said, in perfect idiomatic English,
"we can get through to each other and find out what's what."

Carpenter stared at her. "Well I must say, you caught on to
my language awful fast!"

"Oh, we didn't learn it," the boy said. "Those are
microtranslators—hearrings. With them on, whatever we say
sounds to you the way you would say it, and whatever you say
sounds to us the way we would say it."

"I forgot I had them with me," said the girl. "They're
standard travelers' equipment, but, not being a traveler in the
strict sense of the word, I wouldn't have happened to have
them. Only I'd just got back from foreign-activities class
when the kidnapers grabbed me. Now," she went on, again
gazing earnestly up into Carpenter's eyes, "I think it will be
best if we take care of the amenities first, don't you? My name
is Marcy, this is my brother Skip, and we are from Greater
Mars. What is *your* name, and where are *you* from, kind sir?"

It wasn't easy, but Carpenter managed to keep his voice
matter-of-fact. It was no more than fair that he should have.
If anything, what he had to say was even more incredible than
what he had just heard. "I'm Howard Carpenter, and I'm
from Earth, A.D. 2156. That's 79,062,156 years from now."
He pointed to the triceratank. "Sam over there is my time
machine—among other things. When powered from an out-

side source, there's practically no limit to his field of operations."

The girl blinked once, and so did the boy. But that was all. "Well," Marcy said presently, "that much is taken care of: you're from Earth Future and we're from Mars Present." She paused, looking at Carpenter curiously. "Is there something you don't understand, Mr. Carpenter?"

Carpenter took a deep breath. He exhaled it. "In point of fact, yes. For one thing, there's the little matter of the difference in gravity between the two planets. Here on Earth you weigh more than twice as much as you weigh on Mars, and I can't quite figure out how you can move around so effortlessly, to say nothing of how you could have shinned up the trunk of that ginkgo tree."

"Oh, I see what you mean, Mr. Carpenter," Marcy said. "And it's a very good point, too. But obviously you're using Mars Future as a criterion, and just as obviously Mars Future is no longer quite the same as Mars Present. I—I guess a lot can happen in 79,062,156 years. Well, anyway, Mr. Carpenter," she continued, "the Mars of Skip's and my day has a gravity that approximates this planet's. Centuries ago, you see, our engineers artificially increased the existent gravity in order that no more of our atmosphere could escape into space, and successive generations have adapted themselves to the stronger pull. Does that clarify matters for you, Mr. Carpenter?"

He had to admit that it did. "Do you kids have a last name?" he asked.

"No, we don't, Mr. Carpenter. At one time it was the custom for Martians to have last names, but when desentimentalization was introduced, the custom was abolished. Before we proceed any further, Mr. Carpenter, I would like to thank you for saving our lives. It—it was very noble of you."

"You're most welcome," Carpenter said, "but I'm afraid if we go on standing here in the open like this, I'm going to have to save them all over again, and my own to boot. So let's the three of us get inside Sam where it's safe. All right?"

Leading the way over to the triceratank, he vaulted up on the snout and reached down for the girl's hand. After pulling her up beside him, he helped her into the driver's compartment. "There's a small doorway behind the driver's seat," he told her. "Crawl through it and make yourself at home in the cabin just beyond. You'll find a table and chairs and a bunk, plus a cupboard filled with good things to eat. All the comforts of home."

Before she could comply, a weird whistling sound came from above the plain. She glanced at the sky, and her face went dead-white. "It's them!" she gasped. "They've found us already!"

Carpenter saw the dark winged-shapes of the *Pteranodons* then. There were two of them, and they were homing in on the triceratank like a pair of prehistoric dive bombers. Seizing Skip's hand, he pulled the boy up on the snout, set him in the compartment beside his sister, and told them to get into the cabin fast. Then he jumped into the driver's seat and slammed down the nacelle.

Just in time: the first *Pteranodon* came so close that its right aileron scraped against Sam's frilled head-shield, and the second came so close that its ventral fuselage brushed Sam's back. Their twin tailjets left two double wakes of bluish smoke.

II

Carpenter sat up straight in the driver's seat. Ailerons? Fuselage? Tailjets?

Pteranodons?

He activated Sam's shield-field and extended it to a distance of two feet beyond the armor plating, then he threw the reptivehicle into gear. The pteranodons were circling high overhead. "Marcy," he called, "come forward a minute, will you?"

Her buttercup-colored hair tickled his cheek as she leaned over his shoulder. "Yes, Mr. Carpenter?"

"When you saw the pteranodons, you said, 'They've found us already!' What did you mean by that?"

"They're not pteranodons, Mr. Carpenter. Whatever pteranodons are. They're kidnappers, piloting military-surplus flyabouts that probably look like pteranodons. They abducted Skip and me from the preparatory school of the Greater Martian Technological Apotheosization Institute and are holding us for ransom. Earth is their hideout. There are three of them altogether—Roul and Fritad and Holmer. One of them is probably back in the spaceship."

Carpenter was silent for several moments. The Mars of A.D. 2156 was a desolate place of rubble, sand and wind inhabited by a few thousand diehard colonists from Earth and a few hundred thousand diehard Martians, the former living beneath atmosphere-domes and the latter, save for the few who had intermarried with the colonists, living in deep caves where oxygen could still be obtained. But twenty-second century excavations by the Extraterrestrial Archaeological Society *had* unearthed unquestionable evidence to the effect that an ultra-technological civilization similar to that of Earth Present had existed on the planet over 70,000,000 years ago. Surely it was no more than reasonable to assume that such a civilization had had space travel.

That being the case, Earth, during her uppermost Mesozoic Era, must have presented an ideal hideout for Martian criminals, kidnappers included. Certainly such a theory threw considerable light on the anachronisms that kept cropping up in Cretaceous strata. There was of course another way to explain Marcy's and Skip's presence in the Age of Dinosaurs: they could be A.D. 2156 Earth children, and they could have come back via time machine the same as he had. Or they could have been abducted by twenty-second century kidnappers for that matter, and have been brought back. But, that being so, why should they lie about it?

"Tell me, Marcy," Carpenter said, "do you believe I came from the future?"

"Oh, of course, Mr. Carpenter. And I'm sure Skip does, too. It's—it's kind of *hard* to believe, but I know that someone as nice as you wouldn't tell a fib—especially such a big one."

"Thank you," Carpenter said. "And I believe you came from Greater Mars, which, I imagine, is the planet's largest and most powerful country. Tell me something about your civilization."

"It's a magnificent civilization, Mr. Carpenter. Every day we progress by leaps and bounds, and now that we've licked the instability factor, we'll progress even faster."

" 'The instability factor'?"

"Human emotion. It held us back for years, but it can't any more. Now, when a boy reaches his thirteenth birthday and a girl reaches her fifteenth, they are desentimentalized. And after that, they are able to make calm cool decisions strictly in keeping with pure logic. That way they can achieve maximum efficiency. At the Institute preparatory school, Skip and I are going through what is known as the 'pre-desentimentalization process.' After four more years we'll begin receiving dosages of the desentimentalization drug. Then—"

SKRRRREEEEEEEEEEEK! went one of the pteranodons as it sideswiped the shield-field.

Carpenter watched it as it wobbled wildly for a moment, and before it shot skyward he caught a glimpse of its occupant. All he saw was an expressionless face, but from its forward location he deduced that the man was lying in a prone position between the two twelve-foot wings.

Marcy was trembling. "I—I think they're out to kill us, Mr. Carpenter," she said. "They threatened to if we tried to escape. Now that they've got our voices on the ransom tape, they probably figure they don't need us any more."

He reached back and patted her hand where it lay lightly on his shoulder. "It's all right, pumpkin. With old Sam here protecting you, you haven't got a thing to worry about."

"Is—is that really his name?"

"It sure is. Sam Triceratops, Esquire. Sam, this is Marcy. You take good care of her and her brother—do you hear me?" He turned his head and looked into the girl's wide blue eyes. "He says he will. I'll bet you haven't got anybody like him on Mars, have you?"

She shook her head—as standard a Martian gesture, apparently, as it was a terrestrial—and for a moment he thought that a tremulous smile was going to break up on her lips. It didn't, though—not quite. "Indeed we haven't, Mr. Carpenter."

He squinted up through the nacelle at the circling pteranodons (he still thought of them as pteranodons, even though he knew they were not). "Where's this spaceship of theirs, Marcy? Is it far from here?"

She pointed to the left. "Over there. You come to a river, and then a swamp. Skip and I escaped this morning when Fritad, who was guarding the lock, fell asleep. They're a bunch of sleepyheads, always falling asleep when it's their turn to stand guard. Eventually the Greater Martian Space Police will track the ship here; we thought we could hide out until they got here. We crept through the swamp and floated across the river on a log. It—it was awful, with big snakes on legs chasing us, and—and—"

His shoulder informed him that she was trembling again. "Look, I'll tell you what, pumpkin," he said. "You go back to the cabin and fix yourself and Skip something to eat. I don't know what kind of food you're accustomed to, but it can't be too different from what Sam's got in stock. You'll find some square, vacuum-containers in the cupboard—they contain sandwiches. On the refrigerator shelf just above, you'll find some tall bottles with circlets of little stars—they contain pop. Open some of each, and dig in. Come to think of it, I'm hungry myself, so while you're at it, fix me something, too."

Again, she almost smiled. "All right, Mr. Carpenter. I'll fix you something special."

Alone in the driver's compartment, he surveyed the Cretaceous landscape through the front, lateral and rear viewscopes. A range of young mountains showed far to the left. To the right was the distant line of cliffs. The rear viewscope framed scattered stands of willows, fan palms and dwarf magnolias, beyond which the forested uplands, wherein lay his entry area, began. Far ahead, volcanos smoked with Mesozoic abandon.

79,061,889 years from now, this territory would be part of the state of Montana. 79,062,156 years from now, a group of paleontologists digging somewhere in the vastly changed terrain would unearth the fossil of a modern man who had died 79,062,156 years before his disinterment.

Would the fossil turn out to be his own!

Carpenter grinned, and looked up at the sky to where the two pteranodons still circled. It *could* have been the fossil of a Martian.

He turned the triceratank around and started off in the opposite direction. "Come on, Sam," he said. "Let's see if we can't find a good hiding place where we can lay over for the night. Maybe by morning I'll be able to figure out what to do. Who'd ever have thought we'd wind up playing rescue-team to a couple of kids?"

Sam grunted deep in his gear box and made tracks for the forested uplands.

The trouble with going back in time to investigate anachronisms was that frequently you found yourself the author of the anachronism in question. Take the classic instance of Professor Archibald Quigley.

Whether the story was true or not, no one could say for certain, but, true or not, it pointed up the irony of time travel as nothing else could. A stanch Coleridge admirer, Professor Quigley had been curious for years—or so the story went—as to the identity of the visitor who had called at the farmhouse in Nether Stowey in the county of Somersetshire, England in the year 1797 and interrupted Coleridge while the poet was writing down a poem which he had just composed in his sleep. The visitor had hung around for an hour, and afterward Coleridge hadn't been able to remember the rest of the poem. As a result, *Kubla Khan* was never finished. Eventually, Professor Quigley's curiosity grew to such proportions that he could no longer endure it, and he applied at the Bureau of Time Travel for permission to return to the place-time in order that he might set his mind at ease. His request was granted, whereupon he handed over half his life-savings without a qualm in exchange for a trip back to the morning in question. Emerging near the farmhouse, he hid in a clump of bushes, watching the front door; then, growing impatient when no one showed up, he went to the door himself, and knocked. Coleridge answered the knock personally, and even though he asked the professor in, the dark look that he gave his visitor was something which the professor never forgot to the end of his days.

Recalling the story, Carpenter chuckled. It wasn't really anything for him to be chuckling about, though, because what had happened to the professor could very well happen to him. Whether he liked it or not, there was a good chance that the fossil which the North American Paleontological Society had sent him back to the Mesozoic Era to investigate might turn out to be his own.

Nevertheless, he refused to let the possibility bother him. For one thing, the minute he found himself in a jam, all he had to do was to contact his two assistants, Miss Sands and Peter Detritus, and they would come flying to his aid in Edith

the theropod or one of the other reptivehicles which NAPS
kept on hand. For another, he had already learned that
outside forces were at work in the Cretaceous Period. He
wasn't the only candidate for fossildom. Anyway, worrying
about such matters was a waste of time: what was going to
happen had already happened, and that was all there was to
it.

Skip crawled out of the cabin and leaned over the back of
the driver's seat. "Marcy sent you up a sandwich and a bottle
of pop, Mr. Carpenter," he said, handing over both items.
And then, "Can I sit beside you, sir?"

"Sure thing," Carpenter said, moving over.

The boy climbed over the backrest and slid down into the
seat. No sooner had he done so than another buttercup-
colored head appeared. "Would—would it be all right, Mr.
Carpenter, if—if—"

"Move over and make room for her in the middle, Skip."

Sam's head was a good five feet wide, hence the driver's
compartment was by no means a small one. But the seat itself
was only three feet wide, and accommodating two half-grown
kids and a man the size of Carpenter was no small accomplishment, especially in view of the fact that all three of them
were eating sandwiches and drinking pop. Carpenter felt like
an indulgent parent taking his offspring on an excursion
through a zoo.

And such a zoo! They were in the forest now, and around
them Cretaceous oaks and laurels stood; there were willows,
too, and screw pines and ginkgos galore, and now and then
they passed through incongruous stands of fan palms.
Through the undergrowth they glimpsed a huge and lumbering creature that looked like a horse in front and a kangaroo
in back. Carpenter identified it as an *Anatosaurus*. In a
clearing they came upon a *Struthiomimus* and startled the
ostrichlike creature half out of its wits. A spike-backed
Ankylosaurus glowered at them from behind a clump of
sedges, but discreetly refrained from questioning Sam's right
of way. Glancing into a treetop, Carpenter saw his first
Archaeopteryx. Raising his eyes still higher, he saw the
circling pteranodons.

He had hoped to lose them after entering the forest, and to
this end he held Sam on an erratic course. Obviously,

however, they were equipped with matter detectors. A more sophisticated subterfuge would be necessary. There was a chance that he might bring them down with a barrage of stun-charges, but it was a slim one and he decided not to try it in any event. The kidnappers undoubtedly deserved to die for what they had done, but he was not their judge. He would kill them if he had to, but he refused to do it as long as he had an ace up his sleeve.

Turning toward the two children, he saw that they had lost interest in their sandwiches and were looking apprehensively upward. Catching their eye, he winked. "I think it's high time we gave them the slip, don't you?"

"But how, Mr. Carpenter?" Skip asked. "They're locked right on us with their detector-beams. We're just lucky ordinary Martians like them can't buy super Martian weapons. They've got melters, which are a form of iridescers; but if they had real iridescers, we'd be goners."

"We can shake them easy, merely by jumping a little ways back in time. Come on, you two—finish your sandwiches and stop worrying."

Their apprehension vanished, and excitement took its place. "Let's jump back six days," Marcy said. "They'll never find us then because we won't be here yet."

"Can't do it, pumpkin—it would take too much starch out of Sam. Time-jumping requires a tremendous amount of power. In order for a part-time time-machine like Sam to jump any great distance, its power has to be supplemented by the power of a regular time station. The station propels the reptivehicle back to a preestablished entry area, and the time-traveler drives out of the area and goes about his business. The only way he can get back to the present is by driving back into the area, contacting the station and tapping its power supply again, or by sending back a distress signal and having someone come to get him in another reptivehicle. At the most, Sam could make about a four-day round trip under his own power but it would burn him out. Once that happened, even the station couldn't pull him back. I think we'd better settle for an hour."

Ironically, the smaller the temporal distance you had to deal with, the more figuring you had to do. After directing the triceratank via the liaison ring on his right index finger to

continue on its present erratic course, Carpenter got busy
with pad and pencil, and presently he began punching out
arithmetical brain twisters on the compact computer that was
built into the control panel.

Marcy leaned forward, watching him intently. "If it will
expedite matters, Mr. Carpenter," she said, "I can do simple sums, such as those you're writing down, in my
head. For instance, 828,464,280 times 4,692,438,921 equals
3,887,518,032,130,241,880."

"It may very well at that, pumpkin, but I think we'd better
check and make sure, don't you?" He punched out the first
two sets of numerals on the calculator, and depressed the
multiplication button. 3,887,518, 032,130,241,880 the answer
panel said. He nearly dropped the pencil.

"She's a mathematical genius," Skip said. "I'm a mechanical genius myself. That's how come we were kidnapped. Our
government values geniuses highly. They'll pay a lot of money
to get us back."

"Your government? I thought kidnappers preyed on parents, not governments."

"Oh, but our parents aren't responsible for us any more,"
Marcy explained. "In fact, they've probably forgotten all
about us. After the age of six, children become the property
of the state. Modern Martian parents are desentimentalized,
you see, and don't in the least mind getting rid of—giving up
their children."

Carpenter regarded the two solemn faces for some time.
"Yes," he said, "I do see at that."

With Marcy's help, he completed the rest of his calculations; then he fed the final set of figures into Sam's frontal
ganglion. "Here we go, you two!" he said, and threw the
jumpback switch. There was a brief shimmering effect and an
almost imperceptible jar. So smoothly did the transition take
place that Sam did not even pause in his lumbering walk.

Carpenter turned his wristwatch back from 4:16 P.M. to
3:16 P.M. "Take a look at the sky now, kids. See any more
pteranodons?"

They peered up through the foliage. "Not a one, Mr.
Carpenter," Marcy said, her eyes warm with admiration.
"Not a single one!"

"Say, you've got our scientists beat forty different ways

from Sunday!" Skip said. "They think they're pretty smart, but I'll bet they've never even thought of trying to travel in time . . . How far can you jump into the future, Mr. Carpenter—in a regular time-machine, I mean?"

"Given sufficient power, to the end of time—if time does have an end. But traveling beyond one's own present is forbidden by law. The powers-that-be in 2156 consider it bad for a race of people to find out what's going to happen to them before it actually happens, and for once I'm inclined to think that the powers-that-be are right."

He discontinued liaison control, took over manually and set Sam on a course at right angles to their present direction. At length they broke free from the forest onto the plain. In the distance the line of cliffs that he had noticed earlier showed whitely against the blue and hazy sky. "How'd you kids like to camp out for the night?" he asked.

Skip's eyes went round. "Camp out, Mr. Carpenter?"

"Sure. We'll build a fire, cook our food over it, spread our blankets on the ground—regular American Indian style. Maybe we can even find a cave in the cliffs. Think you'd like that?"

Both pairs of eyes were round now. "What's 'American Indian style,' Mr. Carpenter?" Marcy asked.

He told them about the Arapaho and the Cheyenne and the Crows and the Apache, and about the buffalo and the great plains and Custer's last stand, and the Conestogas and the frontiersmen (the old ones, not the "new"), and about Geronimo and Sitting Bull and Cochise, and all the while he talked their eyes remained fastened on his face as though it were the sun and they had never before seen day. When he finished telling them about the settling of the West, he told them about the Civil War and Abraham Lincoln and Generals Grant and Lee and the Gettysburg Address and the Battle of Bull Run and the surrender at Appomattox.

He had never talked so much in all his life. He wondered what had come over him, why he felt so carefree and gay all of a sudden and why nothing seemed to matter except the haze-ridden Cretaceous afternoon and the two round-eyed children sitting beside him. But he did not waste much time wondering. He went on to tell them about the signing of the Declaration of Independence and the American Revolution and George Washington and Thomas Jefferson and Benjamin Franklin and John Adams, and about what a wonderful dream the founding fathers had had and about how much better it would have turned out if opportunistic men had not used it to further their own selfish end and about how relatively wonderful it had turned out anyway, despite the many crimes that had been committed in its name. By the time he finished, evening was on hand. The white cliffs rose up before them, shouldering the darkening sky.

At the base of the cliffs they found a jim-dandy of an untenanted cave, large enough to accommodate both Sam and themselves and with enough room left over to build a campfire. Carpenter drove the reptivehicle inside and parked it in the rear; then he extended the shield-field till it included the cave, the side of the cliff and a large semicircular area at the base of the cliff. After checking the "front yard" and finding that it contained no reptiles except several small and harmless lizards, he put the two children to work gathering firewood. Meanwhile, he generated a one-way illusion-field just within the shield-field so that the forthcoming campfire would not be visible from without.

There was plenty of firewood available in the form of dead laurel and dogwood branches. Soon a respectable pile of fuel reposed just within the mouth of the cave. By this time Skip, at least, had shed his reserve. "Can I help build the fire, Mr. Carpenter?" he cried jumping up and down. "Can I—can I—can I?"

"Skip!" Marcy said.

"It's all right, pumpkin," Carpenter told her. "You can help, too, if you like."

The walls of the cave turned red, then rosy, as young flames grew into full-fledged ones.

Carpenter opened three packages of frankfurters and three packages of rolls and showed his charges how to spear the frankfurters on the end of pointed sticks and roast them over the fire. Afterward he demonstrated how to place a frankfurter in a roll and smother it with mustard, pickle relish, and chopped onions. It was as though he had flung wide magic casements opening on enchanted lands that the two children had not dreamed existed. The last vestiges of solemnity departed from their faces, and during the next half hour they created and consumed six hot dogs apiece. Skip got so excited that he nearly fell into the fire, and the smile that had been trying all afternoon to break upon Marcy's lips at last came through, teaching the flames to burn bright.

Carpenter had made a pot of cocoa in Sam's kitchenette, and nothing more was needed to round out the cookout except marshmallows. Was it remotely possible, he wondered, that his efficient chief assistant had included such nostalgic delicacies among the various supplies in Sam's tail-compartment? It was doubtful at best, but he took a look anyway. To his delight, he found a whole box of them.

Again, he performed a demonstration, while the two children looked on in open-mouthed awe. When the two marshmallows which he had speared on his stick turned golden brown he thought for a moment that Skip's eyes were going to fall out of his head. As for Marcy, she just stood there and stared as though Carpenter had said, "Let there be light!" and the first day had come into being.

Laughing, he removed the marshmallows and handed one to each of them. "Skip!" Marcy said when the boy popped his into his mouth and dispatched it with a single gulp, "where are your manners?" She ate hers daintily.

After the marshmallow roast, he went outside and cut enough laurel and dogwood branches for three mattresses. He showed the children how to arrange the branches on the cavern floor and how to cover them with the blankets which he took out of Sam's tail-compartment. Skip needed no further invitation to turn in: exhausted from his enthusiastic activities and becalmed by his full stomach, he collapsed upon his blanket as soon as he had it in place. Carpenter got three more blankets, covered him with one of them and turned to Marcy, "You look tired, too, pumpkin."

"Oh, but I'm not, Mr. Carpenter. Not in the least bit. I'm two years older than Skip, you know. He's just a kid."

He folded the remaining two blankets into impromptu pillows and placed them a few feet from the fire. He sat down on one of them; she sat down on the other. All evening, grunts and growls and groans had been coming sporadically from beyond the shield-field; now they were supplanted by an awesome noise that brought to mind a gigantic road-repair machine breaking up old pavement. The cavern floor trembled, and the firelight flickered wildly on the wall. "Sounds like old *Tyrannosaurus*," Carpenter said. "Probably out looking for a midnight snack in the form of a *Struthiomimus* or two."

"'*Tyrannosaurus*,' Mr. Carpenter?"

He described the ferocious theropod for her. She nodded after he had finished, and a shudder shook her. "Yes," she said, "Skip and I saw one. It was a little while after we crossed the river. We—we hid in a clump of bushes till he passed. What terrible creatures you have here on Earth, Mr. Carpenter!"

"They no longer exist in my day and age," Carpenter said. "We have terrible 'creatures' of another order—'creatures' that would send old *Tyrannosaurus* high-tailing it for the hills like a flushed rabbit. I shouldn't be complaining, though. Our technological debauchery left us with a coldwar hangover—sure; but it paid off in quite a number of things. Time travel, for one. Interplanetary travel, for another." At this point, the road-repair machine struck a bad stretch of pavement, and, judging from the ungodly series of sound that ensued, blew a rod to boot. The girl moved closer to him. "Take it easy, pumpkin. There's nothing to worry about. An army of theropods couldn't break through that shield-field."

"Why do you call me 'pumpkin', Mr. Carpenter? On Mars, a pumpkin is an unpleasant squashy vegetable that grows in swamps and midden-marshes."

He laughed. The sounds from beyond the shield-field diminished, then faded away, as the theropod thundered off in another direction. "On Earth, a pumpkin is quite respectable. But that's beside the point. 'Pumpkin' is what a man calls a girl when he likes her."

There was a silence. Then, "Do you have a real girl Mr. Carpenter?"

"Not actually, Marcy. You might say that figuratively speaking I worship one from afar."

"That doesn't sound like very much fun. Who is she?"

"She's my chief assistant at the North American Paleontological Society where I work—Miss Sands. Her first name is 'Elaine,' but I never call her by it. She sees to it that I don't forget anything when I retro-travel, and she cases the place-times over a timescope before I start out. Then she and my other assistant, Peter Detritus, stand by, ready to come to the rescue if I should send back a can of chicken soup. You see, a can of chicken soup is our distress signal. It's about as big an object as a paleontologivehicle can handle in most cases, and the word 'chicken' in our language connotes fear."

"But why do you worship her from afar, Mr. Carpenter?"

"Well you see," Carpenter said, "Miss Sands isn't just an ordinary run-of-the-mill girl. She's the cool, aloof type—a goddess, if you know what I mean. Although I don't see how you possibly could. Anyway, you simply don't treat goddesses the way you treat mere girls—you keep your distance and worship them from afar and humbly wait for them to bestow favors upon you. I—I worship her so much, in fact, that every time I'm near her I get so flustered that I can hardly say anything. Maybe after I get to know her better it'll be different. So far, I've known her three months."

He fell silent. Marcy's hearrings twinkled in the firelight as she turned and looked gently up into his face. "What's the matter, Mr. Carpenter—cat got your tongue?"

"I was just thinking," Carpenter said. "Three months is quite a long time at that—long enough for a man to tell whether a girl is ever going to like him or not. And Miss Sands isn't ever going to like me—I can see that now. Why, she doesn't even look at me unless she absolutely has to, and she won't say two words to me if she can possibly avoid it. So you see, even if I did stop worshiping her from afar and got up enough nerve to tell her that I love her, she would probably only be annoyed and tell me to get lost."

Marcy was indignant. "She must be out of her mind, Mr. Carpenter—just plain out of her mind. She should be ashamed of herself!"

"No, Marcy—you've got her all wrong. You can't expect a girl as beautiful as she is to go for a good-for-nothing time-bum like me."

"A good-for-nothing time-bum indeed! You know, Mr. Carpenter, I don't think you understand women very well. Why, I'll bet if you told her you love her, she'd throw herself into your arms!"

"You're a romantic, Marcy. In real life, such things don't

happen." He stood up. "Well, young lady, I don't know about you, but I'm tired. Shall we call it a day?"

"If you wish to, Mr. Carpenter."

She was asleep by the time he pulled her blanket up to her chin. As he stood there looking down at her, she turned on her side, and the firelight caught the buttercup-hue fuzz on the back of her neck, where her hair had been cut too short, and tinted it red-gold. All he could think of were buttercup-clad meadows in spring, and the warm clean sun rising and ushering in the dew-jeweled day. . . .

After checking to see if Skip was all right, he went over and stood in the cave mouth and stared out into the darkness. With the tyrannosaur's departure, the lesser Cretaceous creatures had come out of their hiding places and were making their presence known again. He glimpsed the grotesque shapes of several ornithopods; he saw an *Ankylosaurus* standing immobile by a coppice of fan palms; he heard lizards scurrying both inside and outside the shield-field. A moon subtly different from the one he was most accustomed to was climbing into the prehistoric heavens. The difference lay in the number of meteorite craters. There were far fewer of them now than there would be 79,062,156 years in the future.

He realized presently that although he was still looking at the moon he was no longer seeing it. He was seeing the campfire instead, and the girl and the boy enthusiastically roasting marshmallows. Why hadn't he gotten married and had children? he wondered suddenly. Why had he passed up all the pretty girls he had ever known, only to fall hopelessly in love at the age of thirty-two with a beautiful goddess who preferred not to know he was alive? What had given him the notion that the thrill derived from adventure was somehow superior to the contentment derived from loving and being loved?—that getting the bugs out of historical and prehistorical times was more important than getting the bugs out of his own life? That a lonely room in a boarding house was a man's castle and that drinks drank in dim-lit bars with fun-girls he could no longer remember the next day spelled "freedom"?

What treasure had he expected to find in the past that could equal the treasures he had passed up in the future?

The night had grown chill. Before lying down to sleep he added more wood to the fire. He listened to the flames crackle and watched their pale flickerings on the cavern walls. A lizard regarded him with golden eyes out of prehistoric shadows. In the distance, an ornithopod went Waroompf! Beside him in the Mesozoic night the two children breathed softly in their green-bough beds. Presently he slept.

III

The next morning, Carpenter wasted no time in getting the show on the road.

Marcy and Skip were all for remaining in the cave indefinitely, but he explained to them that, were they to stay in one place, the kidnappers would find them that much sooner, and that therefore it would be better if they kept on the move. Thus far, everything he had told them had rung a bell in their language just as everything they had told him had rung a bell in his, but this time, for some reason, he had a hard time getting through to them. Either that, or they just plain didn't want to leave the cave. Leave it they did however—after ablutions performed in Sam's compact lavatory and a breakfast of bacon and eggs cooked in Sam's kitchenette—when he made it clear to them that he was still the boss.

He hadn't as yet decided on a definite plan of action. While trying to make up his mind, he let the triceratank pick its own course over the plain—a feat for which its hypersensitive terrainometer more than qualified.

Actually, he had only two choices: (1)—continue to play big brother to the two children and elude the kidnappers until they gave up or until the cavalry, in the form of the Greater Martian Space Police, arrived on the scene, or (2)—return to the entry-area and signal Miss Sands and Peter Detritus to bring the triceratank back to the present. The second choice was by far the safer course of action. He would have settled for it without hesitation if it had not been for two things: (a) Marcy and Skip, while they undoubtedly would be able to adapt to a civilization as similar to their own as twenty-second century terrestrial civilization was, might never feel completely at home in it, and (b) sooner or later, they would come face to face with the demoralizing information that their own civilization of 79,062,156 years ago, had long since turned to dust and that the technological dreams which they had been taught to regard as gospel had come to nothing. A possible third choice lay in taking them back to Earth Present, keeping them there until such a time as the kidnappers gave up and left or until the Space Police showed up, and then returning them to Earth Past; but such a procedure would involve several round trips to the Cretaceous Period. Carpenter knew without having to ask that, owing to the fantastic expense involved, NAPS's budget couldn't support even one such non-paleontological round trip, to say nothing of several.

Pondering the problem, he became aware that someone was tugging on his sleeve. It was Skip, who had come forward and climbed into the driver's seat. "Can I steer him, Mr. Carpenter? Can I?"

Carpenter surveyed the plain through the front, lateral, and rear viewscopes; then he raised Sam's head and took a long look at the sky through the nacelle. A dark speck hovered high above the line of cliffs they had left less than an hour ago. As he watched, it was joined by two others. "Later on, Skip. Right now, I think we've got company."

Skip's eyes had found the specks, too. "The pteranodons again, Mr. Carpenter?"

"I'm afraid so."

The specks grew rapidly larger, resolved into winged shapes with narrow, pointed heads. Marcy had come forward, and her gaze, too, was directed at the sky. This time, she didn't seem to be in the least bit frightened, and neither did Skip. "Are we going to jump back in time again, Mr. Carpenter?" she asked.

"We'll see, pumpkin," he said.

The pteranodons were clearly visible now. There was no question but what they were interested in Sam. Whether they would try attacking him again was another matter. In any event, Carpenter decided that, even though the triceratank's shield-field was in operation, his best bet would be to head for the nearest stand of trees. It was a stand of palmettos, and about half a mile distant. He threw Sam into high, and took over the controls again. "Come on, Sam," he said, to keep the kids' morale from faltering, "show Marcy and Skip what you can do!"

Sam took off like a twentieth-century locomotive, his

flexible steel legs moving rhythmically, his alloy-hooves pounding the ground in a thunderous cadence. Nevertheless, he was no match for the pteranodons, and they overtook him easily. The foremost one swooped down a hundred yards ahead, released what looked like a big metal egg and soared skyward.

The metal egg turned out to be a bomb. The crater that it created was so wide that it took all of Carpenter's skill to guide Sam around it without rolling the reptivehicle over. Instantly he revved up the engine and shifted into second. "They're not going to get us that way, are they, old timer?" he said.

"URRRRRRRR!" Sam grunted.

Carpenter glanced at the sky. All of the pteranodons were directly overhead now. Circling. One, two, three, he counted. Three . . . yesterday there had been only two. "Marcy," he said, suddenly excited, "how many kidnappers did you say there were?"

"Three, Mr. Carpenter. Roul and Fritad and Holmer."

"Then they're all up there. That means the ship is unguarded—unless there's a crew."

"No, Mr. Carpenter—there's no crew. They did the piloting themselves."

He lowered his gaze from the circling pteranodons. "Do you kids think you could get inside?"

"Easy," Skip said. "It's a military-surplus flyabout-carrier with standard locks, and standard locks are simple for someone with a little mechanical ability to disengage. That's how come Marcy and I were able to escape in the first place. You just leave everything to me, Mr. Carpenter."

"Good," Carpenter said. "We'll be there waiting for them when they come back."

With Marcy doing the figuring, retro coordinate calculus was a breeze. Sam was ready for jump-back in a matter of seconds.

Carpenter waited till they were in the stand of palmettos, then he threw the switch. Again, there was a shimmering effect and a slight jar, and daylight gave way to predawn darkness. Behind them in a cave at the base of the cliffs, another triceratank stood, and another Carpenter and another Marcy and Skip still slept soundly in their green-bough beds.

"How far did we jump back this time, Mr. Carpenter?" Skip asked.

Carpenter turned on Sam's headlights and began guiding him out of the stand of palmettos. "Four hours. That should give us plenty of time to reach the ship and get set before our friends return. We may even reach it before they start out—assuming of course that they haven't been searching for us round the clock."

"But suppose they spot us in this time-phase?" Marcy objected. "Won't we be in the same pickle we just got out of?"

"It's a possibility, pumpkin. But the odds have it overwhelmingly that they didn't spot us. Otherwise they wouldn't have gone on searching for us—right?"

She gazed at him admiringly. "You know something, Mr. Carpenter? You're pretty smart."

Coming from someone who could multiply 4,692,438,921 by 828,464,280 in her head, it was quite a compliment. However, Carpenter managed to take it in his stride. "I hope you kids can find the ship now," he said.

"We're already on the right course," Skip said. "I know, because I've got a perfect sense of direction. It's camouflaged as a big tree."

For the second time that morning, the sun came up. As had been the case yesterday, Sam's size and mien cowed the various Cretaceous creatures they met although whether *Tyrannosaurus* would have been similarly cowed had they come upon him was a moot question at best. In any case, they didn't come upon him. By eight o'clock they were moving over the same terrain that Carpenter had come to not long after leaving the forested uplands the day before. "Look!" Marcy exclaimed presently. "There's the tree we climbed when the long-necked monster chased us!"

"It sure is," Skip said. "Boy, were we scared!"

Carpenter grinned. "He probably thought you were some species of flora he hadn't tried yet. Good thing for his digestive system that I happened along when I did."

They looked at him blankly for a moment, and at first he thought that the barriers of two different languages and two different thought worlds had been too high for his little joke to surmount. Such, however, did not prove to be the case. First Marcy burst out laughing, and then Skip. "Mr. Carpenter, if you aren't the darndest!" Marcy cried.

They went on. The landscape grew more and more open, with coppices of palmettos and clusters of fan palms constituting most of the major plant life. Far to the right, smoking volcanoes added their discolored breath to the hazy atmosphere. In the distances ahead, mountains showed, their heads lost in the Mesozoic smog. The humidity was so high that large globules of moisture kept condensing on Sam's nacelle and rolling down like raindrops. Tortoises, lizards and snakes abounded, and once a real pteranodon glided swiftly by overhead.

At length they came to the river which Marcy had mentioned and which the increasing softness of the ground had been heralding for some time. Looking downstream, Carpenter saw his first full-sized brontosaur.

He pointed it out to the kids, and they stared at it bug-eyed. It was wallowing in the middle of the sluggish stream. Only its small head, its long neck and the upper part of its back were visible. The neck brought to mind a lofty rubbery tower, but the illusion was marred by the frequency with which the head kept dipping down to the ferns and horsetails that lined the river bank. The poor creature was so enormous that it virtually had to keep eating day and night in order to stay alive.

Carpenter found a shallows and guided Sam across the stream to the opposite bank. The ground was somewhat firmer here, but the firmness was deceiving, for the reptivehicle's terrainometer registered an even higher frequency of bogs. (Lord! Carpenter thought. Suppose the two kids had blundered into one!) Ferns grew in abundance, and there were thick carpets of sassafras and sedges. Palmettos and fan palms were still the rule, but there were occasional ginkgos scattered here and there. One of them was a veritable giant of a tree, towering to a height of over one hundred and fifty feet.

Carpenter stared at it. Cretaceous Period ginkgos generally grew on highground, not low, but a ginkgo the size of this one had no business growing in the Cretaceous Period at all. Moreover, the huge tree was incongruous in other respects. Its trunk was far too thick, for one thing. For another, the lower part of it up to a height of about twenty feet consisted of three slender subtrunks, forming a sort of tripod on which the rest of the tree rested.

At this point, Carpenter became aware that his two charges were pointing excitedly at the object of his curiosity. "That's *it!*" Skip exclaimed. "That's the *ship!*"

"Well, no wonder it caught my eye," Carpenter said. "They didn't do a very good job of camouflaging it. I can even see one of the fly-about bays."

Marcy said, "They weren't particularly concerned about how it looks from the ground. It's how it looks from above that counts. Of course, if the Space Police get here in time they'll pick it up sooner or later on their detector-beams, but it will fool them for a while at least."

"You talk as though you don't expect them to get here in time."

"I don't. Oh, they'll get here eventually, Mr. Carpenter, but not for weeks, and maybe even months. It takes a long time for their radar-intelligence department to track a ship, besides which it's a sure bet that they don't even know we've been kidnapped yet. In all previous cases where Institute children have been abducted, the government has paid the ransom first and then notified the Space Police. Of course, even after the ransom has been paid and the children have been returned, The Space Police still launch a search for the kidnappers, and eventually they find their hideout; but naturally the kidnappers are long gone by then."

"I think," Carpenter said, "that it's high time a precedent was established, don't you?"

After parking Sam out of sight in a nearby coppice of palmettos and deactivating the shield-field, he reached in under the driver's seat and pulled out the only hand weapon the triceratank contained—a lightweight but powerful stun-rifle specially designed by NAPS for the protection of time-travel personnel. Slinging it on his shoulder, he threw open the nacelle, stepped out onto Sam's snout and helped the two children down to the ground. The trio approached the ship.

Skip shinned up one of the landing jacks, climbed some distance up the trunk and had the locks open in a matter of seconds. He lowered an aluminum ladder. "Everything's all set, Mr. Carpenter."

Marcy glanced over her shoulder at the palmetto coppice. "Will—will Sam be all right do you think?"

"Of course he will, pumpkin," Carpenter said. "Up with you now."

The ship's air-conditioned interior had a temperature that paralleled Sam's, the lighting was cool, subdued. Beyond the inner lock, a brief corridor led to a spiral steel stairway that gave access to the decks above and to the engine rooms below. Glancing at his watch, which he had set four hours back, Carpenter saw that the time was 8:24. In a few minutes, the pteranodons would be closing in on the Sam and Carpenter and Marcy and Skip of the "previous" time-phase. Even assuming that the three kidnappers headed straight for the ship afterward, there was still time to spare—time enough, certainly, to send a certain message before laying the trap he had in mind. True, he could send the message after Roul and Fritad and Holmer were safely locked in their cabins, but in the event that something went wrong he might not be able to send it at all, so it was better to send it right now. "Okay, you kids," he said, "close the locks and then lead the way to the communications-room."

They obeyed the first order with alacrity, but hedged on the second. Marcy lingered in the corridor, Skip just behind her.

"Why do you want to go the communications-room, Mr. Carpenter?" she asked.

"So you kids can radio our position to the Space Police and tell them to get here in a hurry. You do know how, I hope."

Skip looked at Marcy. Marcy looked at Skip. After a moment, both of them shook their heads. "Now see here," Carpenter said, annoyed, "you know perfectly well you know how. Why are you pretending you don't?"

Skip looked at the deck. "We—we don't want to go home, Mr. Carpenter."

Carpenter regarded first one solemn face and then the other. "But you've got to be home! Where *else* can you go?"

Neither of them answered. Neither of them looked at him. "It boils down to this," he proceeded presently. "If we succeed in capturing Roul and Fritad and Holmer, fine and dandy. We'll sit tight, and when the Space Police get here we'll turn them over. But if something goes wrong and we don't capture them, we'll at least have an ace up our sleeve in the form of the message you're going to send. Now I'm familiar with the length of time it takes to get from Mars to Earth in the spaceships of my day, but I don't of course know how long your spaceships take. So maybe you two can give me some idea of the length of time that will elapse between the Space Police's receipt of our message and their arrival here on Earth," he asked.

"With the two planets in their present positions, just over four days," Marcy said. "If you like, Mr. Carpenter, I can figure it out for you right down to a fraction of a—"

"That's close enough, pumpkin. Now, up the stairs with you, and you too, Skip. Time's a-wasting!"

They complied glumly. The communications-room was on the second deck. Some of the equipment was vaguely familiar to Carpenter, but most of it was Greek. A wide, deck-to-ceiling viewport looked out over the Cretaceous plain, and, glancing down through the ersatz foliage, he found that he could see the palmetto coppice in which Sam was hidden. He scanned the sky for signs of the returning pteranodons. The sky was empty. Turning away from the viewport, he noticed that a fourth party had entered the room. He unslung his stun-rifle and managed to get it halfway to his shoulder; then, ZZZZZZTTT! a metal tube in the fourth party's hand went, and the stun-rifle was no more.

He looked incredulously down at his hand.

IV

The fourth party was a tall, muscular man clad in clothing similar to Marcy's and Skip's, but of a much richer material. The expression on his narrow face contained about as much feeling as a dried fig, and the metal tube in his hand was now directed at the center of Carpenter's forehead. Carpenter didn't need to be told that if he moved so much as one iota he would suffer a fate similar to that suffered by his rifle, but the man vouchsafed the information anyway. "If you move, you melt," he said.

"No, Holmer!" Marcy cried. "Don't you dare harm him. He only helped us because he felt sorry for us."

"I thought you said there were only three of them, pumpkin," Carpenter said, not taking his eyes from Holmer's face.

"That *is* all there are, Mr. Carpenter. Honest! The third pteranodon must have been a drone. They tricked us!"

Holmer should have grinned, but he didn't. There should have been triumph in his tone of voice when he addressed Carpenter, but there wasn't.

"You had to be from the future, friend," he said. "Me and my buddies cased this place some time ago, and we knew you couldn't be from now. That being so, it wasn't hard for us to figure out that when that tank of yours disappeared yesterday you either jumped ahead in time or jumped back in it, and the odds were two to one that you jumped back. So we gambled on it, figured you'd try the same thing again if you were forced into it, and rigged up a little trap for you, which we figured you'd be smart enough to fall for. You were. The only reason I don't melt you right now is because Roul and Fritad aren't back yet. I want them to get a look at you first. I'll melt you then but good. And the brats, too. We don't need them any more."

Carpenter recoiled. The dictates of pure logic had much in common with the dictates of pure vindictiveness. Probably the pteranodons had been trying to "melt" Marcy, Skip, Sam and himself almost from the beginning, and if it hadn't been for Sam's shield-field, they undoubtedly would have succeeded. Oh well, Carpenter thought, logic was a two-edged blade, you too could wield it as well as one. "How soon will your buddies be back, Holmer?"

The Martian regarded him blankly. Carpenter tumbled to the fact that the man wasn't wearing hearrings then.

He said to Marcy: "Tell me, pumpkin, if this ship were to fall on its side, would either the change in its position or its impact with the ground be liable to set off an explosion? Answer me with a 'yes' or a 'no' so that our friend here won't know what we're talking about."

"No, Mr. Carpenter."

"And is the structure of the ship sturdy enough to prevent the bulkheads from caving in on us?"

"Yes, Mr. Carpenter."

"How about the equipment in this room. Is it bolted down securely enough to prevent its being torn loose?"

"Yes, Mr. Carpenter."

"Good. Now, as surreptitiously as you can, you and Skip

start sidling over to that steel supporting pillar in the center of the deck. When the ship starts to topple, you hold on for dear life."

"What's he saying to you kid?" Holmer demanded.

Marcy stuck her tongue out at him. "Wouldn't you like to know!" she retorted.

Obviously, the ability to make calm, cool decisions strictly in keeping with pure logic did not demand a concomitant ability to think fast, for it was not until that moment that the desentimentalized Martian realized that he alone of the four persons present was not wearing hearrings.

Reaching into the small pouch that hung at his side, he withdrew a pair. Then, keeping his melter directed at Carpenter's forehead with one hand, he began attaching them to his ears with the other. Meanwhile, Carpenter ran his right thumb over the tiny, graduated nodules of the liaison-ring on his right index finger, and when he found the ones he wanted, he pressed them in their proper sequence. On the plain below, Sam stuck his snout out of the palmetto coppice.

Carpenter concentrated, his thoughts riding the tele-circuit that now connected his mind with Sam's sacral ganglion: *Retract your horn-howitzers and raise your nacelle-shield, Sam.* Sam did so. *Now, back off, get a good run, charge the landing-jack on your right, and knock it out. Then get the hell out of the way!*

Sam came out of the coppice, turned and trotted a hundred yards out on the plain. There he turned again, aligning himself for the forthcoming encounter. He started out slowly, geared himself into second. The sound of his hoofbeats climbed into a thunderous crescendo and penetrated the bulkhead of the communications-room, and Holmer, who had finally gotten his hearrings into place, gave a start and stepped over to the viewport.

By this time Sam was streaking toward the ship like an ornithischian battering ram. No one with an IQ in excess of 75 could have failed to foresee what was shortly going to happen.

Holmer had an IQ considerably in excess of 75, but sometimes having a few brains is just as dangerous as having a little knowledge. It was so now. Forgetting Carpenter completely, the Martian threw a small lever to the right of the viewscope, causing the thick, unbreakable glass to retract into the bulkhead; then he leaned out through the resultant aperture and directed his melter toward the ground. Simultaneously, Sam made contact with the landing-jack, and Holmer went flying through the aperture like a jet-propelled Darius Green.

The two kids were already clinging to the supporting pillar. With a leap, Carpenter joined them. "Hang on, you two!" he shouted, and proceeded to practice what he preached. The downward journey was slow at first, but it rapidly picked up momentum. Somebody should have yelled, "TIMBER!" Nobody did, but that didn't dissuade the ginkgo from fulfilling its destiny. Lizards scampered, tortoises scrambled and sauropods gaped for miles around. KRRRRRRUUUUUUMMMP! The impact tore both Carpenter and the children from the pillar, but he managed to grab them and cushion their fall with his body. His back struck the bulkhead, and his breath blasted from his lungs. Somebody turned out the lights.

At length, somebody turned them back on again. He saw Marcy's face hovering like a small pale moon above his own. Her eyes were like autumn asters after the first frost.

She had loosened his collar and she was patting his cheeks and she was crying. He grinned up at her, got gingerly to his feet and looked around. The communications-room hadn't changed any, but it looked different. That was because he was standing on the bulkhead instead of on the deck. It was also because he was still dazed.

Marcy, tears running down her cheeks, wailed, "I was afraid you were dead, Mr. Carpenter!"

He rumpled her buttercup-colored hair. "Fooled you, didn't I?"

At this point, Skip entered the room through the now horizontal doorway, a small container clutched in his hand. His face lit up when he saw Carpenter. "I went after some recuperative gas, but I guess you don't need it after all. Gee, I'm glad you're all right, Mr. Carpenter!"

"I take it you kids are, too," Carpenter said.

He was relieved when both of them said they were. Still somewhat dazed, he clambered up the concave bulkhead to the viewport and looked out. Sam was nowhere to be seen. Remembering that he was still in tele-circuit contact, he ordered the triceratank to home in, after which he climbed through the viewport, lowered himself to the ground and began looking for Holmer's body. When he failed to find it he thought at first that the man had survived the fall and had made off into the surrounding scenery.

Then he came to one of the bogs with which the area was infested, and saw its roiled surface. He shuddered. Well, anyway, he knew who the fossil was.

Or rather, who the fossil had been.

Sam came trotting up, circumventing the bog in response to the terrainometer's stimuli. Carpenter patted the reptivehicle's head, which was not in the least damaged from its recent collision with the landing-jack; then he broke off liaison and returned to the ship. Marcy and Skip were standing in the viewport, staring at the sky. Turning, Carpenter stared at the sky, too. There were three specks in it.

His mind cleared completely then, and he lifted the two children down to the ground. "Run for Sam!" he said. "Hurry!"

He set out after them. They easily outmatched his longer but far-slower strides, gaining the reptivehicle and clambering into the driver's compartment before he had covered half the distance. The pteranodons were close now, and he could see their shadows rushing toward him across the ground. Unfortunately, however, he failed to see the small tortoise that was trying frantically to get out of his way. He tripped over it and went sprawling on his face.

Glancing up, he saw that Marcy and Skip had closed Sam's nacelle. A moment later, to his consternation the triceratank disappeared.

Suddenly another shadow crept across the land, a shadow so vast that it swallowed those cast by the pteranodons.

Turning on his side, Carpenter saw the ship. It was settling down on the plain like an extraterrestrial Empire State Building, and, as he watched, three rainbow-beams of light shot forth from its upper section and the three pteranodons went PFFFFFFTTT! PFFFFFFTT! PFFFFFFTTT! and were no more.

The Empire State Building came solidly to rest, opened its street doors and extended a gangplank the width of a Fifth Avenue sidewalk. Through the doors and down the sidewalk came the cavalry. Looking in the other direction, Carpenter saw that Sam had reappeared in exactly the same spot from which he had vanished. His nacelle had reopened, and Marcy and Skip were climbing out of the driver's compartment in the midst of a cloud of bluish smoke. Carpenter understood what had happened then, and he kissed the twenty-second century good-bye.

The two kids came running up just as the commander of the cavalry stepped to the forefront of his troops. Actually, the troops were six tall Martians wearing deep-purple togas and stern expressions and carrying melters, while the commander was an even taller Martian wearing an even purpler toga and an even sterner expression and carrying what looked like a fairy godmother's wand. The dirty look which he accorded Carpenter was duplicated a moment later by the dirty look which he accorded the two children.

They were helping Carpenter to his feet. Not that he needed help in a physical sense. It was just that he was so overwhelmed by the rapid turn of events that he couldn't quite get his bearings back. Marcy was sobbing.

"We didn't want to burn Sam out, Mr. Carpenter," she said, all in a rush, "but jumping back four days, two hours, sixteen minutes and three and three-quarter seconds and sneaking on board the kidnapper's ship and sending a message to space Police Headquarters was the only way we could get them here in time to save your life. I told them what a pickle you'd be in, and to have their iridescers ready. Then, just as we were about to come back to the present Sam's time-travel unit broke down and Skip had to fix it, and then Sam went and burned out anyway, and oh, Mr. Carpenter, I'm so sorry! Now, you'll never be able to go back to the year 79,062,156 again and see Miss Sands, and—"

Carpenter patted her on the shoulder. "It's all right, pumpkin. It's all right. You did the right thing, and I'm proud of you for it." He shook his head in admiration. "You sure computed it to a T, didn't you?"

A smile broke through the rain of tears, and the rain went away. "I'm—I'm pretty good at computations, Mr. Carpenter."

"But *I* threw the switch," Skip said. "And *I* fixed Sam's time-travel unit when it broke down."

Carpenter grinned. "I know you did, Skip. I think the two of you are just wonderful." He faced the tall Martian with the fairy-godmother wand, noted that the man already had a pair of hearrings attached to his ears. "I guess I'm almost as beholden to you as I am to Marcy and Skip," Carpenter said, "and I'm duly grateful. And now I'm afraid I'm going to impose on your good will still further and ask you to take me to Mars with you. My reptivehicle's burned out and can't possibly be repaired by anyone except a group of technological specialists working in an ultramodern machine shop with all the trimmings, which means I have no way either of contacting the era from which I came, or of getting back to it."

"My name is Hautor," the tall Martian said. He turned to Marcy. "Recount to me with the maximum degree of conciseness of which you are capable, the events beginning with your arrival on this planet and leading up to the present moment."

Marcy did so. "So you see, sir," she concluded, "in helping Skip and me, Mr. Carpenter has got himself in quite a pickle. He can't return to his own era, and he can't survive in this one. We simply have to take him back to Mars with us, and that's all there is to it!"

Hautor made no comment. Almost casually, he raised his fairy-godmother wand, pointed it toward the kidnappers' prostrate ship and did something to the handle that caused the wand proper to glow in brilliant greens and blues. Presently a rainbow beam of light flashed forth from the Empire State Building, struck the kidnappers' ship and relegated it to the same fate as that suffered by the three pteranodons. Turning, Hautor faced two of his men.

"Put the children on board the police cruiser and see to it that they are suitably cared for." Finally, he turned back to Carpenter. "The government of Greater Mars is grateful for the services you have rendered it in the preserving of the lives of two of its most valuable citizens-to-be. I thank you in its behalf. And now, Mr. Carpenter, good-bye."

Hautor started to turn away. Instantly Marcy and Skip ran to his side. "You can't leave him here!" Marcy cried. "He'll die!"

Hautor signaled to the two Martians whom he had spoken

to a moment ago. They leaped forward, seized the two children and began dragging them toward the Empire State Building. "Look," Carpenter said, somewhat staggered by the new turn of events, but still on his feet, "I'm not begging for my life, but I can do you people some good if you'll make room for me in your society. I can give you time travel, for one thing. For another—"

"Mr. Carpenter, if we had wanted time travel, we would have devised it long ago. Time travel is the pursuit of fools. The pattern of the past is set, and cannot be changed; and in it, that has not already been done. Why try? And as for the future, who but an imbecile would want to know what tomorrow will bring?"

"All right," Carpenter said. "I won't invent time travel then, I'll keep my mouth shut and settle down and be a good solid citizen."

"You wouldn't and you know it, Mr. Carpenter—unless we desentimentalized you, And I can tell from the expression on your face that you would never voluntarily submit to such a solution. You would rather remain here in your prehistoric past and die."

"Now that you mentioned it, I would at that," Carpenter said. "Compared to you people, *Tyrannosaurus rex* is a Salvation Army worker, and all the other dinosaurs, saurischians and ornithischians alike, have hearts of purest gold. But it seems to me that there is one simple thing which you could do in my behalf without severely affecting your desentimentalized equilibrium. You could give me a weapon to replace the one that Holmer disintegrated."

Hautor shook his head. "That is one thing I cannot do, Mr. Carpenter, because a weapon could conceivably become a fossil, and thereby make me responsible for an anachronism. I am already potentially responsible for one in the form of Holmer's irretrievable body, and I refuse to risk being responsible for any more. Why do you think I iridesced the kidnappers' ship?"

"Mr. Carpenter," Skip called from the gangplank, up which two Martians were dragging him and his sister, "maybe Sam's not completely burned out. Maybe you can rev up enough juice to at least send back a can of chicken soup."

"I'm afraid not, Skip," Carpenter called back. "But it's all right, you kids," he went on. "Don't you worry about me—I'll get along okay. Animals have always liked me, so why shouldn't reptiles! They're animals, too."

"Oh, Mr. Carpenter!" Marcy cried. "I'm so sorry this happened! Why didn't you take us back to 79,062,156 with you. We wanted you to all along, but we were afraid to say so."

"I wish I had, pumpkin—I wish I had." Suddenly, he couldn't see very well, and he turned away. When he looked back, the two Martians were dragging Marcy and Skip through the locks. He waved. "Good-bye, you kids," he called. "I'll never forget you."

Marcy made a last desperate effort to free herself. She almost, but not quite, succeeded. The autumn asters of her eyes were twinkling with tears like morning dew. "I love you, Mr. Carpenter!" she cried, just before she and Skip were dragged out of sight. "I'll love you for the rest of my life!"

With two deft movements, Hautor flicked the hearrings from Carpenter's ears; then he and the rest of the cavalry climbed the gangplank and entered the ship. Some cavalry! Carpenter thought. He watched the street doors close, saw the Empire State Building quiver.

Presently it lifted and hovered majestically, stabbed into the sky just above the ground on a wash of blinding light. It rose, effortlessly, and became a star. It wasn't a falling star, but he wished upon it anyway. "I wish both of you happiness," he said, "and I wish that they never take your hearts away, because your hearts are one of the nicest things about you."

The star faded then, and winked out. He stood all alone on the vast plain.

The ground trembled. Turning, he caught a great dark movement to the right of a trio of fan palms. A moment later, he made out the huge head and the massive, upright body. He recoiled as two rows of saberlike teeth glittered in the sun.

Tyrannosaurus!

V

A burned-out reptivehicle was better than no reptivehicle at all. Carpenter made tracks for Sam.

In the driver's compartment, with the nacelle tightly closed, he watched the theropod's approach. There was no question but what it had seen him, and no question but what it was headed straight for Sam. Marcy and Skip had retracted the nacelle-shield, which left Carpenter pretty much of a sitting duck; however, he didn't retreat to Sam's cabin just yet, for they had also re-projected the horn-howitzers.

Although the howitzers were no longer maneuverable, they were still operable. If the *Tyrannosaurus* came within their fixed range it could be put temporarily out of action with a volley of stun-charges. Right now, it was approaching Sam at right angles to the direction in which the howitzers were pointing, but there was a chance that it might pass in front of them before closing in. Carpenter considered it a chance worth taking.

He crouched low in the driver's seat, his right hand within easy reaching distance of the trio of triggers. With the air-conditioning unit no longer functioning, the interior of the triceratank was hot and stuffy. To add to his discomfort, the air was permeated with the acrid smell of burned wiring. He shut his mind to both annoyances, and concentrated on the task at hand.

The theropod was so close now that he could see its atrophied forelegs. They dangled down from the neck-width shoulders like the wizened legs of a creature one tenth its size. Over them, a full twenty-five feet above the ground and attached to a neck the girth of a tree trunk, loomed the huge head; below them, the grotesque torso swelled out and down to the hind legs. The mighty tail dragged over the landscape, adding the cracking and splitting noises of crushed shrubbery to the thunder thrown forth each time the enormous bird-claw feet came into contact with the terrain. Carpenter should have been terrified. He was at a loss to understand why he wasn't.

Several yards from the triceratank, the *Tyrannosaurus*

came to a halt and its partially opened jaws began opening wider.

The foot-and-a-half-high teeth with which they were equipped could grind through Sam's nacelle as though it was made of tissue paper, and from all indications, that was just what they were going to do. Carpenter prepared himself for a hasty retreat into Sam's cabin; then just when things looked blackest, the theropod, as though dissatisfied with its present angle of attack, moved around in front of the reptivehicle, providing him with the opportunity he had been hoping for. His fingers leaped to the first of the trio of triggers, touched, but did not squeeze it. Why wasn't he afraid?

He looked up through the nacelle at the horrendous head. The huge jaws had continued to part, and now the whole top of the skull was raising into a vertical position. As he stared, a pretty head of quite another nature appeared over the lower row of teeth and two bright blue eyes peered down at him.

"Miss Sands!" he gasped, and nearly fell out of the driver's seat.

Recovering himself, he threw open the nacelle, stepped out on Sam's snout and gave the tyrannosaurus an affectionate pat on the stomach. "Edith," he said. "Edith, you doll, you!"

"Are you all right, Mr. Carpenter?" Miss Sands called down.

"Just fine," Carpenter said. "Am I glad to see *you*, Miss Sands!"

Another head appeared beside Miss Sands. The familiar chestnut-haired head of Peter Detritus. "Are you glad to see me too, Mr. Carpenter?"

"Well, I guess, Pete old buddy!"

Miss Sands lowered Edith's lip ladder, and the two of them climbed down. Peter Detritus was carrying a tow cable, and presently he proceeded to affix it to Sam's snout and Edith's tail respectively. Carpenter lent a hand. "How'd you know I was in a pickle?" he asked. "I didn't send back any soup."

"We had a hunch," Peter Detritus said. He turned to Miss Sands. "There, she's all set, Sandy."

"Well, let's be on our way then," Miss Sands said. She looked at Carpenter, then looked quickly away, "If, of course, your mission is completed, Mr. Carpenter."

Now that the excitement was over he was finding her

presence just as disconcerting as he usually found it. "It's completed all right, Miss Sands," he said to the left pocket of her field blouse. "You'll never believe how it turned out, either."

"Oh, I wouldn't say that. Sometimes the most unbelievable things of all turn out to be the most believable ones. I'll fix you something to eat, Mr. Carpenter."

She climbed agilely up the ladder. Carpenter followed, and Peter Detritus brought up the rear. "I'll take the controls, Mr. Carpenter," the latter said, pulling in the ladder. "You look bushed."

"I am," Carpenter said.

In Edith's cabin, he collapsed on the bunk. Miss Sands went over to the kitchenette and put water on to boil for coffee and took a boiled ham down from the refrigerator shelf. Up in the driver's compartment, Peter Detritus closed the nacelle and threw Edith into gear.

He was a good driver, Peter Detritus was, and he would rather drive than eat. Not only that, he could take a paleontologivehicle apart and put it back together again blindfolded. Funny, why he and Miss Sands had never gone for each other. They were both so attractive, you'd have thought they would have fallen in love long ago. Carpenter was glad that they hadn't of course—not that it was ever going to do him any good.

He wondered why they had made no mention of the Space Police ship. Surely, they must have seen it when it blasted off . . .

Edith was moving over the plain in the direction of the uplands now, and through the cabin viewport he could see Sam shambling along behind on motion-provoked legs. In the kitchenette, Miss Sands was slicing ham. Carpenter concentrated on her, trying to drive away the sadness he felt over his parting with Marcy and Skip. His eyes touched her slender shapely legs, her slender waist, rose to her cupreous head, lingering for a moment on the silken fuzz that grew charmingly on the back of her neck where her hair had been cut too short. Strange, how people's hair got darker when they grew older—

Carpenter lay motionlessly on the bunk. "Miss Sands," he said suddenly, "how much is 499,999,991 times 8,003,432,111?"

"4,001,715,983,469,111,001," Miss Sands answered.

Abruptly she gave a start. Then she went on slicing ham.

Slowly, Carpenter sat up. He lowered his feet to the floor. A tightness took over in his chest and he could barely breathe.

Take a pair of lonely kids. One of them a mathematical genius, the other a mechanical genius. A pair of lonely kids who have never known what it is like to be loved in all their lonely lives. Now, transport them to another planet and put them in a reptivehicle that for all its practicality is still a huge and delightful toy, and treat them to an impromptu Cretaceous camping trip, and show them the first affection they have ever known. Finally, take these things away from them and simultaneously provide them with a supreme motivation for getting them back—the need to save a human life—and include in that motivation the inbuilt possibility that by saving that life they can—in another but no less real sense—save their own.

But 79,062,156 years! 49,000,000 miles! It *couldn't* be!

Why couldn't it?

They could have built the machine in secret at the preparatory school, all the while pretending to go along with the "pre-desentimentalization process"; then, just before they were scheduled to begin receiving doses of the desentimentalization drug, they could have entered the machine and time-jumped far into the future.

Granted, such a time-jump would have required a vast amount of power. And granted, the Martian landscape they would have emerged on would have given them the shock of their lives. But they were resourceful kids, easily resourceful enough to have tapped the nearest major power source, and certainly resourceful enough to have endured the climate and the atmosphere of Mars Present until they located one of the Martian oxygen caves. The Martians would have taken care of them and have taught them all they needed to know to pass themselves off as terrestrials in one of the domed colonies. As for the colonists, they wouldn't have asked too many questions because they would have been overjoyed to add two newcomers to their underpopulated community. After that, it would merely have been a matter of the two children's biding their time till they grew old enough to work and earn their passage to Earth. Once on earth, it would merely have been a matter of acquiring the necessary education to equip them for paleontological work.

Sure, it would have taken them years to accomplish such a mission, but they would have anticipated that, and have time-jumped to a point in time far enough in advance of the year A.D. 2156 to have enabled them to do what they had to do. They had played it pretty close at that, though. Miss Sands had only been with NAPS for three months, and as for Peter Detritus, he had been hired a month later. On Miss Sands's recommendation, of course.

They had simply come the long way around—that was all. Traveled 49,000,000 miles to Mars Past, 79,062,156 years to Mars Present, 49,000,000 miles to Earth Present, and 79,062,156 years to Earth Past.

Carpenter sat there, stunned.

Had they known they were going to turn out to be Miss Sands and Peter Detritus? he wondered. They must have— or, if not, they must have gambled on it and taken the names when they joined the colonists. All of which created something of a paradox. But it was a minor one at best, not worth worrying about. In any event, the names certainly fitted them.

But why had they passed themselves off as strangers?

Well, they had been strangers, hadn't they? And if they had told him the truth, would he have believed them?

Of course he wouldn't have.

None of which explained why Miss Sands disliked him.

But *did* she dislike him? Maybe her reaction to him resulted from the same cause that was responsible for his reaction to her. Maybe *she* worshiped *him* as much as he worshiped her, and became as tongue-tied in his presence as he did in hers. Maybe the reason she had never looked at him any longer than was absolutely necessary was that she had been afraid of betraying the way she felt before he learned the truth about her.

He found it suddenly hard to see.

The smooth purring of Edith's battery-powered motor filled the cabin. For quite some time now there had been no other sound.

"What's the matter?" Miss Sands said suddenly out of clear blue sky. "Cat got your tongue, Mr. Carpenter?"

He stood up then. She had turned, and was facing him. Her eyes were misted, and she was looking at him gently, adoringly . . . the way she had looked at him last night, in one sense and 79,062,156 years ago in another, by a Mesozoic campfire in an upper Cretaceous cave. *Why I'll bet if you told her you loved her, she'd throw herself into your arms!*

"I love you, pumpkin," Carpenter said.

And Miss Sands did.

POOR LITTLE WARRIOR!

Brian Aldiss

Promoting dinosaur hunts is one possible way time-travel companies may support themselves. But in this bitter little tale of the late Jurassic, Brian Aldiss suggests that the actual experience may be far from the romantic ideal. His hunter, Claude Ford, appears to be disgusted by the personal habits of the brontosaur, as well as those of the primitive birds that forage through its spoor and the crawling mass of lobsterlike parasites that cover its body.* Actually, however, he is lucky to encounter flowering plants, which most experts believe did not develop in the lowlands until the lower Cretaceous, and to avoid the swarms of insects, which were prevalent at that time.

Claude Ford knew exactly how it was to hunt a brontosaurus.* You crawled heedlessly through the mud among the willows, through the little primitive flowers with petals as green and brown as a football field, through the beauty-lotion mud. You peered out at the creature sprawling among the reeds, its body as graceful as a sock full of sand. There it lay, letting the gravity cuddle it nappy-damp to the marsh, running its big rabbit-hole nostrils a foot above the grass in a sweeping semicircle, in a snoring search for more sausagy reeds. It was beautiful: here horror had reached its limits, come full circle and finally disappeared up its own sphincter. Its eyes gleamed with the liveliness of a week-dead corpse's big toe, and its compost breath and the fur in its crude aural

---

*Eds. note: Here, brontosaur is being used, as it sometimes is, for the technical terms of sauropod or saurischian rather than for the particular type of sauropod now known as *Apatosaurus*.

cavities were particularly to be recommended to anyone who might otherwise have felt inclined to speak lovingly of the work of Mother Nature.

But as you, little mammal with opposed digit and .65 selfloading, semiautomatic, dual-barrelled, digitally computed, telescopically sighted, rustless, high-powered rifle gripped in your otherwise-defenseless paws, slide along under the bygone willows, what primarily attracts you is the thunder lizard's hide. It gives off a smell as deeply resonant as the bass note of a piano. It makes the elephant's epidermis look like a sheet of crinkled lavatory paper. It is gray as the Viking seas, daft-deep as cathedral foundations. What contact possible to bone could allay the fever of that flesh? Over it scamper—you can see them from here!—the little brown lice that live in those gray walls and canyons, gay as ghosts, cruel as crabs. If one of them jumped on you, it would very likely break your back. And when one of those parasites stops to cock its leg against one of the bronto's vertebrae, you can see it carries in its turn its own crop of easy-livers, each as big as a lobster, for you're near now, oh, so near that you can hear the monster's primitive heart-organ knocking, as the ventricle keeps miraculous time with the auricle.

Time for listening to the oracle is past: you're beyond the stage for omens, you're now headed in for the kill, yours or his; superstition has had its little day for today, from now on only this windy nerve of yours, this shaky conglomeration of muscle entangled untraceably beneath the sweat-shiny carapace of skin, this bloody little urge to slay the dragon, is going to answer all your orisons.

You could shoot now. Just wait till that tiny steam-shovel head pauses once again to gulp down a quarry-load of bulrushes, and with one inexpressibly vulgar bang you can show the whole indifferent Jurassic world that it's standing looking down the business end of evolution's sex-shooter. You know why you pause, even as you pretend not to know why you pause; that old worm conscience, long as a baseball pitch, longlived as a tortoise, is at work; through every sense it slides, more monstrous than the serpent. Through the passions: saying here is a sitting duck, O Englishman! Through the intelligence: whispering that boredom, the kite-hawk who never feeds, will settle again when the task is done. Through the nerves: sneering that when the adrenalin currents cease to flow the vomiting begins. Through the maestro behind the retina: plausibly forcing the beauty of the view upon you.

Spare us that poor old slipper-slopper of a word, *beauty;* holy mom, is this a travelogue, nor are we out of it? "*Perched now on this titanic creature's back, we see a round dozen—and, folks, let me stress that round—of gaudily plumaged birds, exhibiting between them all the colour you might expect to find on lovely, fabled Copacabana Beach. They're so round because they feed from the droppings that fall from the rich man's table. Watch this lovely shot now! See the bronto's tail lift. . . . Oh, lovely, yep, a couple of hayricks-full at least emerging from his nether end. That sure was a beauty, folks, delivered straight from consumer to consumer. The birds are fighting over it now. Hey, you, there's enough to go round, and anyhow, you're round enough already . . . And nothing to do now but hop back up onto the old rump steak and wait for the next round. And now as the sun sinks in the Jurassic West, we say 'Fare well on that diet' . . .*"

No, you're procrastinating, and that's a life work. Shoot the beast and put it out of your agony. Taking your courage in your hands, you raise it to shoulder level and squint down its sights. There is a terrible report; you are half stunned. Shakily, you look about you. The monster still munches, relieved to have broken enough wind to unbecalm the Ancient Mariner.

Angered (or is it some subtler emotion?), you now burst from the bushes and confront it, and this exposed condition is typical of the straits into which your consideration for yourself and others continually pitches you. Consideration? Or again something subtler? Why should you be confused just because you come from a confused civilization? But that's a point to deal with later, if there is a later, as these two hog-wallow eyes pupiling you all over from spitting distance tend to dispute. Let it not be by jaws alone, O monster, but also by huge hooves and, if convenient to yourself, by mountainous rollings upon me! Let death be a saga, sagacious, Beowulfate.

Quarter of a mile distant is the sound of a dozen hippos springing boisterously in gymslips from the ancestral mud, and next second a walloping great tail as long as Sunday and as thick as Saturday night comes slicing over your head. You duck as duck you must, but the beast missed you anyway because it so happens that its coordination is no better than yours would be if you had to wave the Woolworth Building at a tarsier. This done, it seems to feel it has done its duty by itself. It forgets you. You just wish you could forget yourself as easily; that was, after all, the reason you had to come the long way here. *Get Away from It All,* said the time travel brochure, which meant for you getting away from Claude Ford, a husbandman as futile as his name with a terrible wife called Maude. Maude and Claude Ford. Who could not adjust to themselves, to each other, or to the world they were born in. It was the best reason in the as-it-is-at-present-constituted world for coming back here to shoot giant saurians—if you were fool enough to think that one hundred and fifty million years either way made an ounce of difference to the muddle of thoughts in a man's cerebral vortex.

You try and stop your silly, slobbering thoughts, but they have never really stopped since the coca-collaborating days of your growing up; God, if adolescence did not exist it would be unnecessary to invent it! Slightly, it steadies you to look again on the enormous bulk of this tyrant vegetarian into whose presence you charged with such a mixed death-life wish, charged with all the emotion the human orga(ni)sm is capable of. This time the bogeyman is real, Claude, just as you wanted it to be, and this time you really have to face up to it before it turns and faces you again. And so again you lift Ole Equalizer, waiting till you can spot the vulnerable spot.

The bright birds sway, the lice scamper like dogs, the marsh groans, as bronto sways over and sends his little cranium snaking down under the bile-bright water in a forage for roughage. You watch this; you have never been so jittery before in all your jittered life, and you are counting on this catharsis wringing the last drop of acid fear out of your system forever. OK, you keep saying to yourself insanely over and over, your milliondollar twenty-second-century education going for nothing, OK, OK. And as you say it for the umpteenth time, the crazy head comes back out of the water like a renegade express and gazes in your direction.

Grazes in your direction. For as the champing jaw with its big blunt molars like concrete posts works up and down, you see the swamp water course out over rimless lips, lipless rims, splashing your feet and sousing the ground. Reed and root, stalk and stem, leaf and loam, all are intermittently visible in that masticating maw and, struggling, straggling or tossed among them, minnows, tiny crustaceans, frogs—all destined in that awful, jaw-full movement to turn into bowel movement. And as the glump-glump-glumping takes place, above it the slime-resistant eyes again survey you.

These beasts live up to two hundred years, says the time travel brochure, and this beast has obviously tried to live up to that, for its gaze is centuries old, full of decades upon decades of wallowing in its heavyweight thoughtlessness until it has grown wise on twitterpatedness. For you it is like looking into a disturbing misty pool; it gives you a psychic shock, you fire off both barrels at your own reflection. Bang-bang, the dum-dums, big as paw-paws, go.

With no indecision, those century-old lights, dim and sacred, go out. These cloisters are closed till Judgment Day. Your reflection is torn and bloodied from them for ever. Over their ravaged panes nictitating membranes slide slowly upwards, like dirty sheets covering a cadaver. The jaw continues to munch slowly, as slowly the head sinks down. Slowly, a squeeze of cold reptile blood toothpastes down the wrinkled flank of one cheek. Everything is slow, a creepy Secondary Era slowness like the drip of water, and you know that if you had been in charge of creation you would have found some medium less heartbreaking than Time to stage it all in.

Never mind! Quaff down your beakers, lords, Claude Ford has slain a harmless creature. Long live Claude the Clawed!

You watch breathless as the head touches the ground, the long laugh of neck touches the ground, the jaws close for good. You watch and wait for something else to happen, but nothing ever does. Nothing ever would. You could stand here watching for an hundred and fifty million years, Lord Claude, and nothing would ever happen here again. Gradually your bronto's mighty carcass, picked loving clean by predators, would sink into the slime, carried by its own weight deeper; then the waters would rise, and old Conqueror Sea come in with the leisurely air of a cardsharp dealing the boys a bad hand. Silt and sediment would filter down over the mighty grave, a slow rain with centuries to rain in. Old bronto's bed might be raised up and then down again perhaps half a dozen times, gently enough not to disturb him, although by now the sedimentary rocks would be forming thick around him.

Finally, when he was wrapped in a tomb finer than any Indian rajah ever boasted, the powers of the Earth would raise him high on their shoulders until, sleeping still, bronto would lie in a brow of the Rockies high above the waters of the Pacific. But little any of that would count with you, Claude the Sword; once the midget maggot of life is dead in the creature's skull, the rest is no concern of yours.

You have no emotion now. You are just faintly put out. You expected dramatic thrashing of the ground, or bellowing; on the other hand, you are glad the thing did not appear to suffer. You are like all cruel men, sentimental; you are like all sentimental men, squeamish. You tuck the gun under your arm and walk round the dinosaur to view your victory.

You prowl past the ungainly hooves, round the septic white of the cliff of belly, beyond the glistening and how-thought-provoking cavern of the cloaca, finally posing beneath the switch-back sweep of tail-to-rump. Now your disappointment is as crisp and obvious as a visiting card: the giant is not half as big as you thought it was. It is not one half as large, for example, as the image of you and Maude is in your mind. Poor little warrior, science will never invent anything to assist the titanic death you want in the contraterrene caverns of your fee-fi-fo fumblingly fearful id!

Nothing is left to you now but to slink back to your time mobile with a belly full of anticlimax. See, the bright dung-consuming birds have already cottoned on to the true state of affairs; one by one, they gather up their hunched wings and fly disconsolately off across the swamp to other hosts. They know when a good thing turns bad, and do not wait for the vultures to drive them off; all hope abandon, ye who entrail here. You also turn away.

You turn, but you pause. Nothing is left but to go back, no, but 2181 A.D. is not just the home date; it is Maude. It is Claude. It is the whole awful, hopeless, endless business of trying to adjust to an overcomplex environment, of trying to turn yourself into a cog. Your escape from it into *the Grand Simplicities of the Jurassic,* to quote the brochure again, was only a partial escape, now over.

So you pause, and as you pause, something lands socko on your back, pitching you face forward into tasty mud. You struggle and scream as lobster claws tear at your neck and throat. You try to pick up the rifle but cannot, so in agony you roll over, and next second the crab-thing is greedying it on your chest. You wrench at its shell, but it giggles and pecks your fingers off. You forgot when you killed the bronto that its parasites would leave it, and that to a little shrimp like you they would be a deal more dangerous than their host.

You do your best, kicking for at least three minutes. By the end of that time there is a whole pack of the creatures on you. Already they are picking your carcass loving clean. You're going to like it up there on top of the Rockies; you won't feel a thing.

DAY OF THE HUNTERS

Isaac Asimov

Why did the dinosaurs disappear at the end of the Mesozoic Era? Was it a rapid temperature drop due to dust from a giant asteroid strike or volcanic activity, egg-sucking mammals, or perhaps something else? Many theories exist, but no one knows for certain. In the first of three stories to touch upon this theme, Isaac Asimov suggests that the reason may have been that dinosaurs were much more human than we supposed. And while his solution may seem farfetched, the supporting logic of selective fossilization (that is, not all things are equally likely to become fossils) is quite valid. Indeed, some flowering plants such as magnolia and breadfruit which appear as early Cretaceous fossils are believed to have developed during the Jurassic in upland environments from which no fossils have been preserved.

It began the same night it ended. It wasn't much. It just bothered me; it still bothers me.

You see, Joe Bloch, Ray Manning, and I were squatting around our favorite table in the corner bar with an evening on our hands and a mess of chatter to throw it away with. That's the beginning.

Joe Bloch started it by talking about the atomic bomb, and what he thought ought to be done with it, and how who would have thought it five years ago. And I said lots of guys thought it five years ago and wrote stories about it and it was going to be tough on them trying to keep ahead of the newspapers now. Which led to a general palaver on how lots of screwy things might come true and a lot of for-instances were thrown about.

Ray said he heard from somebody that some big-shot scientist had sent a block of lead back in time for about two seconds or two minutes or two thousandths of a second—he didn't know which. He said the scientist wasn't saying anything to anybody because he didn't think anyone would believe him.

So I asked, pretty sarcastic, how *he* came to know about it. —Ray may have lots of friends but I have the same lot and none of them know any big-shot scientists. But he said never mind how he heard, take it or leave it.

And then there wasn't anything to do but talk about time machines, and how supposing you went back and killed your own grandfather or why didn't somebody from the future come back and tell us who was going to win the next war, or if there was going to be a next war, or if there'd be anywhere on Earth you could live after it, regardless of who wins.

Ray thought just knowing the winner in the seventh race while the sixth was being run would be something.

But Joe decided different. He said, "The trouble with you guys is you got wars and races on the mind. Me, I got curiosity. Know what I'd do if I had a time machine?"

So right away we wanted to know, all ready to give him the old snicker whatever it was.

He said, "If I had one, I'd go back in time about a couple or five or fifty million years and find out what happened to the dinosaurs."

Which was too bad for Joe, because Ray and I both thought there was just about no sense to that at all. Ray said who cared about a lot of dinosaurs and I said the only thing they were good for was to make a mess of skeletons for guys who were dopey enough to wear out the floors in museums; and it was a good thing they did get out of the way to make room for human beings. Of course Joe said that with *some* human beings he knew, and he gives us a hard look, we should've stuck to dinosaurs, but we pay no attention to that.

"You dumb squirts can laugh and make like you know something, but that's because you don't ever have any imagination," he says. "Those dinosaurs were big stuff. Millions of all kinds—big as houses, and dumb as houses, too—all over the place. And then, all of a sudden, like that," and he snaps his fingers, "there aren't any anymore."

How come, we wanted to know.

But he was just finishing a beer and waving at Charlie for another with a coin to prove he wanted to pay for it and he just shrugged his shoulders. "I don't know. That's what I'd find out, though."

That's all. That would have finished it. I would've said something and Ray would've made a crack, and we all would've had another beer and maybe swapped some talk about the weather and the Brooklyn Dodgers and then said so long, and never think of dinosaurs again.

Only we didn't, and now I never have anything on my mind but dinosaurs, and I feel sick.

Because the rummy at the next table looks up and hollers, "Hey!"

We hadn't seen him. As a general rule, we don't go around looking at rummies we don't know in bars. I got plenty to do keeping track of the rummies I do know. This fellow had a bottle before him that was half empty, and a glass in his hand that was half full.

He said, "Hey," and we all looked at him, and Ray said, "Ask him what he wants, Joe."

Joe was nearest. He tipped his chair backward and said, "What do you want?"

The rummy said, "Did I hear you gentlemen mention dinosaurs?"

He was just a little weavy, and his eyes looked like they were bleeding, and you could only tell his shirt was once white by guessing, but it must've been the way he talked. It didn't *sound* rummy, if you know what I mean.

Anyway, Joe sort of eased up and said, "Sure. Something you want to know?"

He sort of smiled at us. It was a funny smile; it started at the mouth and ended just before it touched the eyes. He said, "Did you want to build a time machine and go back to find out what happened to the dinosaurs?"

I could see Joe was figuring that some kind of confidence game was coming up. I was figuring the same thing. Joe said, "Why? You aiming to offer to build one for me?"

The rummy showed a mess of teeth and said. "No, sir, I could but I won't. You know why? Because I built a time machine for myself a couple of years ago and went back to the Mesozoic Era and found out what happened to the dinosaurs."

Later on, I looked up how to spell "Mesozoic," which is why I got it right, in case you're wondering, and I found out that the Mesozoic Era is when all the dinosaurs were doing whatever dinosaurs do. But of course at the time this is just so much double-talk to me, and mostly I was thinking we had a lunatic talking to us. Joe claimed afterward that he knew about this Mesozoic thing, but he'll have to talk lots longer and louder before Ray and I believe him.

But that did it just the same. We said to the rummy to come over to our table. I guess I figured we could listen to him for a while and maybe get some of the bottle, and the others must have figured the same. But he held his bottle tight in his right hand when he sat down and that's where he kept it.

Ray said, "Where'd you build a time machine?"

"At Midwestern University. My daughter and I worked on it together."

He sounded like a college guy at that.

I said, "Where is it now? In your pocket?"

He didn't blink; he never jumped at us no matter how wise we cracked. Just kept talking to himself out loud, as if the whiskey had limbered up his tongue and he didn't care if we stayed or not.

He said, "I broke it up. Didn't want it. Had enough of it."

We didn't believe him. We didn't believe him worth a darn. You better get that straight. It stands to reason, because if a guy invented a time machine, he could clean up millions—he could clean up all the money in the world, just knowing what would happen to the stock market and the races and elections. He wouldn't throw all that away, I don't care what reasons he had. —Besides, none of us were going to believe in time travel anyway, because what if you *did* kill your own grandfather.

Well, never mind.

Joe said, "Yeah, you broke it up. Sure you did. What's your name?"

But he didn't answer that one, ever. We asked him a few more times, and then we ended up calling him "Professor."

He finished off his glass and filled it again very slow. He didn't offer us any, and we all sucked at our beers.

So I said, "Well, go ahead. What happened to the dinosaurs?"

But he didn't tell us right away. He stared right at the middle of the table and talked to it.

"I don't know how many times Carol sent me back—just a few minutes or hours—before I made the big jump. I didn't care about the dinosaurs; I just wanted to see how far the machine would take me on the supply of power I had available. I suppose it was dangerous, but is life so wonderful? The war was on then—one more life?"

He sort of coddled his glass as if he was thinking about things in general, then he seemed to skip a part in his mind and keep right on going.

"It was sunny," he said, "sunny and bright; dry and hard. There were no swamps, no ferns. None of the accoutrements of the Cretaceous we associate with dinosaurs,"—anyway, I think that's what he said. I didn't always catch the big words, so later on I'll just stick in what I can remember. I checked all the spellings, and I must say that for all the liquor he put away, he pronounced them without stutters.

That's maybe what bothered us. He sounded so familiar with everything, and it all just rolled off his tongue like nothing.

He went on, "It was a late age, certainly the Cretaceous. The dinosaurs were already on the way out—all except those little ones, with their metal belts and their guns."

I guess Joe practically dropped his nose into the beer altogether. He skidded halfway around the glass, when the professor let loose that statement sort of sadlike.

Joe sounded mad. "*What* little ones, with whose metal belts and which guns?"

The professor looked at him for just a second and then let his eyes slide back to nowhere. "They were little reptiles, standing four feet high. They stood on their hind legs with a thick tail behind, and they had little forearms with fingers. Around their waists were strapped wide metal belts, and from these hung guns. —And they weren't guns that shot pellets either; they were energy projectors."

"They were what?" I asked. "Say, when was this? Millions of years ago?"

"That's right," he said. "They were reptiles. They had scales and no eyelids and they probably laid eggs. But they used energy guns. There were five of them. They were on me as soon as I got out of the machine. There must have been millions of them all over Earth—millions. Scattered all over. They must have been the Lords of Creation then."

I guess it was then that Ray thought he had him, because he developed that wise look in his eyes that makes you feel like conking him with an empty beer mug, because a full one would waste beer. He said, "Look P'fessor, millions of them, huh? Aren't there guys who don't do anything but find old bones and mess around with them till they figure out what some dinosaur looked like? The museums are full of these here skeletons, aren't they? Well, where's there one with a metal belt on him. If there were millions, what's become of them? Where are the bones?"

The professor sighed. It was a real, sad sigh. Maybe he realized for the first time he was just speaking to three guys in overalls in a barroom. Or maybe he didn't care.

He said, "You don't find many fossils. Think how many animals lived on Earth altogether. Think how many billions and trillions. And then think how few fossils we find. —And these lizards were intelligent. Remember that. They're not going to get caught in snow drifts or mud, or fall into lava, except by big accident. Think how few fossil men there are—even of these subintelligent apemen of a million years ago."

He looked at his half-full glass and turned it round and round.

He said, "What would fossils show anyway? Metal belts rust away and leave nothing. Those little lizards were warm-blooded. I *know* that, but you couldn't prove it from petrified bones. What the devil? A million years from now could you tell what New York looks like from a human skeleton? Could you tell a human from a gorilla by the bones and figure out which one built an atomic bomb and which one ate bananas in a zoo?"

"Hey," said Joe, plenty objecting, "any simple bum can tell

a gorilla skeleton from a man's. A man's got a larger brain. Any fool can tell which one was intelligent."

"Really?" The professor laughed to himself, as if all this was so simple and obvious, it was just a crying shame to waste time on it. "You judge everything from the type of brain human beings have managed to develop. Evolution has different ways of doing things. Birds fly one way; bats fly another way. Life has plenty of tricks for everything. —How much of your brain do you think you use. About a fifth. That's what the psychologists say. As far as they know, as far as anybody knows, eighty percent of your brain has no use at all. Everybody just works on way-low gear, except maybe a few in history. Leonardo da Vinci, for instance. Archimedes, Aristotle, Gauss, Galois, Einstein—"

I never heard of any of them except Einstein, but I didn't let on. He mentioned a few more, but I've put in all I can remember. Then he said, "Those little reptiles had tiny brains, maybe quarter-size, maybe even less, but they used it all—every bit of it. Their bones might not show it, but they were intelligent; intelligent as humans. And they were boss of all Earth."

And then Joe came up with something that was really good. For a while I was sure that he had the professor and I was awfully glad he came out with it. He said, "Look, P'fessor, if those lizards were so damned hot, why didn't they leave something behind? Where are their cities and their buildings and all the sort of stuff we keep finding of the cavemen, stone knives and things. Hell, if human beings got the heck off of Earth, think of the stuff we'd leave behind us. You couldn't walk a mile without falling over a city. And roads and things."

But the professor just couldn't be stopped. He wasn't even shaken up. He just came right back with, "You're still judging other forms of life by human standards. We build cities and roads and airports and the rest that goes with us—but they didn't. They were built on a different plan. Their whole way of life was different from the ground up. They didn't live in cities. They didn't have our kind of art. I'm not sure what they did have because it was so alien I couldn't grasp it—except for their guns. Those would be the same. Funny, isn't it. —For all I know, maybe we stumble over their relics every day and don't even know that's what they are."

I was pretty sick of it by that time. You just *couldn't* get him. The cuter you'd be, the cuter he'd be.

I said, "Look here. How do you know so much about those things? What did you do; live with them? Or did they speak English? Or maybe you speak lizard talk. Give us a few words of lizard talk."

I guess I was getting mad, too. You know how it is. A guy tells you something you don't believe because it's all cock-eyed, and you can't get him to admit he's lying.

But the professor wasn't mad. He was just filling the glass again, very slowly. "No," he said, "I didn't talk and they didn't talk. They just looked at me with their cold, hard, staring eyes—snake's eyes—and I knew what they were thinking, and I could see that they knew what I was thinking. Don't ask me how it happened. It just did. Everything. I knew that they were out on a hunting expedition and I knew they weren't going to let me go."

And we stopped asking questions. We just looked at him, then Ray said, "What happened? How did you get away?"

"That was easy. An animal scurried past on the hilltop. It was long—maybe ten feet—and narrow and ran close to the ground. The lizards got excited. I could feel the excitement in waves. It was as if they forgot about me in a single hot flash of blood lust—and off they went. I got back in the machine, returned, and broke it up."

It was the flattest sort of ending you ever heard. Joe made a noise in his throat. "Well, what happened to the dinosaurs?"

"Oh, you don't see? I thought it was plain enough. —It was those little intelligent lizards that did it. They were hunters—by instinct and by choice. It was their hobby in life. It wasn't for food; it was for fun."

"And they just wiped out all the dinosaurs on the Earth?"

"All that lived at the time, anyway; all the contemporary species. Don't you think it's possible? How long did it take us to wipe out bison herds by the hundred million? What happened to the dodo in a few years? Supposing we really put our minds to it, how long would the lions and the tigers and the giraffes last? Why, by the time I saw those lizards there wasn't any big game left—no reptile more than fifteen feet maybe. All gone. Those little demons were chasing the little, scurrying ones, and probably crying their hearts out for the good old days."

And we all kept quiet and looked at our empty beer bottles and thought about it. All those dinosaurs—big as houses—killed by little lizards with guns. Killed for fun.

Then Joe leaned over and put his hand on the professor's shoulder, easylike, and shook it. He said, "Hey, P'fessor, but if that's so, what happened to the little lizards with the guns? Huh? —Did you ever go back to find out?"

The professor looked up with the kind of look in his eyes that he'd have if he were lost.

"You still don't see! It was already beginning to happen to them. I saw it in their eyes. They were running out of big game—the fun was going out of it. So what did you expect them to do? They turned to other game—the biggest and most dangerous of all—and really had fun. They hunted that game to the end."

"What game?" asked Ray. He didn't get it, but Joe and I did.

"Themselves," said the professor in a loud voice. "They finished off all the others and began on themselves—till not one was left."

And again we stopped and thought about those dinosaurs —big as houses—all finished off by little lizards with guns. Then we thought about the little lizards and how they had to keep the guns going even when there was nothing to use them on but themselves.

Joe said, "Poor dumb lizards."

"Yeah," said Ray, "poor crackpot lizards."

And then what happened really scared us. Because the professor jumped up with eyes that looked as if they were trying to climb right out of their sockets and leap at us. He shouted, "You damned fools. Why do you sit there slobbering over reptiles dead a hundred million years. That was the first intelligence on Earth and that's how it ended. That's *done*. But we're the second intelligence—and how the devil do you think *we're* going to end?"

He pushed the chair over and headed for the door. But then he stood there just before leaving altogether and said: *"Poor dumb humanity!* Go ahead and cry about that."

HERMES TO THE AGES

Frederick D. Gottfried

In this story, Frederick D. Gottfried examines four physical attributes (besides the brain) that man needed to become dominant—upright walking to free the forelimbs, "hands that could grasp and hold tools, depth perception to utilize those tools, and a voicebox for speech and communication." He concludes that besides primates, only one other evolutionary line possessed similar characteristics—the saurischian carnivorous dinosaurs. Of course, Tyrannosaurus, Deinonychus, Dromaeosaurus, and Stenonychosaurus are known, but were there other intelligent subspecies which are yet undiscovered? And if so, then why did they, as well as all the other dinosaurs, disappear? Or are there, indeed, some things which man is not meant to know?

"What you're suggesting, Professor's, absurd."

"How can you say that, Dr. Tereskevitch, after what your cosmonauts found on the moon?"

The Russian glowered at Professor Lars Hansen. At least it seemed that way to the professor's young associate, Eleanor Mercer. Tereskevitch was commander of *Gagaringrad*, the first permanent Soviet space station. Sue suspected that he wasn't used to having his work challenged in his domain. Certainly not by Americans.

"Your reputation preceded your flight up. You Americans have a rather unflattering term—cracked pot or crashed pot or something similar. I'm never quite sure with your imprecise English."

Now he was being deliberately rude. Lars, however, merely shrugged.

"Still your government did agree to let this particular crackpot look at your find."

"Why do you keep insisting that anything was brought back other than some unusual rocks?"

"Can I ask the crew members themselves? They're still all up here in isolation—along with whatever it was they dug up."

The look Tereskevitch shot Lars Hansen was as withering as some Ellie used to receive when she had the temerity to ask questions in her freshman classes—from nearly every professor but Lars.

The Russian turnabout was as baffling as it had been unexpected. Everything was supposed to have been arranged. But instead of being welcomed upon their arrival, Lars and Ellie were treated as intruders.

That seemed to confirm the suspicion that *Gagaringrad* was more military than scientific. But another reason the Soviets were reluctant to permit outsiders aboard their station soon suggested itself. *Gagaringrad*, for all its technical innovations, proved crude in many respects. True, they could stand normally thanks to centrifugal force, but they were surrounded by nuts-and-bolts boilerplate. And all the considerable Soviet accomplishment in Earth orbit could not wipe out the fact that they had been beaten to the moon by some twenty years.

"I didn't consent to your coming," growled Tereskevitch. "Why anyone down there thought we needed an *American* paleontologist is more than I can understand."

"Perhaps because my theory finds more credence among your people than my own," said Lars. "*Your* colleagues sent for us, Doctor. They want it confirmed—especially considering the alternative."

Good for you, Lars, thought Ellie.

Tereskevitch pursed his lips. "You would have it that our lunar expedition found a *body* on the moon?"

"Uh-huh. At least, that's what their transmissions indicated—until you clamped down security."

"And you further insist that this—this creature, or whatever you call it, is millions of years old?"

"I'm only guessing, but I have good reasons for believing so."

"Sheer fantasy! Millions of years! Do you seriously think,

Professor, there'd be even a trace of such a thing after so much time?"

"In the vacuum of space, yes—with all the body fluids evaporated, shielded from radiation, no decay, nothing to disturb its rest."

"But you'd have us believe that this creature is not extraterrestrial? That it's some sort of man?"

"No. Not if it dates back some 65 million years. This marks the transition from the Mesozoic to the Cenozoic era in Earth's geological history. In other words, from the age of reptiles to the age of mammals."

"Professor Hansen, if I understand you correctly—"

"You do. Although the creature your cosmonauts found on the moon may be humanoid in appearance, it is definitely not related to *Homo sapiens*. It's not even mammalian. It is an intelligent *dinosaur*."

Frowning, Tereskevitch turned to the two military men accompanying him and spoke rapidly in Russian. Both their visitors knew that this was not mere translation, particularly when one man obviously disagreed with what Tereskevitch was saying to him.

That was encouraging. Unanimous opinion usually meant rejection. They were used to that, along with a lot of forced politeness. Lars Hansen's scientific credentials were too impressive for rudeness—at least to his face. Besides, Lars was a huge bear of a man who filled the cramped quarters Tereskevitch had picked for their meeting. His patience for lesser mortals was quite incongruous to his commanding presence.

Ellie Mercer, by contrast, had neither his bearing nor patience. She was short and stout—a decided advantage for field work but not in most social situations—and she had little tolerance for fools.

"All this is merely academic," said Tereskevitch to his guests, "since intelligent dinosaurs are a scientific impossibility."

"About as impossible," Ellie put in, "as what you found on the moon?"

Instantly, she was sorry. She'd promised herself to stay out of the discussions. Not to get riled up this time or lash back at their critics. But the smugness of the man was just too much.

Glancing apologetically at Lars, she was surprised how tickled he was by what she'd said.

Tereskevitch decidedly was not. "I regret I wasn't informed in advance of your coming. My people mentioned only your shuttle flight. They should stick to their own business and let me do mine."

Lars grinned sheepishly. "Well, since we *are* here. . . ."

"But you come at a most inopportune time, Professor. We're in the midst of some, ah, delicate matters which require my immediate attention. So I'm afraid you're going to have to go back. At once."

"Dr. Tereskevitch—" Lars protested, rising to his full height—and promptly bumped his head against the upper bulkhead.

"Professor," said Tereskevitch. "Are you hurt?" There was genuine concern.

"No, no. It's nothing. *Nothing.* But surely you can't be serious? Leave now? When we just got here?"

The same Soviet official who disagreed with Tereskevitch before also objected. When Tereskevitch grew adamant, the other man became more insistant—and his Russian had the ring of authority to it.

"Well, Professor," said Tereskevitch, smiling without humor, "it seems that some of us would like to hear more about your, ah, rather amazing hypothesis—assuming that it won't take too long."

Visibly relieved, Lars said, "Perhaps if we had an opportunity to examine—"

"There's nothing for you to examine," declared Tereskevitch, "unless I say there is. Now, if you'll please proceed. My time here is extremely limited. Oh, and Professor, do try to restrain your enthusiasm. We'd like to keep these walls intact awhile longer."

Ellie bristled, but Lars didn't mind a bit. She knew that the only thing important to him was his—their—theory. All he had to do was present it and there would be immediate access to the *specimen.*

Ellie said nothing. But she thought she knew better.

For such occasions, Lars had two set speeches. The first, for the scientific community, was impressive in its technical detail. The second, for lay audiences, stressed the more sensational. As much as he professed distaste for such "pandering," it was this latter presentation that Lars found himself delivering far more often.

Ellie had no doubt which one he would give to their Russian hosts.

"Despite his name 'terrible lizard,' the dinosaur comprises a distinct branch of the reptilian family, unrelated to present-day lizards. It was during the 150-million-odd years of the Mesozoic that the dinosaur arose, flourished and then—very mysteriously—died out. Although other forms of reptiles then living—notably crocodiles and turtles—survive down to our own times, no member of the dinosaur branch lived beyond the end of the Mesozoic, approximately 65 million years ago.

"There simply is no adequate explanation for this mass extinction. Every theory so far proposed has its defects. But the most glaring is the assumption that the cause could only have been *natural*."

At this, even the seemingly disinterested Tereskevitch perked up.

"If you accept the fact that mammals have been the dominant life form on Earth for something less than 65 million years and evolved man in such a relatively short period, why couldn't a similar intelligent creature have emerged during the dinosaur age—a period at least twice as long?"

"A romantic notion," Tereskevitch interrupted, "except that the reptiles are lower on the evolutionary scale."

"Mammals are not so much a higher form of life," Lars replied, "as one more suitably adapted to an environment of rigorous temperature variations. Evolution, Doctor, is hardly a straight-line progression. During the Permian age more than 250 million years ago—a period of climatic extremes comparable to our own—a line of mammallike reptiles evolved with fatty layers under their skin and possibly even fur to keep themselves warm. Their line declined when the climate of the Mesozoic that followed warmed to one more compatible to conventional reptiles.

"And what splendid creatures evolved in the warm and even temperatures of the Mesozoic! The rich variety of specialization of the dinosaur rivals those of present-day mammals!"

Ellie knew what effort it took for the exuberant professor not to wave his arms wildly about in the narrow confines the way he did in class.

"Yes, yes, yes," growled Tereskevitch impatiently. "But still just brutes, for all of that. Nothing comparable to man."

Lars smiled. "Let me tell you something about revered *Homo sapiens*. He did not become what he is today by virtue of his brain alone. No, he required four additional physical attributes: walking upright to free the forelimbs for uses other than locomotion, hands that could grasp and hold tools, depth perception to utilize those tools, and a voicebox for speech and communication. Now this may surprise you, but in all evolution there's only one other class of creatures besides primates that possesses similar characteristics—the saurischian carnivorous dinosaur.

"Take one example I'm sure you're familiar with—the fearsome *Tyrannosaurus rex*. He walked upright. Had shortened forelimbs, very similar to the human arm, used to grasp and hold prey. His eye sockets were set more forward in his skull than to the side, giving him binocular vision. Of course, we don't know his internal physiology, since all we possess are fossilized skeletons. But he could have had some structure capable of emitting distinctive sounds. It needn't have been like our vocal cords. The modern parrot imitates the human voice quite neatly using the syrinx near the juncture of the trachea leading into its lungs."

"Professor, you have a knack for skipping over the most important points," said Tereskevitch. "You should have been a politician. But I would still like to know about the brain. If I remember rightly, all the dinosaurs were like the one with a brain no bigger than a walnut—the one with the plates on its back and the spiked tail. I forget its name—"

"*Stegosaurus*," supplied Lars. "Yes, I agree with you that there were many dinosaurs like that. But we're not talking about the plant-eaters—the sheep and cattle of their day. We must look instead to the carnivores—and not the hulking monsters like *Tyrannosaurus* that didn't need intelligence to survive. But dinosaurs, like mammals, came in all sizes. It's the smaller, more agile ones that prove the most promising."

"Such as what?"

"Such as *Deinonychus*, with a nervous system so sophisticated that it had the coordination to stand on one leg while attacking its prey with the other. And *Dromaeosaurus*, with its greatly enlarged braincase. And *Stenonychosaurus*, which had a large brain, binocular vision, and opposable fingers. The fossil record supports the existence of these. There are more recent finds"—Lars glanced knowingly at Ellie—"which are still being bitterly disputed.

"Don't forget that man developed from the smaller, more intelligent primates. Just as we are not descended from the bison, Dr. Tereskevitch, don't look to *Stegosaurus* and his ilk for proof that intelligence could not have existed contemporaneously."

"What proof do you offer that it did?" asked the Russian.

Ellie caught Lars' questioning glance. She shook her head. Not yet. Tereskevitch still doubted too much.

"It, uh, would be very surprising if I had any at all," Lars hedged. "Paleontology depends on fossils. On land, the process which creates them is extremely rare. So rare, in fact, that out of the millions of individual members of some species, we possess only a couple of complete skeletons. Less than one one-hundredth of the total species that lived in past eons—that's all we estimate that we know of."

Ellie's judgment was borne out by Tereskevitch's obvious incredulity.

"An example," said Lars, "out of my field, perhaps, but true nonetheless. All we know about certain types of ancient man comes from what, four or five specimens? That's because the number of individuals living at one time was always small. And the time span involved—only one to two million years compared to the tens of millions for most species of dinosaur —if there's any evolutionary parallel, the creature your cosmonauts found may not have existed long enough to leave a permanent geological record!"

"Interesting, your example of prehistoric man," said Tereskevitch, "only there's just one problem: today man numbers in the billions. Our presence at this stage would hardly go unnoticed by any curious future anthropologists."

"Maybe our intelligent dinosaurs were never very numerous. Remember how comparatively small human population was until recent centuries."

"What about their civilization itself? Their buildings, artifacts?"

"Gone. Vanished. All traces obliterated."

"That, I cannot accept."

"There are modern parallels. A hundred years ago, what did we know of Sumeria outside the Bible? Troy itself was just a legend. The Maya of Mexico—we knew nothing of abandoned cities *miles* long."

"But once discovered," said Tereskevitch, "there was a wealth of archeological finds."

"And much more that had been destroyed forever by the natural processes of nature. Doctor, we're not talking about hundreds or thousands of years. Nor just a million. Can you conceive of the result of *tens* of millions of years of erosion, decay, seas flooding dry land, mountains thrust up and worn down, the very continents torn apart and reshaped?"

"Surely something would remain," Tereskevitch said. "Tools of some kind—even if only like those found with primitive man?"

"Tools are barely distinguishable from the rocks in which they're found. It takes a trained eye to recognize them for what they are—something extremely unlikely if one has no reason to be looking for them."

There was a definite change in Tereskevitch. No longer was he openly skeptical. He was carefully considering everything Lars said.

"Even if I concede the possibility of such creatures—not to mention their entire civilization—escaping detection, one thing would not: their effect on the environment. Any civilization capable of putting one of its members on the moon—as you suggest—would require extensive use of coal or petroleum: Obviously, our present supplies have not been depleted by anyone other than ourselves."

Ellie might have pointed out that the era they were discussing was the source for today's oil. Coal, however, was formed in the Carboniferous, long before, so the point was probably well-taken.

But Lars didn't bother. "Why assume," he asked instead, "that they relied on fossil fuels, the way we've so foolishly done?"

"Now we're in *my* expertise, and I tell you that fire is essential to technology. Without it, man would still be living in caves."

"Ah, but what drove man into those caves in the first place? The Ice Age. Whatever else, fire became essential for survival against the cold. But there were no ice ages in the Mesozoic. With a warm and uniform climate, there wouldn't have been the overriding need for intelligent creatures to become dependent—fixated actually—upon fire."

"Maybe not in the primitive stages. But how could they possibly develop industry without fire to forge their metals?" Tereskevitch countered.

"I don't know," Lars admitted. "A substitute for the metals we know? A different source of power? You tell me. That's your field. Only I can't help wondering if you're letting your expertise blind you to different possibilities. Who says the way *we* did it is the only way? Cities, metals—all those things you find so essential—they've been around for only the last 5,000 years. Man became the master of Earth long before the rise of modern civilization. And there are cultures today—the Australian aborigines, for one—said to have societies more complex than our own, all without the trappings of so-called modern man. Could *that* be the model for our intelligent dinosaurs—rather than your country or mine?"

"Perhaps," said the Russian. "if we were talking about a body found in Australia. Maybe you can enlighten me, sir, on how an aborigine—without metals or other technological innovations—made it to the moon?"

"You mean, how could he do it the way we did it?"

"How else?"

"How else, indeed? Wouldn't it be wonderful to search for the answer here on Earth—rather than in some far-off and unknown solar system?"

Tereskevitch obviously agreed. "All this is very intriguing. A pity you have no evidence to support your theory."

"I never said that."

"What?"

"I've only tried to give you an idea how difficult it would be to find such evidence. Shall I go on, Doctor?"

Before Tereskevitch could say anything a loudspeaker blared out his name.

The Russian words were indecipherable, but there was no mistaking the urgent tone.

"Excuse, please, Professor," Tereskevitch said quietly. "A brief moment. We'll be back as soon as possible."

As soon as the three had shut the hatch they passed through, Lars cried out happily, "By God, we've got them hooked, Ellie!"

Ellie wasn't so sure. Interested, yes. But so far it had all been one-sided. They'd listened to what Lars told them but promised nothing in return.

Poor Lars. So trusting. Never could understand that poeple could be mean or jealous because that's the way they are. Or that envy could be just as important in the rejection of their theory as honest skepticism.

"You ought to be the one to tell them about *Herman*," said Lars.

"Oh, no, Lars. I—I shouldn't say anything more. I almost blew it for us before."

"Not really. You've got to understand Tereskevitch. He'd have reacted the same no matter what either of us said. I was warned about him: part of the team that orbited Gagarin. Worked as hard as anyone to beat us to the moon. Really believed they could have if the politicians and bureaucrats had stayed out of it. Still thinks they should have. But he's a scientist. A damned good one. That's the side of him we've got to interest."

Lars grinned wickedly. "Besides, if you hadn't asked him that, I would have."

Still Ellie hesitated.

"After all, you discovered him," Lars pointed out. "And I can't help feeling I've monopolized the conversation long enough."

Ellie recalled every detail on the sun-baked plains of western Australia five years before. That, the skeptics could never take from her—the magical moment of discovery.

She had been a mere undergraduate, chosen by her favorite professor to accompany his fossil-hunting expedition during summer vacation (winter, fortunately, in the searing climes of the outback). What she lacked in confidence, she more than made up for in hard work. That was what originally brought her to Lars' attention and what qualified her for the expedition. It was also what led to her discovery.

It had been Ellie who put in the extra few minutes digging at dusk that uncovered the precious bones.

The new find had been unclassified. Its skeleton lay in a fetal position, with the shortened forelegs drawn up to the skull. Compared to the typical dinosaur death pose of head arched back due to post-mortem tightening of the neck ligaments, this posture appeared extremely manlike.

Good-naturedly, Lars—then still "Professor Hansen"—suggested designating the new creature *Homosaurus mercer.*

Ellie preferred her own nickname for it: "Herman."

The more important discovery came the next morning. Ellie had awakened before dawn, long before any of the others, to be with *her* find. She had come a long way from a nondescript small town and the misery of being an unpopular and overweight girl in high school, who, to make matters worse, was smarter than any of her teachers. Now none of that mattered. How could anything human beings concerned themselves with compare to the 65 million years Herman had lain undisturbed?

As first light crept over the eastern hills, Ellie knelt in awe and pride before the partially exposed bones. Almost the entire left side of the specimen lay uncovered. As she watched, the shadows lifted in the morning sunlight from its small tail bones, then from the larger bones of the hips.

Frowning, Ellie looked more closely at one of the lower vertebrae. She bent over, whisking her tiny brush across the fossilized bone.

With a yelp, she leaped to her feet.

"Professor Hansen, Professor Hansen!"

Frantically, she raced back to camp.

Only the professor could confirm the impossible.

The Russians were all apologies when they returned. Perhaps Lars' intuition was correct. Ellie sensed renewed impatience, but it would have been much more difficult for them to be rude to her.

Any resentment she felt vanished as she described what it had been that so astonished the expedition, changing the course of Lars' and her lives. "The long rays of the morning sun made it stand out," she concluded. "An enormous swelling in the lower vertebrae. Even I—the greenest of all—could tell that the tiny lump that lodged there was not a bone fragment or anything similar. Most of it had broken off, but there was no mistaking what was still imbedded—the tip of a *spear* or *arrow*."

Ellie paused. Usually at this point came the denunciations. She was especially sensitive about this since she had been alone for some period of time with the specimen and the implication was clear. One so-called expert even went so far as to accuse her of fabricating the point and sticking it into Herman herself.

Instead, Tereskevitch thoughtfully chewed his lip. "What sort of collaborative evidence did you find?"

"None," she had to say, "at least not at this site."

"But once the notion took hold that there might have been intelligent creatures predating man," said Lars, "we began to accumulate from all over the world items no one has been able to explain. This, for instance."

From his pocket, Lars removed a vial containing what appeared to be a piece of blackened egg shell. "This dinosaur egg came from Mongolia. Your people were quite helpful in supplying information about it. Apparently, this sat on the shelf unrecognized for years. Certainly, we in the West had no idea of its existence. Look at the markings on the outer surface."

One by one each of the Soviet officials viewed the object carefully.

"You are looking at what may be the egg of one of *their* young."

Tereskevitch looked up sharply from his examination.

Lars said, "Our theoretical creatures, being reptilian, probably laid eggs rather than bear their young alive. This is no reason to believe they didn't lavish the same care and affection upon their children as we do. And I quite imagine that they would look upon an unprotected fetus carried for months in the womb with equal astonishment, if not outright disgust."

"These markings," Tereskevitch muttered, "could be natural."

"One straight line in nature," said Lars, "maybe even two could be explained. But six—interwoven to fit what could be a geometric pattern? If these eggs remained for any extended period unhatched, intelligent creatures might wish to designate and distinguish them. Perhaps what we're looking at represents the future child's name."

"You do have a tendency to humanize them, Professor. Forgive me if I say that I find this quite—quite disconcerting. Did you find any specimens of these creatures that had, ah, hatched?"

"No. And this leads to the most startling discovery of all."

Before Lars could go on, the third military man—the one who had not protested earlier when Tereskevitch wanted to end the discussion—whispered something to Tereskevitch. Irritated, Tereskevitch looked at his watch, then shook his head no.

"Forgive the interruption, Professor. Please continue."

"Generally reptile eggs are porous, permitting transfer of air from outside while retaining sufficient resilience to protect the developing individual inside. Detailed examination of the microstructure shows this particular eggshell lacks such properties. Whatever was inside could not have survived."

"So? A piece from a single egg?"

"Not just one egg," Ellie said. "Every single egg your people claim was found with this one was similarly affected."

"And all date from the same period," Lars added. "The late Cretaceous, the last period in the Mesozoic—the very end of the age of dinosaurs."

Tereskevitch frowned. "What are you trying to say?"

"There are certain things that could do this," Lars said. "Disease, for one. Some sort of chemical poison. Or radioactivity. Short, but intense. Such as in a major war."

"You—how do you say it?—jump to conclusions. Very unscientific, Professor."

"They had the ability to use weapons. That's the significance of Ellie's find. And we come back to the initial question: what single catastrophic event could have wiped out an entire line of creatures such as the dinosaurs? Do we ignore a possibility all too real in our own times?"

"Still you have no proof that these hypothetical creatures of yours possessed anywhere near a technology capable of such a thing."

"That's what I thought too," said Lars, "until your discovery on the moon. If the creature brought back turns out to be one of them, that would be such proof."

"How could you show any connection whatsoever?"

"If the skull has certain openings behind the eyes characteristic of the dinosaur branch of reptiles, we would know for sure."

Again the third Soviet officer touched Tereskevitch on the shoulder. This time Tereskevitch nodded his head.

The officer who had supported them before did nothing.

"What then, Professor?"

"We could tell the world."

"Why should we do that?" Tereskevitch's voice hardened.

"The knowledge it would bring—"

"There's no need to tell anyone at this time. *If* things were as you say, it could wait until confirmed by *our own* scientists."

Never had Ellie seen such dismay on Lars' face. "But this discovery belongs to all humanity."

"Assuming there was such a find," said Tereskevitch, "it would still be within the province of *Soviet* scientists to release it. Don't you agree?"

Ellie knew it. It always amounted to the same thing. What made Lars think it would have been any different with Tereskevitch?

"I see," said Lars, the defeat so heavy in his voice that Ellie wanted to cry in anger. "But—how soon will you make the announcement? That much at least you'll tell us?"

"It has not been decided," said Tereskevitch, "when, *if at all.*"

"What do you mean," exclaimed Lars, " 'if at all'? "

"I mean just that. How can there be an announcement if there is nothing to announce?"

"How can you say that? What have we been discussing all this time?"

"Your theory, Professor. And we've found it quite instructive. However, this interview now must end."

"Wait," Lars pleaded. "Let me prove it to you. Just a quick examination—"

"Examination of what? No body was found on the moon. If you must know, our cosmonauts did find some strange rocks. But, unfortunately, when they were brought on board and exposed to the air, *they crumbled into dust and are no more.*"

The Soviet scientist smiled patronizingly. "So you may go

back to Earth, secure in the knowledge that there's nothing for you—or any western scientist—to examine."

The shuttle orbiter backed off from *Gagaringrad*. Lars and Ellie sat in the two rear couches on the flight deck, still dressed in the pressure suits, minus helmets, required for the short EVA to and from the space station. It was much easier just to keep them on the short time it would take to return to Earth—particularly considering the effort it took to get the bulky professor into his in the first place.

They stared dejectedly at the slowly rotating dumbbell that seemed to shrink in the blackness as distance increased between them.

"I feel so—so used," said Ellie angrily. "We gave them everything. And then to tell us that they—they destroyed *him*—"

"Don't believe that for a moment," muttered Lars. "Someone else, maybe. Mistakes happen. Specimens get damaged or destroyed. But not Tereskevitch. He's too careful for that. No, he's got *Herman II* over there. Safe. But he intends to suppress any knowledge of his existence. That's what's so appalling."

It would be several minutes before they attained the point in orbit for firing their reentry rockets. Captain Bradley, command pilot of the orbiter, turned from his controls and asked, "'Herman II,' sir?"

Despite everything, Lars had to smile. "Just our name for the Russian find. 'Herman I' was the fossil in Australia—the one Ellie thinks was killed in some form of intertribal warfare."

"Oh, I know you think he was just some animal being hunted," she retorted. "A more primitive stage in their evolution. But why couldn't the intelligent ones have retained their tails? They didn't have to be *exactly* like exalted *Homo sapiens*."

Ellie thought she detected the familiar twinkle in Lars's eye. Often he'd bring up points like this, delighting in drawing out the not-so-scientific basis for her insistence. He wanted her to learn to laugh more at things that bothered her. Was he doing that now—for both of them?

"Mind telling me one thing?" Bradley asked. "Just exactly what was it you think killed off the dinosaurs?"

Ellie cringed. That part of their theory Lars wished had never been raised. Sensationalism at its worse. Probably more than anything else the cause of most of the ridicule they'd received. She'd have ignored the question, told the captain to just go back to his controls, get them back to Earth as fast as possible.

But then, when could Lars *ever* give up an opportunity to lecture?

"Had to be a biological war," Lars told Bradley.

"You seem so positive," Bradley said.

Bradley was everything Ellie expected a shuttle pilot to be: stalwart, self-assured, moderately intelligent. He could have been her high school quarterback. She hadn't cared much for him either.

"Process of elimination," said Lars, "*if* you assume intelligent beings had anything to do with it at all. Nuclear weapons? No, they'd have destroyed indiscriminately all forms of life. Yet we find a continuity among the plants and animals other than dinosaurs. Chemical agents? Possibly. Except that the devastation was planetwide, affecting reptilian life in the seas as well as on land. The effect must have been multigenerational. This implies the ability to reproduce. So we come down to some type of living agent—a highly selective but worldwide plague."

"You make them sound a lot like us," Bradley said.

"I suppose so. A natural tendency for people who look upon the past as alive. You ought to see the pets Ellie's made of some of our specimens."

"Lots better," said Ellie, "than some of the things alive today."

"There is one way I hope they were like us," Lars said. "I keep wondering what we'd do if we'd survived the initial outbreak. Try to leave some sort of record—something to warn of the tragedy that befell us for whatever the future might bring. And someday we'll come across that—whatever their Rosetta Stone might be."

Bradley shook his head. "You've got me again, Professor."

Patiently, Lars explained, "In 1799 a piece of black basalt was found near the mouth of the Nile which bore inscriptions in an ancient Greek and Egyptian. Before its discovery, no one could interpret the hieroglyphics of ancient Egypt. The

Rosetta Stone became literally the key to unlocking the secrets of a hitherto unknown world."

"And you think your intelligent dinosaurs left one of those?"

"I thought we had its equivalent over there." Lars gestured toward *Gagaringrad*, and Ellie saw the sigh—a small gesture that someone who did not know him well would have missed. "Well, whatever comes of that, Ellie and I will spend the rest of our lives looking for other traces that must be somewhere. Right, Ellie?"

So Lars had reconciled himself to the loss. And probably lost none of his faith in human nature. Ellie knew what he'd say about the way Russians treated them: "They had their reasons"—as if that was enough. Damn it, why did he always have to be so generous? Hadn't he ever been kicked in the teeth? Big as he was, did he always have to be so far removed from ordinary human cussedness?

Difficult as it was, Ellie managed a fleeting smile.

"You know," Bradley went on in his obtuse fashion, "what you suggest sounds inefficient as hell. I mean, you'd think your dinosaurs would've tried something better than stone inscriptions to pass on their secrets."

"Well, I didn't mean that literally," Lars said.

"Yeah. Sure'd been interesting if they had some of the techniques NASA's been experimenting with."

"Such as?"

"Oh, things to cut down long duration flight. Takes centuries to go even to the nearest stars with what we've got now. They're working with test animals. Freezing them. Dehydrating them. Trying to find find some practical form of *suspended animation*."

"Aii—yeeeeeeeee!" Ellie's shriek cut through the cabin.

Lars was a half-step behind her. "The lifeless, eternal moon! No need to worry about the world changing about you! A landscape that's been the same for billions of years and would be for billions more!"

"Until intelligent life reestablishes itself on Earth," cried Ellie, "and finally develops the capability to get back to the moon and—and—and finds what's been left up there for them to find!"

"Oh, how close you were in naming him 'Herman'! Herman—*Hermes*—Hermes, the messenger of the gods!"

"What—What's got into you two?" said Bradley.

"Don't you see, man?" Lars said. *"That's* why they wouldn't let us see him. Not that they didn't find anything. Or destroyed what they found. No, they found more than they realized. All that activity, the impatience to be rid of us. They found out he's alive. And they didn't want any Americans around while they *revived* him!"

"The bastards!" Ellie exploded. "Leading us on like that! Laughing behind our backs! All the time knowing—"

"Wait, Ellie. The one thing we didn't have a chance to tell them—our theory about the plague. What if the specimen's *still* contagious?"

Lars told Bradley: "Contact the station! Immediately!"

"Professor, you can't be serious. A plague? Why, the thing over there's what, a reptile? You don't get disease from animals."

"Oh, you don't? Ever heard of anthrax, Captain? Bovine or poultry tuberculosis? Salmonella, that you catch from turtles? Or maybe you've forgotten that the carriers of the bubonic plague that wiped out a third of Europe were rats?"

"You've made your point," said Bradley. "But surely they've taken precautions. Decontamination procedures of some kind?"

"You mean like we did after the Apollo splashdowns?" said Ellie. "Scrubbing the capsule down by hand while it bobbed up and down in the middle of the most fertile natural medium in the whole damned world!"

"Captain, we don't know what the hell they're doing over there," Lars said. "Would you please just send a message?"

"All right," said the haggard shuttle commander.

Orbiter and space station continued in their joint orbit hundreds of meters apart. But the radio from *Gagaringrad* remained silent.

"They refuse to even acknowledge my signal," said Bradley.

"They must be going ahead with their experiment," Lars said.

"It is rather inhospitable," said Bradley grimly. "They can't know it's not an emergency over here."

"We can't wait any longer," Lars said. "Anybody got any ideas?"

Ellie did: "Ram them!"

"What!" Bradley protested.

"Well, that'd sure slow down whatever they're doing," she said.

"Captain, somebody's got to get on board before they have a chance to get into it. What about taking this ship close enough to let me try to sneak inside without being seen?"

"Professor, you're both talking crazy. Much as I wouldn't mind ramming this ship down those bastards' throats, that's obviously out of the question. In fact, *any* EVA's much too dangerous."

"We did it before," Lars said.

"Sure. On a line, with me guiding you at this end and a big smiling Russian on their side. Don't think there'll be too many of them smiling now."

Ellie watched Lars stare at the station so tantalizingly close. He was calculating the risks, and she thought she'd better start doing the same thing. One way or another, Lars was going across.

"Hell, let the Russians kill themselves," said Bradley, "if that's what they insist on doing."

"Don't you see the real danger?" Lars said. "Suppose the disease organism can't be controlled? We don't know how it's spread or whether it can be isolated to *Gagaringrad*—especially if the Russians refuse to believe us about the cause. And if they somehow manage to spread it to Earth. . . ."

"Damn, you make sense even when you don't make sense," Bradley said. "Only *I'll* be the one to make the EVA. My copilot can take the ship in close. It'll be a bit tricky for one man, but I think—"

"But I'm already dressed for it," said Lars. "Besides, what would you tell the Russians once you got over? At least I can make a convincing case. You still only half believe it yourself."

"And you're the last person who should go, Professor. You don't know how to handle yourself in weightless space."

"Captain, as a paleontologist, I've climbed some places in my field work you wouldn't believe possible."

"It's a different ball game out here. You haven't the training. You'll just end up getting yourself killed."

"I have to go."

"We'll both go," Ellie declared.

Lars started to protest.

"Oh don't be so impossibly noble," she told him. "You couldn't possibly make it by yourself—even with the fate of all mankind riding on those big broad shoulders."

That settled the matter.

Quickly Bradley helped Lars and Ellie put their helmets back on, and handed them safety lines. He gave what instructions he could, ending with an impassioned, "Most important of all, don't lose your heads. Especially you, Professor."

The two novices entered the tiny airlock to the rear of the flight deck. Lars managed to float down to the outer door without difficulty. But when Bradley fired the ship's main engines for a short burst, he banged against Ellie's space-suited figure.

Ellie knew this was insanity. Even if they did get across, why should the Russians listen to them? Didn't Lars learn anything about Tereskevitch before?

Still, they had to do something. And maybe this time they would gain access to the specimen.

They heard Bradley's voice through their suit radios: "Mayday! Mayday! This is Shuttle *Constitution*. We have a misfiring rocket."

"*Constitution*," came an alarmed Russian voice, "you are on a collision course. Turn or reverse power."

"Negative," said Bradley. "No other system functioning. Wait, I have powered down the malfunctioning engine."

Awkwardly with her gloved hands, Ellie had followed the instructions of Bradley in fashioning a wide noose in her safety line. It hung stiffly in the weightless space just beyond the open hatch. The idea was to somehow catch it on some projection from the space station.

Ellie was a lousy swimmer, but she could float in water indefinitely. She'd already decided that they would never make it across if she tried to "swim." But if she let the safety line do the work while she simply drifted with the motion of her body, there was a chance.

The hardest thing would be to ignore what was happening to Lars.

"Stand by," said Bradley to Lars and Ellie only. "I'm going to kill all forward velocity."

Gagaringrad's spin in space to provide artificial gravity was

slow. Bradley had aimed toward the almost stable central hub
to minimize the possibility of collision. "Get ready," he
radioed, and Lars and Ellie braced themselves as best they
could against the seal of the opened hatch.

The station's dull-gray hull filled the blackness ahead.
Concentrating on the row of external hatches with their
various extensions, Ellie grasped the line tightly. She couldn't
throw it. She had to transfer to it the motion she would gain
by kicking free from the orbiter, keep its loop wide, get close
enough to the station to trail it across the hull.

She didn't want to think about the possibility that the
Soviets' inhospitality included locked doors. Extremely unlikely, considering the intended use of the hatches, but
still . . .

Through their suit radio, Ellie heard Lars mutter hopefully,
"Maybe the near-miss itself will be enough."

Oh, Christ, Lars, she said in silent exasperation. *Do you
want to go back now?*

No, she felt him crowding close to the hatchway. Come
what may, he was going.

*All right. Only please, if you don't do anything else, just stay
out of my way until I can get us across.*

The entire fabric of the orbiter shuddered as all forward
reaction control engines ignited.

The deceptive gentleness of their approach must have
deceived Lars. Unprepared, he found himself propelled out
the open hatch by his own immense inertia.

Ellie couldn't stop him without being thrown out herself.

Ignoring his tumbling figure, Ellie kicked out as hard as she
dared directly toward the slowly turning space station. So far
so good. She remembered everything Bradley'd told her
about keeping herself in line with her center of gravity. The
noose was still wide, extended ahead of her toward the hull of
Gagaringrad.

Damn, it was exhausting moving within her spacesuit! She
began to puff. At least she was in good shape from her field
work. And she didn't have to fight the direction she was
coasting.

Keep floating, Ellie! she told herself. *Don't swim.*

Abruptly, her own motion stopped.

Even as she oriented herself, the snagged line brought her
down to *Gagaringrad*'s hull. And since her kicking had given

her greater exit velocity, she had passed Lars on the way over. His slowly turning spacesuit, with its tangle of arms and legs, was coming her way.

Even the rotation of *Gagaringrad* was cooperating, bringing her toward him rather than away.

Ellie was not about to tempt luck any further. Before kicking off again, she resecured her line around the nearest support she could find.

As it was, she almost missed Lars as he drifted past in his desperate efforts to stop his tumbling, huffing and wheezing from the effort.

Her gloved hand just barely caught a thrashing foot and tugged.

"Lars, you big oaf, *relax*! Stop fighting me! You're too blasted strong! I'll pull us in. Just don't do anything!"

Like a caught fish, Lars let Ellie reel them both toward the hatch to which she had attached her line.

Within moments they were safely inside. Lars placed one gigantic gloved hand on Ellie's shoulder and, with a quick squeeze, said all that had to be said between them.

"Where now?" Ellie asked as they both caught their breath.

"Good question. Their labs must be located in the end opposite from where we met before. But damned if I can tell one from the other."

"Lars!"

Sounds of people approaching emanated from the central hub, which, because of the slight pull of centrifugal force at their present location, was "above" them.

"They just made up our minds," said Lars. "'Down' we go."

The two Americans pushed themselves along a ladder, passing through a series of compartments with hatches that sealed each from the other. The farther down the passageway they traveled, the greater became their apparent weight, until they had to use the rungs of the ladder.

"Are we going the right way?" Ellie wondered.

"Fifty-fifty. But we haven't met anyone this way yet. Figures they wouldn't allow many people nearby when they started their experiment. They like to keep secrets, even from themselves."

The bottom compartment was much wider than those

above. They had arrived at one of the two large personnel spheres located at each end of *Gagaringrad*.

Waiting for them were Tereskevitch and the same two as before.

"So, Professor Hansen, I suppose I should ask what the meaning of all this is."

The Russian scientist had his anger somewhat under control. The same could not be said for his two scowling comrades.

Ellie was first to remove her helmet. "You've got to stop what you're doing."

"Indeed? And just what, Miss Mercer, do you think that is?"

"You're going to revive Herm—the specimen. You can't do that."

"You *are* mad. I was just saying it before. But this. Do you have any idea the damage you almost caused this station? Or the repercussions?"

Finally Lars got his helmet off.

"Doctor, please listen to us."

"They want to have you shot," said Tereskevitch. "They're quite serious. Fortunately—for you—we don't have an armory up here."

"Dr. Tereskevitch," Lars snapped, "while we stand here bickering, you may be destroying yourselves—and maybe the entire human race!"

"Huh?"

"You wouldn't listen to all our theory. How the dinosaurs destroyed themselves. We believe that the type of war they waged was biological. If the individual you found was placed in suspended animation after that conflict, every part of him—every organ, every cell—must have been preserved intact. *And every living thing that might have been inside his body.*"

Tereskevitch's jaw dropped.

Ellie reacted to the horror in Tereskevitch's face. "Oh, my God, Lars! We're too late!"

"No, no," stammered Tereskevitch. "Not yet. Maybe—"

He moved toward a sealed chamber. "Wait!" Lars said. "If that's where you've got him, you can't go in there now."

Resigned, the Russian turned back. "No, of course not. I wouldn't have anyway. The chamber's not supposed to be opened at all during the course of the experiment. My own orders . . ."

"When did it start?" Lars asked.

"We—activated the pumps only a few moments before we got the call about your ship. Now it's into the moisture cycle." Tereskevitch smiled ruefully. "You should've been more prompt, Professor."

Lars sighed. "The damage's already done. You'd better radio Earth and advise what's happened."

Tereskevitch hesitated. "I'd prefer, ah, not to have to contact anyone down there just yet. The creature's isolated in the vacuum chamber. Surely, there's no danger."

"We can't be sure. If it's the actual biological agent, we have to presume—if only from what it did before—that it's extremely virulent and easily spread. Perhaps even through the seal of that door."

"I'd still prefer to wait, Professor, please try to understand. The decision to proceed was—not unanimous."

"Further delay may be too late. What if we're unable to get word out because we've *already* been infected?"

Tereskevitch turned to his companions and again spoke in Russian.

"Tell them every second we delay may be crucial," Lars urged.

"How can we believe *you*?" spoke up the third officer, the one most opposed to their previous visit. "This is all some sort of capitalist plot to destroy us and our station. Just as your unauthorized boarding was in clear violation of our sovereignty and—"

Tereskevitch cringed at the man's words.

Lars did better. He voiced what must have been his Soviet counterpart's thoughts: "Oh, don't be an ideological ass! Anything happens up here, you think your leaders'll let any American spacecraft near? It'll be *your* cosmonauts transmitting the disease down to *your* country first."

Tereskevitch resumed arguing in Russian. The other man wavered, then rushed to the ladder and speedily clambered upward.

"He's going to the communications center," said Tereskevitch.

"But will he send the message?" said Lars.

"Dr. Tereskevitch," Ellie asked, "how did you discover that the specimen was actually alive?"

Grateful for the diversion, Tereskevitch said, "When our cosmonauts brought the body on board their craft, I sent specific instructions to keep it exposed to the vacuum. I was afraid of deterioration. Once they got it back here, we stored it in this vacuum chamber. Conducted all preliminary tests in the chamber. We placed tissue samples in a sealed air tank. Nothing happened then. It was only a few days ago—we were interested in the dehydration—we added water. To our utter astonishment, the tissue not only absorbed the fluid but retained it, and—incredibly—began to *use* it. It gave all the appearance of cellular division, growth."

"But what precautions did you take during all this?" Lars insisted.

"Professor—we are not peasants sticking our boots in manure to hear them squish. Whatever you Americans think of our scientific methods, we took what we considered appropriate precautions. We were concerned about contamination. From us, of course, not from it. But it amounts to the same thing. Everything was handled by remote instrumentation, the way we do radioactive materials. So even if you hadn't come thundering onto the scene like your beloved cavalry, there probably would've been no direct exposure anyway."

"Probably?"

"All right. Maybe we'd have sent someone inside eventually. Only not without proper testing first. I don't work that way, Professor. Nobody—and I mean not one person aboard this station, whatever his authority"—Tereskevitch glanced significantly at the man who earlier argued to hear Lars and Ellie out—"would dare enter that chamber without my direct permission and supervision. I don't care what's going on inside. And up to this point, nothing of note has."

"So far as you know. Since you commenced the tests on the tissue sample, has anyone returned to Earth?"

"No, Professor. I can assure you of that. In fact, your ship was the first to leave *Gagaringrad* since then."

"Which means *we* could have been the ones to spread the contagion!"

There was nothing Tereskevitch could say to that.

Instead, he took refuge in his explanation. "When we removed the water and air, the tissue sample stopped its activities. But it didn't die. Exposed to a vacuum, the only appreciable effect was to allow the fluid to exit without apparent damage to the cellular structure. So, becoming dormant, it resumed growing when again placed in air and water.

"Obviously, this was a process totally unknown to our science. The implications were staggering. After much deliberation up here—ground control knew as little as you did, Professor—we determined that there really was only one course for us to follow: place the entire creature in an environment that offered the best chance to revive it."

"Of course," added Lars, "you had no intention of sharing this experiment with anyone from the United States. Hence the secrecy, even from your own people."

The degree of bitterness shocked Ellie. How often had she tried to get Lars to see people as they truly were? Now she realized what a real loss that would be.

Tereskevitch sensed it too. "I could say that events dictated what we've done. We had no way of knowing what effect removing the body from its resting place would have. The fact that the experiment had to be conducted up here in a true vacuum. Time working against us . . ."

"But that wouldn't be the whole story, would it, Dr. Tereskevitch?"

"Why should we have shared this discovery with you?" Tereskevitch became increasingly defensive. "Would you Americans have been any more generous in our place? Besides—twenty years ago you had your chance on the moon. Now it's our turn."

Ellie couldn't stand this any longer. Besides, there was something much more important going on.

"Dr. Tereskevitch," she said, "is there some way to observe what's taking place inside the chamber?"

"We have television cameras inside. Over here's a monitor. I haven't yet been able to switch it on. Your untimely arrival—"

"Do so, man!" Lars cried, all resentment vanishing immediately.

The television screen wavered as Tereskevitch focused on a shape lying on a padded table. Then the camera dollied inward. Ellie's intake of breath was the only sound as Soviets and Americans crowded in front of the monitor.

At first it was difficult to observe. Clouds of steam filled the chamber, wreathed about the figure like the mists it may once have walked among 65 million years before on Earth.

It had wide saurischian hips, thick legs, and a full dinosaur tail—a victory for Ellie's position earlier—but the arms and shoulders were proportioned like those of a man. The one hand in view, though oversized, had no claws and one of the three fingers opposed the others. More they could not tell because of the wrinkled, dried-out appearance of the body. Yet as they watched, the contours began to fill out, the wrinkles slowly disappear, the body take on weight and color, changing from dead ash to living flesh.

"It seems to be rejuvinating itself from the moist air alone," said Lars.

"You see," Tereskevitch said to his companion, "your worries were all for nothing." To Lars and Ellie: "We're basing this procedure on numerous tests with the tissue samples. The air inside is saturated with as much humidity as possible. The body cells are refilling with water at a greatly accelerated, but not dangerous, rate. Total immersion in water would have been too much. Caused the cells to burst."

"Is it possible to focus for a closeup view?" Ellie requested.

"I'm not sure what we'll see with all that steam, but . . . " The Soviet scientist complied, and the upper body filled the screen.

Most saurian characteristics were muted. The snout was greatly foreshortened, the mouth shrunk to less than twice the width of a human's. The large oval eyes—actually the eyesockets, the most prominent reptilian characteristic retained—were set close together in the center of the face, the enlarged cranium above promising a brain the equal to man's—if not greater.

"Despite everything, so much like us," Lars marveled. "He resembles his reptilian forebears as little as we do the ape."

"I wonder if he really is male," said Ellie.

When the Russians glanced at her, she declared, "Well, it's a logical question. Reptiles don't have external genitalia, male or female. And it certainly wouldn't have breasts. It's not mammalian, after all."

Tereskevitch became embarrassed.

Stifling a laugh, Lars said, "For now, he's officially—if tentatively—male. Don't want to complicate things too much."

"Dr. Tereskevitch!" the other Russian exclaimed.

Slowly the creature began to clench his fists.

"He seems to be stretching," said Lars. "Like awakening from a long sleep. Doctor, do you have an intercom into the chamber?"

"Of course. Stupid. How could I forget?"

Quickly Tereskevitch flicked a switch.

From inside the chamber came sounds of movement. The creature stirred, tried to rise, fell back. *Almost painfully*, thought Ellie.

Now, a kind of chirping. There was nothing else in the chamber that could be causing it. It had to be coming from the creature.

"Speech?" said Lars. "Listen how strained it sounds."

The creature stopped moving. But the same sound kept being repeated, growing louder, more insistent.

Lars turned to Ellie. The two paleontologists realized the same thing: "Something's wrong with him!"

"Not necessarily," said Tereskevitch. "We'll keep watching."

"No, dammit!" snapped Lars. "Look at him."

The face in the monitor. Tereskevitch hadn't worked with fossils, never reconstructed what they must have looked like. He couldn't see the agony that Lars and Ellie did.

"It must be water, Lars," said Ellie. "He's not getting enough from the air."

"There is some in the chamber?" Lars asked Tereskevitch.

"Of course. I'll get it to him."

Tereskevitch grasped two handles below the monitor. On the screen, two mechanical arms appeared. One moved toward the creature on the table, a clear beaker clutched in its metal claw.

Both the creature's eyes snapped open. He saw the approaching arm through the clouds of steam, drew back feebly.

"He doesn't understand," Lars said.

"No, that can't be," said Tereskevitch. "He's intelligent. He's got to know we're only trying to help."

"But he doesn't," Lars said. "Maybe there's nothing in his experience anything like what you're putting him through."

Now the creature raised a three-fingered hand toward the beaker.

"There, you see," Tereskevitch started to say.

"No. Don't," Ellie cried.

He wasn't trying to reach for the container. He was trying to push it away.

Swearing, Tereskevitch grasped with both hands the left handle, trying to regain control of the mechanical arm and pull it back.

"We can't help him *this way*," said Lars.

It was the way he said it. Ellie turned toward him hoping she was wrong.

"Lars, you're not thinking of going inside there with him?"

"Somebody has to."

"But the disease—"

"That's why it has to be only one of us. The rest of you clear out. Seal off the entire area."

Tereskevitch protested, "I can't let you do that."

"Precautions be damned. You started this. Now that he's revived, we've got to do whatever we can to save him."

"I didn't mean that. *You*, Professor. I can't let you kill yourself."

Lars ignored him. "Ellie, use your suit radio to contact Bradley. Tell him what's happened. Have him relay it back to Earth."

"I can't just leave you," she said helplessly.

"You must. That message has got to get through. We don't know if their man sent anything. You're the only person I can trust to do it and make them understand. Now please go. *All of you!*"

Tereskevitch's associate slipped behind Ellie to the ladder. She couldn't make herself leave. All she could do was stare at big, clumsy generous Lars, who wouldn't even be there if it hadn't been for her.

Suddenly she was running to him, throwing her arms about him, the tears streaming down her cheeks.

Without any idea whether she made it to the ladder by herself or with Lars' help, Ellie began the long climb upward. All she knew was that Lars was right. The message had to get out. Otherwise, she'd still be there with him.

Passing through the ceiling hatch, she saw that the first Russian had already reached the next compartment. How many more after that? Ten? Twelve?

As the hatch beneath slammed shut and locked, Ellie suddenly realized that Tereskevitch had not come up with either of them.

He was still down by the chamber with Lars.

Descending from the ladder, Tereskevitch asked, "Why are you doing this?"

Lars had been studying the complicated pump handle to the chamber door. "Get the hell out of here!" he said, without looking up.

"Not without knowing why you're so set on becoming a martyr," said Tereskevitch. "If you think your death will give your country some sort of claim to our find—? But no, it's not that with you, is it?"

"The door," said Lars, "how do I get it open the quickest way?"

"Personal glory then? Your name attached to what happens today? Your own life vindication for everything you've stood for?"

Lars straightened to his full height. Between the two men was the monitor, with the creature's tormented face a visage even Tereskevitch could now understand.

"Isn't that reason enough?"

Tereskevitch glanced at the monitor, then slowly nodded.

"And you," said Lars. "Why are you still here?"

"Because," said Tereskevitch, "it takes *two* people to get that damned door open in time."

Lars looked at him. "Who in blazes designed such a monstrosity?"

Tereskevitch shrugged. "A time and efficiency study committee. Who else?"

Lars began to laugh. Heartily, uproariously. And Tereskevitch, after only a moment's hesitation, joined in.

Both men were still laughing as they worked together to open the chamber door.

"There really wasn't any danger after all."

Lars and Ellie were relaxing in the small cabin assigned to them in their first moments alone after Lars' release from the chamber. The statement he'd just made was one of the few things he could say with any degree of certainty.

"But we were right about it being some sort of disease," said Ellie.

"Yes, even though the exact type of pathogen still hasn't been determined. But at least we have an idea how it worked. It didn't kill or cripple. Just attacked the sex cells, making it impossible for his species to reproduce."

"As well as any other species," added Ellie.

"Of dinosaur. That limitation's important. Not merely for the clue it provided us. But as an added safeguard. Whether it would affect mammals—particularly man—is an open question. One we'll never have to find out. Thank God."

"Can we really be sure?"

"Based on what we've learned, yes. We know that it thrived only on *living* gametes and that it had no dormant cycle. Once it completed its horrid work, there was nothing further to sustain it. So when our guest entered suspended animation, any residue in his body *had* to be dead."

Ellie could tell by the off-hand manner he spoke that Lars was trying to minimize what he'd done. But she knew better. "You couldn't have known that *before* entering that chamber."

"No. But we should've guessed it. After all, precautions surely would have been taken to insure that the disease didn't spread any more after he was found and revived."

"Maybe," said Ellie, thinking of all those other species that vanished—the ones without intelligence.

"Anyway, the Soviet doctors went to great pains to make sure that there wasn't anything in our bloodstreams not easily identifiable before releasing Serge and me. *Our* pains, that is." Lars grinned, again making light of what took place for Ellie's benefit.

So now it's 'Serge,' thought Ellie. She'd come to doubt that Dr. Tereskevitch had a first name.

Despite the present atmosphere of camaraderie, she still didn't trust their Soviet hosts. All the Americans, Bradley and his copilot included, were temporarily quarantined aboard *Gagaringrad*. Ellie had insisted upon staying with Lars. Quite a few Russian eyebrows had been raised at this.

"With all their testing," said Ellie, "I just hope they don't forget one thing: *You* were the one who saved his life. Don't deny it, Lars. Dr. Tereskevitch never would have gone in there if it hadn't been for you. You know that's true."

"Oh, I'm not so sure about that," Lars disputed. "Serge's pretty hardheaded. But he did the right thing when it counted. And I think he'd have done it whether I was there or not. You ought to get to know him, Ellie. I think you two would get along just fine."

"Ugh! I'd rather spend my time with—Herman. I guess we can call him that—now, that we know he's definitely male—until we find out his real name."

"That won't be for some time. Between the shock of revival and all he tried to do, he'll probably be sleeping for days. He tried to tell us so much. Tried to get across so much more we couldn't grasp."

"I still can't believe that you actually *talked* with him!"

"Don't credit us with that. It was entirely his doing. Learned enough of our language from the few words we were using to start conversing after just half an hour!" Lars shook his head in renewed amazement.

Lars had already related to Ellie how they managed to communicate. The "trilling" had originated from lower in the throat than the human voicebox. Lars' earlier analogy to the parrot's syrinx had been close. But the range of sounds produced surpassed even a human's. And they were spoken at a much faster rate.

It was the being who recognized this and adjusted his own speech patterns to the comparative slowness of the lower-pitched words spoken by Lars and Tereskevitch.

"W-a-a-a-a-ter-r-r-r-r," he had uttered, exaggerating the syllables with an underlying "hissing"—precisely the type of sound one would have associated with a reptile.

From this, he picked up human speech rapidly, never forgetting a word once he'd spoken it. Within minutes, he had acquired a sufficiently large vocabulary to assure his rescuers that they had nothing to fear from him.

"I suppose we shouldn't have been too surprised," said Lars to Ellie. "There are people with photographic memories. Math geniuses. Why shouldn't *he* have turned out to be some sort of language genius? After all, what would've been the purpose of sending a messenger if he couldn't communicate!"

He grinned wickedly. "Of course, Serge couldn't help being a bit miffed. We were speaking English, in deference to me, and *that's* the language he picked up on. I don't think he learned a single word of Russian the whole time!"

Ellie burst out laughing. She hadn't realized how much she needed to. And she didn't give a damn if it were picked up by any of the microphones she was certain the Russians had stashed about the cabin.

"Actually, I doubt if Serge cared all that much. He was really interested in one thing. Couldn't wait until there were enough words learned to ask him how he got to the moon. Herman—oh, that doesn't fit him, Ellie; *Hermes* is much more appropriate—Hermes couldn't answer at that point. Guess I'd have trouble too, if I'd only been speaking English for an hour!"

Ellie envied him—both of them—for those precious moments at the very beginning—when a new day for science had dawned and dark clouds not yet settled.

"The only way we could continue," Lars said, "was by explaining to him how we got there ourselves. Help him build up his vocabulary. Yet we couldn't get beyond the basics of rocketry. He kept on interrupting. Couldn't seem to understand why we'd ignored the greatest power source available—our own planet!"

"What could he have meant by that?"

"Serge's the engineer. He figures some sort of antigravity drive. Only Hermes didn't have the capability to supply a lot of detail. We're reasonably certain it wasn't done through any instrumentation we're familiar with. Throughout the discussion, he kept pointing to his head."

"Sounds like he just willed himself to go to the moon."

"No. That's not it either. Obviously, they needed protection from the vacuum of space, same as us. And they did use spacecraft of some type, although apparently quite different from what we have. It seems that their minds formed a vital component."

"Oh, Dr. Tereskevitch must have loved *that*."

"Actually, Serge was quite impressed. Don't forget, the Soviets have done much more in the fields of psychic energy, Kirlian photography, ESP, than we have. If there's a way, mentally, to tap the energy fields of Earth, you can be sure they wouldn't reject it out of hand. Not the way most Western scientists rejected our theory."

Lars hesitated. Obviously, there was a great need in him to go on. But also great reluctance. Usually Ellie would have resented such protectiveness. Now she wasn't so sure.

"You can see the difficulties we were getting into already. The English language, Ellie, is such a marvelous tool. With just one hundred fifty words, you can make yourself understood in most common situations. Trouble is the intricacies after that point. What I've told you so far—however sketchy —at least there's little doubt what he was trying to get across. But the rest of it—well, you've got to bear in mind the handicap Hermes was working under, not being familiar with the wide variety of meanings that attach to words. And maybe a lot of it's merely Serge's or my interpretation. I don't know. In a way, I almost hope . . ."

Ellie understood. "The reason they destroyed themselves?"

Lars nodded. "Some of it makes sense. Much of it doesn't. The way they went about it: if you *are* going to eliminate someone, can you think of a more *benevolent* way of doing it? No death or destruction. Just stop all their births.

"But the destruction of other life forms—the *universality* of the tragedy—they couldn't have deliberately intended that. Not from what I've learned about them from Hermes."

Oh, sure, thought Ellie. A *little miscalculation. Happens all the time. Sorry.*

"Maybe that was the most horrifying thing of all to them," said Lars. "His people really were closely attuned to the natural processes of their world at one time. That comes out of almost everything he says. But gradually that changed. They turned away from what had previously sustained them. Began modifying their environment. Became more mechanical."

"In other words," said Ellie, "their civilization became more like ours?"

"I suppose so—although I wouldn't quite characterize it like that."

Ellie wasn't surprised. "And that, naturally enough, led to the war?"

"No. Not a war. At least, not the way we think of one.

Something happened. Whether a single catastrophic event or a whole series of them, we're not sure. We know that the net result was so terrible that Hermes won't speak of it other than to acknowledge that it did occur. That led to the decision on their part. He wouldn't—perhaps couldn't—say who made it or how it was arrived at. But this much we do know: What they did was to commit *deliberate racial suicide.*"

Ellie shuddered at his words.

"It would help if I could believe I misunderstood him," said Lars. "How can anyone come to the conclusion—as they apparently did—that all intelligence is an aberration? Maybe you can make sense out of that, Ellie. I can't," he said helplessly.

Ellie studied the cold metal walls about them. Very little made sense now. More questions than answers. Each new discovery more terrible in its implications. The dark clouds in this new day of science had indeed descended.

She knew that Lars had to find some way to reconcile this. He'd devote the rest of his life—in any event—helping and studying this being whose life he'd saved. But for Lars this—this anomaly could not stand.

For Ellie there was a much more vital concern.

"Why did Hermes survive? A messenger from their time? I can't believe that, Lars. Why would people who destroyed all intelligence—and almost their entire world as well—*care* about the future?"

"Maybe he was sent to guide us," suggested Lars. "Insure that we don't make the same mistakes they did."

Ellie expected Lars to say something like that. Why should he think the worse of anyone—or anything?

"What if it's more than that?" she said.

"What else could it be?"

"To *judge* us."

Lars looked at her. He had been closest to their Hermes. Closer probably than Tereskevitch. Ellie knew what was going through his mind. Why had he failed to detect that? Because of what he truly observed? Or because of the type of person he was?

"What do we do then, Lars? We don't know the full extent of the powers he has. What he's capable of. He could destroy *us,* just like—"

"The answer's simple, Ellie. We'll just have to convince him that we are worthy. And maybe we've already made a big step in that direction, Serge and me."

The smile on Lars Hansen's face made Ellie almost forget her fears.

Almost.

A STATUE FOR FATHER

Isaac Asimov

Assuming that dinosaurs were alive today, for what would we use them? In another story, Robert Silverberg suggests study and tourism. Other possibilities include hunting and movie work. But the most palatable choice we've seen appears in the following little tale. Ironically, Isaac Asimov had trouble deciding on its title; originally he called it "Benefactor of Humanity." Leo Margulies, the purchasing editor, renamed it "A Statue for Father," and only after much soul-searching did Asimov decide that he liked the substitution more. However, it has occurred to us that the perfect label might be "A Taste for Fame."

First time? Really? But of course you have heard of it. Yes, I was sure you had.

If you're really interested in the discovery, believe me, I'll be delighted to tell you. It's a story I've always liked to tell, but not many people give me the chance. I've even been advised to keep the story under wraps. It interferes with the legends growing up about my father.

Still, I think the truth is valuable. There's a moral to it. A man can spend his life devoting his energies solely to the satisfaction of his own curiosity and then, quite accidentally, without ever intending anything of the sort, find himself a benefactor of humanity.

Dad was just a theoretical physicist, devoted to the investigation of time travel. I don't think he ever gave a thought to what time travel might mean to *Homo sapiens*. He was just curious about the mathematical relationships that governed the universe, you see.

Hungry? All the better. I imagine it will take nearly half an hour. They will do it properly for an official such as yourself. It's a matter of pride.

To begin with, Dad was poor as only a university professor can be poor. Eventually, though, he became wealthy. In the last years before his death he was fabulously rich, and as for myself and my children and grandchildren—well, you can see for yourself.

They've put up statues to him, too. The oldest is on the hillside right here where the discovery was made. You can just see it out the window. Yes. Can you make out the inscription? Well, we're standing at a bad angle. No matter.

By the time Dad got into time-travel research the whole problem had been given up by most physicists as a bad job. It had begun with a splash when the Chrono-funnels were first set up.

Actually, they're not much to see. They're completely irrational and uncontrollable. What you see is distorted and wavery, two feet across at the most, and it vanishes quickly. Trying to focus on the past is like trying to focus on a feather caught in a hurricane that has gone mad.

They tried poking grapples into the past but that was just as unpredictable. Sometimes it was carried off successfully for a few seconds with one man leaning hard against the grapple. But more often a pile driver couldn't push it through. Nothing was ever obtained out of the past until— Well, I'll get to that.

After fifty years of no progress, physicists just lost interest. The operational technique seemed a complete blind alley; a dead end. I can't honestly say I blame them as I look back on it. Some of them even tried to show that the funnels didn't actually expose the past, but there had been too many sightings of living animals through the funnels—animals now extinct.

Anyway, when time travel was almost forgotten, Dad stepped in. He talked the government into giving him a grant to set up a Chrono-funnel of his own, and tackled the matter all over again.

I helped him in those days. I was fresh out of college, with my own doctorate in physics.

However, our combined efforts ran into bad trouble after a year or so. Dad had difficulty in getting his grant renewed.

Industry wasn't interested, and the university decided he was besmirching their reputation by being so single-minded in investigating a dead field. The dean of the graduate school, who understood only the financial end of scholarship, began by hinting that he switch to more lucrative fields and ended by forcing him out.

Of course, the dean—still alive and still counting grant-dollars when Dad died—probably felt quite foolish, I imagine, when Dad left the school a million dollars free and clear in his will, with a codicil canceling the bequest on the ground that the dean lacked vision. But that was merely posthumous revenge. For years before that—

I don't wish to dictate, but please *don't have any more of the breadsticks. The clear soup, eaten slowly to prevent a too-sharp appetite, will do.*

Anyway, we managed somehow. Dad kept the equipment we had bought with the grant money, moved it out of the university and set it up here.

Those first years on our own were brutal, and I kept urging him to give up. He never would. He was indomitable, always managing to find a thousand dollars somewhere when we needed it.

Life went on, but he allowed nothing to interfere with his research. Mother died; Dad mourned and returned to his task. I married, had a son, then a daughter, couldn't always be at his side. He carried on without me. He broke his leg and worked with the cast impeding him for months.

So I give him all the credit. I helped, of course. I did consulting work on the side and carried on negotiation with Washington. But *he* was the life and soul of the project.

Despite all that, we weren't getting anywhere. All the money we managed to scrounge might just as well have been poured into one of the Chrono-funnels—not that it would have passed through.

After all, we never once managed to get a grapple through a funnel. We came near on only one occasion. We had the grapple about two inches out the other end when focus changed. It snapped off clean, and somewhere in the Mesozoic there is a man-made piece of steel rod rusting on a riverbank.

Then one day, the crucial day, the focus held for ten long minutes—something for which the odds were less than one in-a trillion. Lord, the frenzies of excitement we experienced as we set up the cameras. We could see living creatures just the other side of the funnel, moving energetically.

Then, to top it off, the Chrono-funnel grew permeable, until you might have sworn there was nothing but air between the past and ourselves. The low permeability must have been connected with the long holding of focus, but we've never been able to prove that it did.

Of course, we had no grapple handy, wouldn't you know. But the low permeability was clear enough because something just fell through, moving from the *Then* into the *Now*. Thunderstruck, acting simply on blind instinct, I reached forward and caught it.

At that moment we lost focus, but it no longer left us embittered and despairing. We were both staring in wild surmise at what I held. It was a mass of caked and dried mud, shaved off clean where it had struck the borders of the Chrono-funnel, and on the mud cake were fourteen eggs about the size of duck eggs.

I said, "Dinosaur eggs? Do you suppose they really are?"

Dad said, "Maybe. We can't tell for sure."

"Unless we hatch them," I said in sudden, almost uncontrollable excitement. I put them down as though they were platinum. They felt warm with the heat of the primeval sun. I said, "Dad, if we hatch them, we'll have creatures that have been extinct for over a hundred million years. It will be the first case of something actually brought out of the past. If we announce this—"

I was thinking of the grants we could get, of the publicity, of all that it would mean to Dad. I was seeing the look of consternation on the dean's face.

But Dad took a different view of the matter. He said firmly, "Not a word, son. If this gets out, we'll have twenty research teams on the trail of the Chrono-funnels, cutting off my advance. No, once I've solved the riddle of the funnels, you can make all the announcements you want. Until then—we keep silent. Son, don't look like that. I'll have the answer in a year. I'm sure of it."

I was a little less confident, but those eggs, I felt convinced, would arm us with all the proof we'd need. I set up a large oven at blood-heat; I circulated air and moisture. I rigged up an alarm that would sound at the first signs of motion within the eggs.

They hatched at 3 A.M. nineteen days later, and there they were—fourteen wee kangaroos with greenish scales, clawed hindlegs, plump little thighs, and thin, whiplash tails.

I thought at first they were *Tyrannosauri,* but they were too small for that species of dinosaur. Months passed, and I could see they weren't going to grow any larger than moderate-sized dogs.

Dad seemed disappointed, but I held on, hoping he would let me use them for publicity. One died before maturity and one was killed in a scuffle. But the other twelve survived—five males and seven females. I fed them on chopped carrots, boiled eggs, and milk, and grew quite fond of them. They were fearfully stupid and yet gentle. And they were truly beautiful. Their scales—

Oh, well, it's silly to describe them. Those original publicity pictures have made their rounds. Though, come to think of it, I don't know about Mars— Oh, there, too. Well, good.

But it took a long time for the pictures to make an impression on the public, let alone a sight of the creatures in the flesh. Dad remained intransigent. A year passed, two, and finally three. We had no luck whatsoever with the Chrono-funnels. The one break was not repeated, and still Dad would not give in.

Five of our females laid eggs and soon I had over fifty of the creatures on my hands.

"What shall we do with them?" I demanded.

"Kill them off," he said.

Well, I couldn't do that, of course.

Henri, is it almost ready? Good.

We had reached the end of our resources when it happened. No more money was available. I had tried everywhere, and met with consistent rebuffs. I was even glad because it seemed to me that Dad would have to give in now. But with a chin that was firm and indomitably set, he coolly set up another experiment.

I swear to you that if the accident had not happened the truth would have eluded us forever. Humanity would have been deprived of one of its greatest boons.

It happens that way sometimes. Perkin spots a purple tinge in his gunk and comes up with aniline dyes. Remsen puts a contaminated finger to his lips and discovers saccharin. Goodyear drops a mixture on the stove and finds the secret of vulcanization.

With us, it was a half-grown dinosaur wandering into the main research lab. They had become so numerous I hadn't been able to keep track of them.

The dinosaur stepped right across two contact points which happened to be open—just at the point where the plaque immortalizing the event is now located. I'm convinced that such a happenstance couldn't occur again in a thousand years. There was a blinding flash, a blistering short circuit, and the Chrono-funnel which had just been set up vanished in a rainbow of sparks.

Even at the moment, really, we didn't know exactly what we had. All we knew was that the creature had short-circuited and perhaps destroyed two hundred thousand dollars worth of equipment and that we were completely ruined financially. All we had to show for it was one thoroughly roasted dinosaur. We were slightly scorched ourselves, but the dinosaur got the full concentration of field energies. We could smell it. The air was saturated with its aroma. Dad and I looked at each other in amazement. I picked it up gingerly in a pair of tongs. It was black and charred on the outside, but the burnt scales crumbled away at a touch, carrying the skin with it. Under the char was white, firm flesh that resembled chicken.

I couldn't resist tasting it, and it resembled chicken about the way Jupiter resembles an asteroid.

Believe me or not, with our scientific work reduced to rubble about us, we sat there in seventh heaven and devoured dinosaur. Parts were burnt, parts were nearly raw. It hadn't been dressed. But we didn't stop until we had picked the bones clean.

Finally I said, "Dad, we've got to raise them gloriously and systematically for food purposes."

Dad had to agree. We were completely broke.

I got a loan from the bank by inviting the president to dinner and feeding him dinosaur.

It has never failed to work. No one who has once tasted what we now call "dinachicken" can rest content with ordinary fare. A meal without dinachicken is a meal we choke down to keep body and soul together. Only dinachicken is *food*.

Our family still owns the only herd of dinachickens in existence and we are the only suppliers for the worldwide chain of restaurants—this is the first and oldest—which has grown up about it.

Poor Dad! He was never happy, except for those unique moments when he was actually eating dinachicken. He continued working on the Chrono-funnels and so did twenty other research teams which, as he had predicted would happen, jumped in. Nothing ever came of any of it, though, to this day. Nothing *except* dinachicken.

Ah, Pierre, thank you. A superlative job! Now, sir, if you will allow me to carve. No salt, now, and just a trace of the sauce. That's right. . . . Ah, that is precisely the expression I always see on the face of a man who experiences his first taste of the delight.

A grateful humanity contributed fifty thousand dollars to have the statue on the hillside put up, but even that tribute failed to make Dad happy.

All he could see was the inscription: The Man Who Gave Dinachicken to the World.

You see, to his dying day, he wanted only one thing, to find the secret of time travel. For all that he was a benefactor of humanity, he died with his curiosity unsatisfied.

WILDCAT

Poul Anderson

Many feel that man has a continuous need for frontiers. Today, the two most likely areas are the oceans and space. But with the development of time machines, the new future may be the past. Poul Anderson develops this possibility in the following story about five hundred men who fight brontosaurs, plesiosaurs (long necked, aquatic dinosaurs), and an unexpected variety of carnosaur in order to pump oil. Now, it may seem strange to send oil workers into the Jurassic; however, the idea is derived from Fred Hoyle, a notable astronomer, who believes that petroleum, on a bonding agent, may have been present since the beginning of earth.

It was raining again, hot and heavy out of a hidden sky, and the air stank with swamp. Herries could just see the tall derricks a mile away, under a floodlight glare, and hear their engines mutter. Farther away, a bull brontosaur cried and thunder went through the night.

Herries's boots resounded hollowly on the dock. Beneath the slicker, his clothes lay sweat-soggy, the rain spilled off his hat and down his collar. He swore in a tired voice and stepped onto his gangplank.

Light from the shack on the barge glimmered off drenched wood. He saw the snaky neck just in time, as it reared over the gangplank rail and struck at him. He sprang back, grabbing for the Magnum carbine slung over one shoulder. The plesiosaur hissed monstrously and flipper-slapped the water. It was like a cannon going off.

Herries threw the gun to his shoulder and fired. The long

155

sleek form took the bullet—somewhere—and screamed. The raw noise hurt the man's eardrums.

. Feet thudded over the wharf. Two guards reached Herries and began to shoot into the dark water. The door of the shack opened and a figure stood black against its yellow oblong, a tommy gun stammering idiotically in its hands.

"Cut it out!" bawled Herries. "That's enough! Hold your fire!"

Silence fell. For a moment only the ponderous rainfall had voice. Then the brontosaur bellowed again, remotely, and there were seethings and croakings in the water.

"He got away," said Herries. "Or more likely his pals are now stripping him clean. Blood smell." A dull anger lifted in him. He turned and grabbed the lapel of the nearest guard. "How often do I have to tell you characters, every gangway has to have a man near it with grenades?"

"Yes, sir. Sorry, sir." Herries was a large man, and the other face looked up at him, white and scared in the wan electric radiance. "I just went off to the head—"

"You'll stay here," said Herries. "I don't care if you explode. Our presence draws these critters, and you ought to know that by now. They've already snatched two men off this dock. They nearly got a third tonight—me. At the first suspicion of anything out there, you're to pull the pin on a grenade and drop it in the water, understand? One more dereliction like this, and you're fired— No." He stopped, grinning humorlessly. "That's not much of a punishment, is it? A week in hack on bread."

The other guard bristled. "Look here, Mr. Herries, we got our rights. The union—"

"Your precious union is a hundred million years in the future," snapped the engineer. "It was understood that this is a dangerous job, that we're subject to martial law, and that I can discipline anyone who steps out of line. Okay— remember."

He turned his back and tramped across the gangplank to the barge deck. It boomed underfoot. With the excitement over, the shack had been closed again. He opened the door and stepped through, peeling off his slicker.

Four men were playing poker beneath an unshaded bulb. The room was small and cluttered, hazy with tobacco smoke and the Jurassic mist. A fifth man lay on one of the bunks, reading. The walls were gaudy with pinups.

Olson riffled the cards and looked up. "Close call, Boss," he remarked, almost casually. "Want to sit in?"

"Not now," said Herries. He felt his big square face sagging with weariness. "I'm bushed." He nodded at Carver, who had just returned from a prospecting trip farther north. "We lost one more derrick today."

"Huh?" said Carver. "What happened this time?"

"It turns out this is the mating season." Herries found a chair, sat down, and began to pull off his boots. "How they tell one season from another, I don't know . . . length of day, maybe . . . but anyhow the brontosaurs aren't shy of us any more—they're going nuts. Now they go gallyhooting around and trample down charged fences or anything else that happens to be in the way. They've smashed three rigs to date, and one man."

Carver raised an eyebrow in his chocolate-colored face. It was a rather sour standing joke here, how much better the Negroes looked than anyone else. A white man could be outdoors all his life in this clouded age and remain pasty. "Haven't you tried shooting them?" he asked.

"Ever try to kill a brontosaur with a rifle?" snorted Herries. "We can mess 'em up a little with .50-caliber machine guns or a bazooka—just enough so they decide to get out of the neighborhood—but being less intelligent than a chicken, they take off in any old direction. Makes as much havoc as the original rampage." His left boot hit the floor with a sullen thud. "I've been begging for a couple of atomic howitzers, but it has to go through channels . . . Channels!" Fury spurted in him. "Five hundred human beings stuck in this nightmare world, and our requisitions have to go through channels!"

Olson began to deal the cards. Polansky gave the man in the bunk a chill glance. "You're the wheel, Symonds," he said. "Why the devil don't you goose the great Transtemporal Oil Company?"

"Nuts," said Carver. "The great benevolent all-wise United States Government is what counts. How about it, Symonds?"

You never got a rise out of Symonds, the human tape

recorder, just a playback of the latest official line. Now he laid his book aside and sat up in his bunk. Herries noticed that the volume was Marcus Aurelius, in Latin yet.

Symonds looked at Carver through steel-rimmed glasses and said in a dusty tone: "I am only the comptroller and supply supervisor. In effect, a chief clerk. Mr. Herries is in charge of operations."

He was a small shriveled man, with thin gray hair above a thin gray face. Even here, he wore a stiff-collared shirt and sober tie. One of the hardest things to take about him was the way his long nose waggled when he talked.

"In charge!" Herries spat expertly into a gobboon. "Sure, I direct the prospectors and the drillers and everybody else on down through the bull cook. But who handles the paperwork —all our reports and receipts and requests? You." He tossed his right boot on the floor. "I don't want the name of boss if I can't get the stuff to defend my own men."

Something bumped against the supervisors' barge; it quivered and the chips on the table rattled. Since there was no outcry from the dock guards, Herries ignored the matter. Some swimming giant. And except for the plesiosaurs and the nonmalicious bumbling bronties, all the big dinosaurs encountered so far were fairly safe. They might step on you in an absent-minded way, but most of them were peaceful and you could outrun those that weren't. It was the smaller carnivores, about the size of a man, leaping out of brush or muck with a skullful of teeth, that had taken most of the personnel lost. Their reptile life was too diffuse: even mortally wounded by elephant gun or grenade launcher, they could rave about for hours. They were the reason for sleeping on barges tied up by this sodden coast, along the gulf that would some day be Oklahoma.

Symonds spoke in his tight little voice: "I send your recommendations in, of course. The project office passes on them."

"I'll say it does," muttered young Greenstein irreverently.

"Please do not blame me," insisted Symonds.

I wonder. Herries glowered at him. Symonds had an in of some kind. That was obvious. A man who was simply a glorified clerk would not be called to Washington for unspecified conferences with unspecified people as often as this one was. But what was he, then?

A favorite relative? No . . . in spite of high pay, this operation was no political plum. FBI? Scarcely . . . the security checks were all run in the future. A hack in the bureaucracy? That was more probable. Symonds was here to see that oil was pumped and dinosaurs chased away and the hideously fecund jungle kept beyond the fence according to the least comma in the latest directive from headquarters.

The small man continued: "It has been explained to you officially that the heavier weapons are all needed at home. The international situation is critical. You ought to be thankful you are safely back in the past."

"Heat, large economy-size alligators, and not a woman for a hundred million years," grunted Olson. "I'd rather be blown up. Who dealt this mess?"

"You did," said Polansky. "Gimme two, and make 'em good."

Herries stripped the clothes off his thick hairy body, went to the rear of the cabin, and entered the shower cubby. He left the door open, to listen in. A boss was always lonely. Maybe he should have married when he had the chance. But then he wouldn't be here. Except for Symonds, who was a widower and in any case more a government than company man, Transoco had been hiring only young bachelors for operations in the field.

"It seems kinda funny to talk about the international situation," remarked Carver. "Hell, there won't be any international situation for several geological periods."

"The inertial effect makes simultaneity a valid approximational concept," declared Symonds pedantically. His habit of lecturing scientists and engineers on their professions had not endeared him to them. "If we spend a year in the past, we must necessarily return to our own era to find a year gone, since the main projector operates only at the point of its own existence which—"

"Oh, stow it," said Greenstein. "I read the orientation manual too," He waited until everyone had cards, then shoved a few chips forward and added: "Druther spend my time a little nearer home. Say with Cleopatra."

"Impossible," Symonds told him. "Inertial effect again. In order to send a body into the past at all, the projector must energize it so much that the minimal time-distance we can cover becomes precisely the one we have covered to arrive here, one hundred and one million, three hundred twenty seven thousand, et cetera, years."

"But why not time-hop into the future? You don't buck entropy in that direction. I mean, I suppose there is an inertial effect there, too, but it would be much smaller, so you could go into the future—"

"—about a hundred years at a hop, according to the handbook," supplied Polansky.

"So why don't they look at the twenty-first century?" asked Greenstein.

"I understand that that is classified information," Symonds said. His tone implied that Greenstein had skirted some unimaginably gross obscenity.

Herries put his head out of the shower. "Sure it's classified," he said. "They'd classify the wheel if they could. But use your reason and you'll see why travel into the future isn't practical. Suppose you jump a hundred years ahead. How do you get home to report what you've seen? The projector will yank you a hundred million years into the past, less the distance you went forward."

Symonds dove back into his book. Somehow he gave an impression of lying there rigid with shock that men dared think after he had spoken the phrase of taboo.

"Uh . . . yes. I get it." Greenstein nodded. He had been recruited only a month ago, to replace a man drowned in a moss-veiled bog. Before then, like nearly all the world, he had had no idea time travel existed. So far he had been too busy to examine its implications.

To Herries it was an old, worn-thin story.

"I daresay they did send an expedition a hundred million years up, so it could come back to the same week as it left," he said. "Don't ask me what was found. Classified: Tip-top Secret, Burn Before Reading."

"You know, though," said Polansky in a reflective tone, "I been thinking some myself. Why are we here at all? I mean, oil is necessary to defense and so forth, but it seems to me it'd make more sense for the U.S. Army to come through, cross the ocean, and establish itself where the enemy nations are going to be. Then we'd have a gun pointed at their heads!"

"Nice theory," said Herries. "I've daydreamed myself. But

there's only one main projector, to energize all the subsidiary ones. Building it took almost the whole world supply of certain rare earths. Its capacity is limited. If we started sending military units into the past, it'd be a slow and cumbersome operation—and not being a security officer, I'm not required to kid myself that Moscow doesn't know we have time travel. They've probably even given Washington a secret ultimatum: 'Start sending back war material in any quantity, and we'll hit you with everything we've got.' But evidently they don't feel strongly enough about our pumping oil on our own territory—or what will one day be our own territory—to make it a, uh, *casus belli*."

"Just as we don't feel their satellite base in the twentieth century is dangerous enough for us to fight about," said Greenstein. "But I suspect we're the reason they agreed to make the moon a neutral zone. Same old stand-off."

"I wonder how long it can last?" murmured Polansky.

"Not much longer," said Olson. "Read your history. I'll see you, Greenstein, boy, and raise you two."

Herries let the shower run about him. At least there was no shortage of hot water. Transoco had sent back a complete nuclear reactor. But civilization and war still ran on oil, he thought, and oil was desperately short up there.

Time, he reflected, was a paradoxical thing. The scientists had told him it was utterly rigid. Perhaps, though of course it would be a graveyard secret, the cloak-and-dagger boys had tested that theory the hard way, going back into the historical past (it could be done after all, Herries suspected, by a round-about route that consumed fabulous amounts of energy) in an attempt to head off the Bolshevik revolution. It would have failed. Neither past nor future could be changed; they could only be discovered. Some of Transoco's men had discovered death, an eon before they were born . . . But there would not be such a shortage of oil in the future if Transoco had not gone back and drained it in the past. A self-causing future. . . .

Primordial stuff, petroleum. Hoyle's idea seemed to be right, it had not been formed by rotting dinosaurs but was present from the beginning. It was the stuff that had stuck the planets together.

And, Herries thought, was sticking to him now. He reached for the soap.

Earth spun gloomily through hours, and morning crept over wide brown water. There was no real day as men understood day; the heavens were a leaden sheet with dirty black rainclouds scudding below the permanent fog layers.

Herries was up early, for a shipment was scheduled. He came out of the bosses' messhall and stood for a moment looking over the mud beach and the few square miles of cleared land, sleazy buildings, and gaunt derricks inside an electric mesh fence. Automation replaced thousands of workers, so that five hundred men were enough to handle everything, but still the compound was the merest scratch, and the jungle remained a terrifying black wall. Not that the trees were so utterly alien. Besides the archaic grotesqueries, like ferns and mosses of gruesome size, he saw cycad, redwood, and gingko, scattered prototypes of oak and willow and birch. But Herries missed wild flowers.

A working party with its machines was repairing the fence the brontosaur had smashed through yesterday, the well it had wrecked, the inroads of brush and vine. A caterpillar tractor hauled a string of loaded wagons across raw red earth. A helicopter buzzed overhead, on watch for dinosaurs. It was the only flying thing. There had been a nearby pterodactyl rookery, but the men had cleaned that out months ago. When you got right down to facts, the most sinister animal of all was man.

Greenstein joined Herries. The new assistant was tall, slender, with curly brown hair and the defenseless face of youth. Above boots and dungarees he wore a blue sports shirt; it offered a kind of defiance to this sullen world. "Smoke?" he invited.

"Thanks." Herries accepted the cigarette. His eyes still dwelt on the drills. Their walking beams went up and down, up and down, like a joyless copulation. Perhaps a man could get used to the Jurassic rain forest and eventually see some dark beauty there, for it was at least life; but this field would always remain hideous, being dead and pumping up the death of men.

"How's it going, Sam?" he asked when the tobacco had soothed his palate.

"All right," said Greenstein. "I'm shaking down. But God, it's good to know today is mail call!"

They stepped off the porch and walked toward the transceiving station. Mud squelched under their feet. A tuft of something, too pale and fleshy to be grass, stood near Herries's path. The yard crew had better uproot that soon, or in a week it might claim the entire compound.

"Girl friend, I suppose," said the chief. "That does make a month into a hell of a long drought between letters."

Greenstein flushed and nodded earnestly. "We're going to get married when my two years here are up," he said.

"That's what most of 'em plan on. A lot of saved-up pay and valuable experience—sure, you're fixed for life." It was on Herries's tongue to add that the life might be a short one, but he suppressed the impulse.

Loneliness dragged at his nerves. No one waited in the future for him. It was just as well, he told himself during the endless nights. Hard enough to sleep without worrying about some woman in the same age as the cobalt bomb.

"I've got her picture here, if you'd like to see it," offered Greenstein shyly.

His hand was already on his wallet. A tired grin slid up Herries's mouth. "Right next to your . . . er . . . heart, eh?" he murmured.

Greenstein blinked, threw back his head, and laughed. The field had not heard so merry a sound in a long while. Nevertheless, he showed the other man a pleasant-faced, unspectacular girl.

Out in the swamp, something hooted and threshed about.

Impulsively, Herries asked: "How do you feel about this operation, Sam?"

"Huh? Why, it's . . . interesting work. And a good bunch of guys."

"Even Symonds?"

"Oh, he means well."

"We could have more fun if he didn't bunk with us."

"He can't help being . . . old," said Greenstein.

Herries glanced at the boy. "You know," he said, "you're the first man in the Jurassic Period who's had a good word for Ephraim Symonds. I appreciate that. I'd better not say whether or not I share the sentiment, but I appreciate it." -

His boots sludged ahead, growing heavier with each step.

"You still haven't answered my first question," he resumed after a while. "I didn't ask if you enjoyed the work, I asked how you feel about it. Its purpose. We have the answers here to questions which science has been asking—will be asking—for centuries. And yet, except for a couple of underequipped paleobiologists, who aren't allowed to publish their findings, we're doing nothing but rape the Earth in an age before it has ever conceived us."

Greenstein hesitated. Then, with a surprise dryness: "You're getting too psychoanalytic for me, I'm afreud."

Herries chuckled. The day seemed a little more alive, all at once. "*Touché!* Well, I'll rephrase Joe Polansky's question of last night. Do you think the atomic standoff in our home era—to which this operation is potentially rather important—is stable?"

Greenstein considered for a moment. "No," he admitted. "Deterrence is a stopgap till something better can be worked out."

"They've said as much since it first began. Nothing has been done. It's improbable that anything will be. Ole Olson describes the international situation as a case of the irresistibly evil force colliding with the immovably stupid object."

"Ole likes to use extreme language," said Greenstein. "So tell me, what else could our side do?"

"I wish to God I had an answer." Herries sighed. "Pardon me. We avoid politics here as much as possible; we're escapists in several senses of the word. But frankly, I sound out new men. I was doing it to you. Because in spite of what Washington thinks, a Q clearance isn't all that a man needs to work here."

"Did I pass?" asked Greenstein, a bit too lightly.

"Sure. So far. You may wish you hadn't. The burning issue today is not whether to tolerate 'privileged neutralism,' or whatever the latest catchword is up there. It's: Did I get the armament I've been asking for?"

The transceiving station bulked ahead. It was a long corrugated-iron shed, but dwarfed by the tanks that gleamed behind it. Every one of those was filled, Herries knew. Today they would pump their crude oil into the future. Or rather, if you wanted to be exact, their small temporal unit would establish a contact and the gigantic main projector in the twentieth century would then "suck" the liquid toward itself.

And in return the compound would get food, tools, weapons, supplies, and mail. Herries prayed for at least one howitzer . . . and no VIP's. That senator a few months ago!

For a moment, contemplating the naked ugliness of tanks and pumps and shed, Herries had a vision of this one place stretching through time. It would be abandoned some day, when the wells were exhausted, and rain and jungle would rapidly eat the last thin traces of man. Later would come the sea, and then it would be dry land again, a cold prairie scoured by glacial winds, and then it would grow warm and . . . on and on, a waste of years until the time projector was invented and the great machine stood on this spot. And afterward? Herries didn't like to think what might be here after that.

Symonds was already present. He popped rabbitlike out of the building, a coded manifest in one hand, a pencil behind his ear. "Good morning, Mr. Herries," he said. His tone gave its usual impression of stiff self-importance.

"Morning. All set in there?" Herries went in to see for himself. A spatter of rain began to fall, noisy on the metal roof. The technicians were at their posts and reported clear. Outside, one by one, the rest of the men were drifting up. This was mail day, and little work would be done for the remainder of it.

Herries laid the sack of letters to the future inside the shed in its proper spot. His chronometer said one minute to go. "Stand by!" At the precise time, there was a dim whistle in the air and an obscure pulsing glow. Meters came to life. The pumps began to throb, driving crude oil through a pipe that faced open-ended into the shed. Nothing emerged that Herries could see. Good. Everything in order. The other end of the pipe awas a hundred million years in the future. The mail sack vanished with a small puff, as air rushed in where it had waited. Herries went back outside.

"Ah . . . excuse me."

He turned around, with a jerkiness that told him his nerves were half unraveled. "Yes?" he snapped.

"May I see you a moment?" asked Symonds. "Alone?" And the pale eyes behind the glasses said it was not a request but an order.

Herries nodded curtly, swore at the men for hanging around idle when the return shipment wasn't due for hours, and led the way to a porch tacked onto one side of the transceiving station. There were some camp stools beneath it. Symonds hitched up his khakis as if they were a business suit and sat primly down, his hands flat on his knees.

"A special shipment is due today," he said. "I was not permitted to discuss it until the last moment."

Herries curled his mouth. "Go tell Security that the Kremlin won't be built for a hundred million years. Maybe they haven't heard."

"What no one knew, no one could put into a letter home."

"The mail is censored anyway. Our friends and relatives think we're working somewhere in Asia." Herries spat into the mud and said: "And in another year the first lot of recruits are due home. Plan to shoot them as they emerge, so they can't possibly talk in their sleep?"

Symonds seemed too humorless even to recognize sarcasm. He pursed his lips and declared: "Some secrets need be kept for a few months only; but within that period, they *must* be kept."

"Okay, okay. Let's hear what's coming today."

"I am not allowed to tell you that. But about half the total tonnage will be crates marked top secret. These are to remain in the shed, guarded night and day by armed men." Symonds pulled a slip of paper from his jacket. "These men will be assigned to that duty, each one taking eight hours a week."

Herries glanced at the names. He did not know everyone here by sight, though he came close, but he recognized several of these. "Brave, discreet, and charter subscribers to *National Review*," he murmured. "Teacher's pets. All right. Though I'll have to curtail exploration correspondingly— either that, or else cut down on escorts and sacrifice a few extra lives."

"I think not. Let me continue. You will get these orders in the mail today, but I will prepare you for them now. A special house must be built for the crates, as rapidly as possible, and they must be moved there immediately upon its completion. I have the specifications in my office safe; essentially, it must be air-conditioned, burglar-proof, and strong enough to with- stand all natural hazards."

"Whoa, there!" Herries stepped forward. "That's going to take reinforced concrete and—"

"Materials will be made available," said Symonds. He did

not look at the other man but stared straight ahead of him, across the rain-smoky compound to the jungle. He had no expression on his pinched face, and the reflection of light off his glasses gave him a strangely blind look.

"But—Judas priest!" Herries threw his cigarette to the ground; it was swallowed in mud and running water. He felt the heat enfold him like a blanket. "There's the labor too, the machinery, and— How the devil am I expected to expand this operation if—"

"Expansion will be temporarily halted," cut in Symonds. "You will simply maintain current operations with skeleton crews. The majority of the labor force is to be reassigned to construction."

"What?"

"The compound fence must be extended and reinforced. A number of new storehouses are to be erected to hold certain supplies which will presently be sent to us. Bunkhouse barges for an additional five hundred are required. This, of course, entails more sick bay, recreational, mess, laundry, and other facilities."

Herries stood dumbly, staring at him. Pale lightning flickered in the sky.

The worst of it was, Symonds didn't even bother to be arrogant. He spoke like a schoolmaster.

"Oh, no!" whispered Herries after a long while. "They're not going to try to establish that Jurassic military base after all!"

"The purpose is classified."

"Yeah. Sure. Classified. Arise, ye duly cleared citizens of democracy, and cast your ballot on issues whose nature is classified, that your leaders whose names and duties are classified may— Great. Hopping. Balls. Of. Muck." Herries swallowed. Vaguely, through his pulse, he felt his fingers tighten into fists.

"I'm going up," he said. "I'm going to protest personally in Washington."

"That is not permitted," Symonds said in a dry, clipped tone. "Read your contract. You are under martial law. Of course," and his tone was neither softer nor harder, "you may file a written recommendation."

Herries stood for a while. Out beyond the fence stood a bulldozer, wrecked and abandoned. The vines had almost

buried it and a few scuttering little marsupials lived there.
Perhaps they were his own remote ancestors. He could take a
.22 and go potshooting at them some day.

"I'm not permitted to know anything," he said at last. "But
is curiosity allowed? An extra five hundred men aren't much.
I suppose, given a few airplanes and so on, a thousand of us
could plant atomic bombs where enemy cities will be. Or
could we? Can't locate them without astronomical studies
first, and it's always clouded here. So it would be practical to
boobytrap only with mass action weapons. A few husky
cobalt bombs, say. But there are missiles available to deliver
those in the twentieth century. So . . . what is the purpose?"

"You will learn the facts in due course," answered Symonds. "At present, the government has certain military
necessities."

"Haw!" said Herries. He folded his arms and leaned
against the roofpost. It sagged a bit—shoddy work, shoddy
world, shoddy destiny. "Military horses' necks! I'd like to get
one of those prawn-eyed brass hats down here, just for a
week, to run his precious security check on a lovesick
brontosaur. But I'll probably get another visit from Senator
Lardhead, the one who took up two days of my time walking
around asking about the possibilities of farming. *Farming!*"

"Senator Wien is from an agricultural state. Naturally he
would be interested—"

"—in making sure that nobody here starts raising food and
shipping it back home to bring grocery prices down to where
people can afford an occasional steak. Sure. I'll bet it cost us a
thousand man-hours to make his soil tests and tell him, yes,
given the proper machinery this land could be farmed. Of
course, maybe I do him an injustice. Senator Wien is also on
the Military Affairs Committee, isn't he? He may have visited
us in that capacity, and soon we'll get a directive to start our
own little victory gardens."

"Your language is close to being subversive," declared
Symonds out of prune-wrinkled lips. "Senator Wien is a
famous statesman."

For a moment the legislator's face rose in Herries's memory; it had been the oldest and most weary face he had ever
known. Something had burned out in the man who fought a
decade for honorable peace; the knowledge that there was no
peace and could be none became a kind of death, and Senator

Wien dropped out of his Free World Union organization to arm his land for Ragnarok. Briefly, his anger fading, Herries pitied Senator Wien. And the President, and the Chief of Staff, and the Secretary of State, for their work must be like a nightmare where you strangled your mother and could not stop your hands. It was easier to fight dinosaurs.

He even pitied Symonds, until he asked if his request for an atomic weapon had finally been okayed, and Symonds replied, "Certainly not." Then he spat at the clerk's feet and walked out into the rain.

After the shipment and guards were seen to, Herries dismissed his men. There was an uneasy buzz among them at the abnormality of what had arrived; but today was mail day, after all, and they did not ponder it long. He would not make the announcement about the new orders until tomorrow. He got the magazines and newspapers to which he subscribed (no one up there "now" cared enough to write to him, though his parents had existed in a section of space-time that ended only a year before he took this job) and wandered off to the boss's barge to read a little.

The twentieth century looked still uglier than it had last month. The nations felt their pride and saw no way of retreat. The Middle Eastern war was taking a decisive turn which none of the great powers could afford. Herries wondered if he might not be cut off in the Jurassic. A single explosion could destroy the main projector. Five hundred womanless men in a world of reptiles— He'd take the future, cobalt bomb and all.

After lunch there fell a quiet, Sunday kind of atmosphere. Men lay on their bunks reading their letters over and over. Herries made his rounds, machines and kitchen and sick bay, inspecting.

"I guess we'll discharge O'Connor tomorrow," said Dr. Yamaguchi. "He can do light work with that Stader on his arm. Next time tell him to duck when a power shovel comes down."

"What kind of sick calls have you been getting?" asked the chief.

Yamaguchi shrugged. "Usual things, very minor. I'd never have thought this swamp country could be so healthful. I guess disease germs that can live on placental mammals haven't evolved yet."

Father Gonzales, one of the camp's three chaplains, but-tonholed Herries as he came out. "Can you spare me a minute?" he said.

"Sure, padre. What is it?"

"About organizing some baseball teams. We need more recreation. This is not a good place for men to live."

"Sawbones was just telling me—"

"I know. No flu, no malaria, oh, yes. But man is more than a body."

"Sometimes I wonder," said Herries. "I've seen the latest headlines. The dinosaurs have more sense than we do."

"We have the capacity to do nearly all things," said Father Gonzales. "At present, I mean in the twentieth century, we seem to do evil very well. We can do as much good, given the chance."

"Who's denying us the chance?" asked Herries. "Just ourselves, H. Sapiens. Therefore I wonder if we really are able to do good."

"Don't confuse sinfulness with damnation," said the priest. "We have perhaps been unfortunate in our successes. And yet even our most menacing accomplishments have a kind of sublimity. The time projector, for example. If the minds able to shape such a thing in metal were only turned toward human problems, what could we not hope to do?"

"But that's my point," said Herries. "We don't do the high things. We do what's trivial and evil so consistently that I wonder if it isn't in our nature. Even this time travel business . . . more and more I'm coming to think there's something fundamentally unhealthy about it. As if it's an invention that only an ingrown mind would have made first."

"First?"

Herries looked up into the steaming sky. A foul wind met his face. "There are stars above those clouds," he said, "and most stars must have planets. I've not been told how the time projector works, but elementary differential calculus will show that travel into the past is equivalent to attaining, momentarily, an infinite velocity. In other words, the basic natural law that the projector uses is one that somehow goes beyond relativity theory. If a time projector is possible, so is a spaceship that can reach the stars in a matter of days, maybe of minutes or seconds. If we were sane, padre, we wouldn't have been so anxious for a little organic grease and the little military advantage involved that the first thing we did was go back into the dead past after it. No, we'd have invented that spaceship first, and gone out to the stars where there's room to be free and to grow. The time projector would have come afterward, as a scientific research tool."

He stopped, embarrassed at himself and trying awkwardly to grin. "Excuse me. Sermons are more your province than mine."

"It was interesting," said Father Gonzales. "But you brood too much. So do a number of men. Even if they have no close ties at home—it was wise to pick them for that—they are all of above-average intelligence, and aware of what the future is becoming. I'd like to shake them out of their depression. If we could get some more sports equipment . . ."

"Sure. I'll see what I can do."

"Of course," said the priest, "the problem is basically philosophical. Don't laugh. You too were indulging in philosophy, and doubtless you think of yourself as an ordinary, unimaginative man. Your wildcatters may not have heard of Aristotle, but they are also thinking men in their way. My personal belief is that this heresy of a fixed, rigid time line lies at the root of their growing sorrowfulness, whether they know it or not."

"Heresy?" The engineer lifted thick sandy brows. "It's been proved. It's the basis of the theory which showed how to build a projector; that much I do know. How could we be here, if the Mesozoic were not just as real as the Cenozoic? But if all time is coexistent, then all time must be fixed— unalterable—because every instant is the unchanging past of some other instant."

"Perhaps so, from God's viewpoint," said Father Gonzales. "But we are mortal men. And we have free will. The fixed-time concept need not, logically, produce fatalism. Remember, Herries, man's will is an important reason why twentieth-century civilization is approaching suicide. If we think we know our future is unchangeable, if our every action is foreordained, if we are doomed already, what's the use of trying? Why go through the pain of thought, of seeking an answer and struggling to make others accept it? But if we really believed in ourselves, we would look for a solution, and find one."

"Maybe," said Herries uncomfortably. "Well, give me a

list of the equipment you want, and I'll put in an order for it the next time the mail goes out."

As he walked off, he wondered if the mail would ever go out again.

Passing the rec hall, he noticed a small crowd before it and veered to see what was happening. He could not let men gather to trade doubts and terrors, or the entire operation was threatened. *In plain English,* he told himself with a growing bitter honesty, *I can't permit them to think.*

But the sound which met him, under the subtly alien rustle of forest leaves and the distant bawl of a thunder lizard, was only a guitar. Chords danced forth beneath expert fingers, and a young voice lilted:

> . . . I traveled this wide world over,
> A hundred miles or more,
> But a saddle on a milk cow,
> I never seen before! . . .

Looking over shoulders, Herries made out Greenstein, sprawled on a bench and singing. He heard chuckles from the listeners. Well deserved: the kid was good; Herries wished he could relax and simply enjoy the performance. Instead, he must note that they were finding it pleasant, and that swamp and war were alike forgotten for a valuable few minutes.

The song ended. Greenstein stood up and stretched. "Hi, Boss," he said.

Hard, wind-beaten faces turned to Herries and a mumble of greeting went around the circle. He was well enough liked, he knew, insofar as a chief can be liked. But that is not much. A leader can inspire trust, loyalty, what have you, but he cannot be humanly liked, or he is no leader.

"That was good," said Herries. "I didn't know you played."

"I didn't bring this whangbox with me, since I had no idea where I was going till I got here," answered Greenstein. "Wrote home for it and it arrived today."

A heavy-muscled crewcut man said, "You ought to be on the entertainment committee." Herries recognized Worth, one of the professional patriots who would be standing guard on Symonds's crates; but not a bad sort, really, after you learned to ignore his rather tedious opinions.

Greenstein said an indelicate word. "I'm sick of committees," he went on. "We've gotten so much into the habit of being herded around—everybody in the twentieth century has—that we can't even have a little fun without first setting up a committee."

Worth looked offended but made no answer. It began to rain again, just a little.

"Go on now, anyway," said Joe Eagle Wing. "Let's not take ourselves so goddam serious. How about another song?"

"Not in the wet." Greenstein returned his guitar to its case. The group began to break up, some to the hall and some back toward their barges.

Herries lingered, unwilling to be left alone with himself. "About that committee," he said. "You might reconsider. It's probably true what you claim, but we're stuck with a situation. We've simply got to tell most of the boys, 'Now is the time to be happy,' or they never will be."

Greenstein frowned. "Maybe so. But hasn't anyone ever thought of making a fresh start? Of unlearning those bad habits?"

"You can't do that within the context of an entire society's vices," said Herries. "And how're you going to get away?"

Greenstein gave him a long look. "How the devil did you ever get this job?" he asked. "You don't sound like a man who'd be cleared for a dishwashing assistantship."

Herries shrugged. "All my life I've liked totalitarianism even less than what passes for democracy. I served in a couple of the minor wars and— No matter. Possibly I might not be given the post if I applied now. I've been here more than a year, and it's changed me some."

"It must," said Greenstein, flickering a glance at the jungle.

"How's things at home?" asked Herries, anxious for another subject.

The boy kindled, "Oh, terrific!" he said eagerly. "Miriam, my girl, you know, she's an artist, and she's gotten a commission to—"

The loudspeaker coughed and blared across the compound, into the strengthening rain: "Attention! Copter to ground, attention! Large biped dinosaur, about two miles away north-northeast, coming fast."

Herries cursed and broke into a run.

Greenstein paced him. Water sheeted where their boots struck. "What is it?" he called.

"I don't know . . . yet . . . but it might be . . . a really big . . . carnivore." Herries reached the headquarters shack and flung the door open. A panel of levers was set near his personal desk. He slapped one down and the "combat stations" siren skirled above the field. Herries went on, "I don't know why anything biped should make a beeline for us unless the smell of blood from the critter we drove off yesterday is attracting it. The smaller carnivores are sure as hell drawn. The charged fence keeps them away, but I doubt if it would do much more than enrage a dinosaur— Follow me!"

Jeeps were already leaving their garage when Herries and Greenstein came out. Mud leaped up from their wheels and dripped back off the fenders. The rain fell harder, until the forest beyond the fence blurred and the earth smoked with vapors. The helicopter hung above the derricks, like a skeleton vulture watching a skeleton army, and the alarm sirens filled the brown air with screaming.

"Can you drive one of these buggies?" asked Herries.

"I did in the Army," said Greenstein.

"Okay, we'll take the lead one. The main thing is to stop that beast before it gets in among the wells." Herries vaulted the right-hand door and planted himself on sopping plastic cushions. A .50-caliber machine gun was mounted on the hood before him, and the microphone of a police car radio hung at the dash. Five jeeps followed as Greenstein swung into motion. The rest of the crew, ludicrous ants across these wide wet distances, went scurrying to defend the most vital installations.

The north gate opened and the cars splashed out beyond the fence. There was a strip several yards across, also kept cleared; then the jungle wall rose, black, brown, dull red, and green and yellow. Here and there along the fence an occasional bone gleamed up out of the muck, some animal shot by a guard or killed by the voltage. Oddly enough, Herries irrelevantly remembered, such a corpse drew enough scavenging insects to clean it in a day, but it was usually ignored by the nasty man-sized hunter dinosaurs that still slunk and hopped and slithered in this neighborhood. Reptiles just did not go in for carrion. However, they followed the odor of blood. . . .

"Farther east," said the helicopter pilot's radio voice. "There. Stop. Face the woods. He's coming out in a minute. Good luck, Boss. Next time gimme some bombs and I'll handle the bugger myself."

"We haven't been granted any heavy weapons." Herries licked lips that seemed rough. His pulse was thick. No one had ever faced a tyrannosaur before.

The jeeps drew into line, and for a moment only their windshield wipers had motion. Then undergrowth crashed, and the monster was upon them.

It was indeed a tyrannosaur, thought Herries in a blurred way. A close relative, at least—he remembered vaguely that the *Tyrannosaurus rex*, belonged in the Cretaceous period, but never mind, this fellow was some kind of early cousin, unknown to science until this moment— It blundered ahead with the overweighted, underwitted stiffness which paleontologists had predicted, and which had led some of them to believe that it must have been a gigantic, carrion-eating hyena.* They forgot that, like the Cenozoic snake or crocodile, it was too dull to recognize dead meat as food; that the brontosaurs it preyed on were even more clumsy; and that sheer length of stride would carry it over the earth at a respectable rate.

Herries saw a blunt head three man-heights above ground, and a tail ending fifteen yards away. Scales of an unfairly beautiful steel gray shimmered in the rain, which made small waterfalls off flanks and wrinkled neck and tiny useless forepaws. Teeth clashed in a mindless reflex, the ponderous belly wagged with each step, and Herries felt the vibration of tons coming down claw-footed. The beast paid no attention to the jeeps, but moved jerkily toward the fence. Sheer weight would drive it through the mesh.

"Get in front of him, Sam!" yelled the engineer.

*Eds. note: For evidence relating to this possibility of undiscovered carnosaurs, see L. Sprague de Camp and Catherine Crook de Camp, *The Day of the Dinosaur* (Garden City, New York: Doubleday and Company, Inc., 1968), 132–133.

He gripped the machine gun. It snarled on his behalf, and a sleet of bullets stitched a bloody seam across the white stomach. The tyrannosaur halted, weaving its head about. It made a hollow, coughing roar. Greenstein edged the jeep closer.

The others attacked from the sides. Tracer streams hosed across alligator tail and bird legs. A launched grenade burst with a little puff on the right thigh. It opened a red ulcer-like crater. The tyrannosaur swung slowly about toward one of the cars.

That jeep dodged aside. "Get in on him!" shouted Herries. Greenstein shifted gears and darted through a fountain of mud. Herries stole a glance. The boy was grinning. Well, it would be something to tell the grandchildren, all right!

His jeep fled past the tyrannosaur, whipped about on two wheels, and crouched under a hammer of rain. The reptile halted. Herries cut loose with his machine gun. The monster standing there, swaying a little, roaring and bleeding, was not entirely real. This had happened a hundred million years ago. Rain struck the hot gun barrel and sizzled off.

"From the sides again," rapped Herries into his microphone. "Two and Three on his right, Four and Five on his left. Six, go behind him and lob a grenade at the base of his tail."

The tyrannosaur began another awkward about face. The water in which it stood was tinged red.

"Aim for his eyes!" yelled Greenstein, and dashed recklessly toward the profile now presented him.

The grenade from behind exploded. With a sudden incredible speed, the tyrannosaur turned clear around. Herries had an instant's glimpse of the tail like a snake before him, then it struck.

He threw up an arm and felt glass bounce off it as the windshield shattered. The noise when metal gave way did not seem loud, but it went through his entire body. The jeep reeled on ahead. Instinct sent Herries to the floorboards. He felt a brutal impact as his car struck the dinosaur's left leg. It hooted far above him. He looked up and saw a foot with talons, raised and filling the sky. It came down. The hood crumpled at his back and the engine was ripped from the frame.

Then the tyrannosaur had gone on. Herries crawled up into

the bucket seat. It was canted at a lunatic angle. "Sam," he croaked. "Sam, Sam."

Greenstein's head was brains and splinters, with half the lower jaw on his lap and a burst-out eyeball staring up from the seat beside him.

Herries climbed erect. He saw his torn-off machine gun lying in the mud. A hundred yards off, at the jungle edge, the tyrannosaur fought the jeeps. It made clumsy rushes, which they sideswerved, and they spat at it and gnawed at it. Herries thought in a dull, remote fashion: *This can go on forever. A man is easy to kill, one swipe of a tail and all his songs are a red smear in the rain. But a reptile dies hard, being less alive to start with. I can't see an end to this fight.*

The Number Four jeep rushed in. A man sprang from it and it darted back in reverse from the monster's charge. The man—"Stop that, you idiot," whispered Herries into a dead microphone, "stop it, you fool"—plunged between the huge legs. He moved sluggishly enough with clay on his boots, but he was impossibly fleet and beautiful under that jerking bulk. Herries recognized Worth. He carried a grenade in his hand. He pulled the pin and dodged claws for a moment. The flabby, bleeding stomach made a roof over his head. Jaws searched blindly above him. He hurled the grenade and ran. It exploded against the tyrannosaur's belly. The monster screamed. One foot rose and came down. The talons merely clipped Worth, but he went spinning, fell in the gumbo ten feet away and tried weakly to rise but couldn't.

The tyrannosaur staggered in the other direction, spilling its entrails. Its screams took on a ghastly human note. Somebody stopped and picked up Worth. Somebody else came to Herries and gabbled at him. The tyrannosaur stumbled in yards of gut, fell slowly, and struggled, entangling itself.

Even so, it was hard to kill. The cars battered it for half an hour as it lay there, and it hissed at them and beat the ground with its tail. Herries was not sure it had died when he and his men finally left. But the insects had long been busy, and a few of the bones already stood forth clean white.

The phone jangled on Herries's desk. He picked it up. "Yeh?"

"Yamaguchi in sickbay," said the voice. "Thought you'd want to know about Worth."

"Well?"

"Broken lumbar vertebra. He'll live, possibly without permanent paralysis, but he'll have to go back for treatment."

"And be held incommunicado a year, till his contract's up. I wonder how much of a patriot he'll be by that time."

"What?"

"Nothing. Can it wait till tomorrow? Everything's so disorganized right now, I'd hate to activate the projector."

"Oh, yes. He's under sedation anyway." Yamaguchi paused. "And the man who died—"

"Sure. We'll ship him back too. The government will even supply a nice coffin. I'm sure his girl friend will appreciate that."

"Do you feel well?" asked Yamaguchi sharply.

"They were going to be married," said Herries. He took another pull from the fifth of bourbon on his desk. It was getting almost too dark to see the bottle. "Since patriotism nowadays . . . in the future, I mean . . . in our own home, sweet home . . . since patriotism is necessarily equated with necrophilia, in that the loyal citizen is expected to rejoice every time his government comes up with a newer gadget for mass-producing corpses . . . I am sure the young lady will just love to have a pretty coffin. So much nicer than a mere husband. I'm sure the coffin will be chrome plated."

"Wait a minute—"

"With tail fins."

"Look here," said the doctor, "you're acting like a case of combat fatigue. I know you've had a shock today. Come see me and I'll give you a tranquilizer."

"Thanks," said Herries, "I've got one." He took another swig and forced briskness into his tone. "We'll send 'em back tomorrow morning, then. Now don't bother me. I'm composing a letter to explain to the great white father that this wouldn't have happened if we'd been allowed one stinking little atomic howitzer. Not that I expect to get any results. It's policy that we aren't allowed heavy weapons down here, and who ever heard of facts affecting a policy? Why, facts might be un-American."

He hung up, put the bottle on his lap and his feet on the desk, lit a cigarette and stared out the window. Darkness came sneaking across the compound like smoke. The rain had stopped for a while, and lamps and windows threw broken yellow gleams off puddles, but somehow the gathering night was so thick that each light seemed quite alone. There was no one else in the headquarters shack at this hour. Herries had not turned on his own lights.

To hell with it, he thought. *To hell with it.*

His cigarette tip waxed and waned as he puffed, like a small dying star. But the smoke didn't taste right when invisible. Or had he put away so many toasts to dead men that his tongue was numbed? He wasn't sure. It hardly mattered.

The phone shrilled again. He picked it up, fumble-handed in the murk. "Chief of operations," he said pleasantly. "To hell with you."

"What?" Symonds' voice rattled a bare bit. Then: "I have been trying to find you. What are you doing there this late?"

"I'll give you three guesses. Playing pinochle? No. Carrying on a sordid affair with a lady *Iguanodon?* No. None of your business? Right! *Give* that gentleman a box of see-gars."

"Look here, Mr. Herries," stated Symonds, "this is no time for levity. I understand that Matthew Worth was seriously injured today. He was supposed to be on guard duty tonight—the secret shipment. This has disarranged all my plans."

"Tsk-tsk-tsk. My nose bleeds for you."

"The schedule of duties must be revised. According to my notes, Worth would have been on guard from midnight until four A.M. Since I do not know precisely what other jobs his fellows are assigned to, I cannot single any one of them out to replace him. Will you do so? Select a man who can then sleep later tomorrow morning?"

"Why?" asked Herries.

"Why? Because . . . because—"

"I know. Because Washington said so. Washington is afraid some nasty dinosaur from what is going to be Russia will sneak in and look at an unguarded crate and hurry home with the information. Sure, I'll do it. I just wanted to hear you sputter."

Herries thought he made out an indignant breath sucked past an upper plate. "Very good," said the clerk. "Make the necessary arrangements for tonight, and we will work out a new rotation of watches tomorrow."

Herries put the receiver back.

The list of tight-lipped, tight-minded types was somewhere in his desk, he knew vaguely. A copy, rather. Symonds had a copy, and no doubt copies would be going to the Pentagon and the FBI and the Transoco personnel office and— Well, look at the list, compare it with the work schedule, see who wouldn't be doing anything of critical importance tomorrow forenoon, and put him on a bit of sentry-go. Simple.

Herries took another swig. He could resign, he thought. He could back out of the whole fantastically stupid, fantastically meaningless operation. He wasn't compelled to work. Of course, they could hold him for the rest of his contract. It would be a lonesome year. Or maybe not; maybe a few others would trickle in to keep him company. To be sure, he'd then be under surveillance the rest of his life. But who wasn't, in a century divided between two garrisons?

The trouble was, he thought, there was nothing a man could do about the situation. You could become a peace-at-any-cost pacifist and thereby, effectively, league yourself with the enemy; and the enemy had carried out too many cold massacres for any halfway sane man to stomach. Or you could fight back (thus becoming more and more like what you fought) and hazard planetary incineration against the possibility of a tolerable outcome. It only took one to make a quarrel, and the enemy had long ago elected himself that one. Now, it was probably too late to patch up the quarrel. Even if important men on both sides wished for a disengagement, what could they do against their own fanatics, vested interests, terrified common people . . . against the whole momentum of history?

Hell take it, thought Herries, *we may be damned but why must we be fools into the bargain?*

Somewhere a brontosaur hooted, witlessly plowing through a night swamp.

Well, I'd better— No!

Herries stared at the end of his cigarette. It was almost scorching his fingers. At least, he thought, at least he could find out what he was supposed to condone. A look into those crates, which should have held the guns he had begged for, and perhaps some orchestral and scientific instruments . . . and instead held God knew what piece of Pentagonal-brained idiocy . . . a look would be more than a blow in Symonds's smug eye. It would be an assertion that he was Herries, a free man, whose existence had not yet been pointlessly spilled from a splintered skull. He, the individual, would know what the Team planned; and if it turned out to be a crime against reason, he could at the very least resign and sit out whatever followed.

Yes. By the dubious existence of divine mercy, yes.

Again a bit of rain, a small warm touch on his face, like tears. Herries splashed to the transceiver building and stood quietly in the sudden flashlight glare. At last, out of blackness, the sentry's voice came: "Oh, it's you, sir."

"Uh-huh. You know Worth got hurt today? I'm taking his watch."

"What? But I thought—"

"Policy," said Herries.

The incantation seemed to suffice. The other man shuffled forth and laid his rifle in the engineer's hands. "And here's the glim," he added. "Nobody came by while I was on duty."

"What would you have done if somebody'd tried to get in?"

"Why, stopped them, of course."

"And if they didn't stop?"

The dim face under the dripping hat turned puzzledly toward Herries. The engineer sighed. "I'm sorry, Thornton. It's too late to raise philosophical questions. Run along to bed."

He stood in front of the door, smoking a damp cigarette, and watched the man trudge away. All the lights were out now, except overhead lamps here and there. They were brilliant, but remote; he stood in a pit of shadow and wondered what the phase of the moon was and what kind of constellations the stars made nowadays.

He waited. There was time enough for his rebellion. Too much time, really. A man stood in rain, fog about his feet and a reptile smell in his nose, and he remembered anemones in springtime, strewn under trees still cold and leafless, with here and there a little snow between the roots. Or he remembered drinking beer in a New England country inn one fall day, when the door stood open to red sumac and yellow beech and a far blue wandering sky. Or he remembered a man snatched under black Jurassic quagmires, a man stepped into red ruin, a man sitting in a jeep and bleeding brains down onto the picture of the girl he had planned to marry. And then he started wondering what the point of it all was, and decided that it was either without any point whatsoever or else had the purpose of obliterating anemones and quiet country inns, and he was forced to dissent somehow.

When Thornton's wet footsteps were lost in the dark, Herries unlocked the shed door and went through. It was smotheringly hot inside. Sweat sprang forth under his raincoat as he closed the door again and turned on his flashlight. Rain tapped loudly on the roof. The crates loomed over him, box upon box, many of them large enough to hold a dinosaur. It had taken a lot of power to ship that tonnage into the past. No wonder taxes were high. And what might the stuff be? A herd of tanks, possibly . . . some knocked-down bombers . . . Lord knew what concept the men who lived in offices, insulated from the sky, would come up with. And Symonds had implied it was a mere beginning; more shipments would come when this had been stored out of the way, and more, and more.

Herries found a workbench and helped himself to tools. He would have to be careful; no sense in going to jail. He laid the flashlight on a handy barrel and stooped down by one of the crates. It was of strong wood, securely screwed together. But while that would make it harder to dismantle, it could be reassembled without leaving a trace. Maybe. Of course, it might be booby trapped. No telling how far the religion of secrecy could lead the office men.

Oh, well, if I'm blown up I haven't lost much. Herries peeled off his slicker. His shirt clung to his body. He squatted and began to work.

It went slowly. After taking off several boards, he saw a regular manufacturer's crate, open-slatted. Something within was wrapped in burlap. A single curved metal surface projected slightly. What the devil? Herries got a crowbar and pried one slat loose. The nails shrieked. He stooped rigid for a while, listening, but heard only the rain, grown more noisy. He reached in and fumbled with the padding. . . . God, it was hot!

Only when he had freed the entire blade did he recognize what it was. And then his mind would not quite function; he gaped a long while before the word registered.

A plowshare.

"But they don't know what to do with the farm surpluses at home," he said aloud, inanely.

Like a stranger's, his hands began to repair what he had torn apart. He couldn't understand it. Nothing seemed altogether real any more. Of course, he thought in a dim way, theoretically anything might be in the other boxes, but he suspected more plows, tractors, discs, combines . . . why not bags of seeds? . . . *What were they planning to do?*

"Ah."

Herries whirled. The flashlight beam caught him like a spear.

He grabbed blindly for his rifle. A dry little voice behind the blaze said: "I would not recommend violence." Herries let the rifle fall. It thudded.

Symonds closed the shed door behind him and stepped forward in his mincing fashion, another shadow among bobbing misshapen shadows. He had simply flung on shirt and pants, but bands of night across them suggested necktie, vest, and coat.

"You see," he explained without passion, "all the guards were instructed *sub rosa* to notify me of anything unusual, even when it did not seem to warrant action on their part." He gestured at the crate. "Please continue reassembling it."

Herries crouched down again. Hollowness filled him; his sole wonder was how best to die. For if he were sent back to the twentieth century, surely, surely they would lock him up and lose the key, and the sunlessness of death was better than that. It was strange, he thought, how his fingers used the tools with untrembling skill.

Symonds stood behind him and held his light on the work. At last he asked primly, "Why did you break in like this?"

I could kill him, thought Herries. *He's unarmed. I could wring his scrawny neck between these two hands, and take a gun, and go into the swamp to live a few days. . . . But it might be easier just to turn the rifle on myself.*

He sought words with care, for he must decide what to do, though it seemed remote and scarcely important. "That's not an easy question to answer," he said.

"The significant ones never are."

Astonished, Herries jerked a glance upward and back. (And was the more surprised that he could still know surprise.) But the little man's face was in darkness. Herries saw a blank glitter off the glasses.

He said, "Let's put it this way. There are limits even to the rights of self-defense. If a killer attacked me, I could fight back with anything I've got. But I wouldn't be justified in grabbing some passing child for a shield."

"So you wished to make sure that nothing you would consider illegitimate was in those boxes?" asked Symonds academically.

"I don't know. What is illegitimate, these days? I was . . . I was disgusted. I liked Greenstein, and he died because Washington had decided we couldn't have bombs or atomic shells. I didn't know how much more I could consent to. I had to find out."

"I see." The clerk nodded. "For your information, it is agricultural equipment. Later shipments will include industrial and scientific material, a large reserve of canned food, and as much of the world's culture as it proves possible to microfilm."

Herries stopped working, turned around and rose. His knees would not hold him. He leaned against the crate and it was a minute before he could get out: "Why?"

Symonds did not respond at once. He reached forth a precise hand and took up the flashlight Herries had left on the barrel. Then he sat down there himself, with the two glowing tubes in his lap. The light from below ridged his face in shadows, and his glasses made blind circles. He said, as if ticking off the points of an agenda:

"You would have been informed of the facts in due course, when the next five hundred people arrive. Now you have brought on yourself the burden of knowing what you would otherwise have been ignorant of for months yet. I think it may safely be assumed that you will keep the secret and not be broken by it. At least, the assumption is necessary."

Herries heard his own breath harsh in his throat. "Who are these people?"

The papery half-seen countenance did not look at him, but into the pit-like reaches of the shed. "You have committed a common error," said Symonds, as if to a student. "You have assumed that because men are constrained by circumstances to act in certain ways, they must be evil or stupid. I assure you, Senator Wien and the few others responsible for this are neither. They must keep the truth even from those officials within the project whose reaction would be rage or panic instead of a sober attempt at salvage. Nor do they have unlimited powers. Therefore, rather than indulge in tantrums about the existing situation, they use it. The very compart-mentalization of effort and knowledge enforced by Security helps conceal their purposes and mislead those who must be given some information."

Symonds paused. A slight frown crossed his forehead, and he tapped an impatient fingernail on a flashlight casing. "Do not misunderstand," he went on. "Senator Wien and his associates have not forgotten their oaths of office, nor are they trying to play God. Their primary effort goes, as it must, to a straightforward dealing with the problems of the twenti-eth century. It is not they who are withholding the one significant datum—a datum which, incidentally, any informed person could reason out for himself if he cared to. It is properly constituted authority, using powers legally granted to stamp certain reports top secret. Of course, the senator has used his considerable influence to bring about the present eventuality, but that is normal politics."

Herries growled: "Get to the point, damn you! What are you talking about?"

Symonds shook his thin gray head. "You are afraid to know, are you not?" he asked quietly.

"I—" Herries turned about, faced the crate and beat it with his fist. The parched voice in the night continued to punish him:

"You know that a time-projector can go into the future about a hundred years at a jump, but can only go pastward in jumps of approximately one hundred megayears. We all realize there is a way to explore certain sections of the historical past, in spite of this handicap, by making enough century hops forward before the one long hop backward. But can you tell me how to predict the historical future? Say, a century hence? Come, come, you are an intelligent man. Answer me."

"Yeah," said Herries. "I get the idea. Leave me alone."

"Team A, a group of well-equipped volunteers, went into the twenty-first century," pursued Symonds. "They recorded what they observed and placed the data in a chemically inert box within a large block of reinforced concrete erected at an agreed-on location: one which a previous expedition to circa one hundred million A.D. had confirmed would remain stable. I presume they also mixed radioactive materials of long half-life into the concrete, to aid in finding the site. Of course, the bracketing of time jumps is such that they cannot now get back to the twentieth century. But Team B went a full hundred-megayear jump into the future, excavated the data, and returned home."

Herries squared his body and faced back to the other man. He was drained, so weary that it was all he could do to keep on his feet. "What did they find?" he asked. There was no tone in his voice or in him.

"Actually, several expeditions have been made to the year one hundred million," said Symonds. "Energy requirements for a visit to two hundred million—A.D. or B.C.—were considered prohibitive. In one hundred million, life is re-evolving on Earth. However, as yet the plants have not liberated sufficient oxygen for the atmosphere to be breathable. You see, oxygen reacts with exposed rock, so that if no biological processes exist to replace it continuously— But you have a better technical education than I."

"Okay," said Herries, flat and hard. "Earth was sterile for a long time in the future. Including the twenty-first century?"

"Yes. The radioactivity had died down enough so that Team A reported no danger to itself, but some of the longer-lived isotopes were still measurably present. By making differential measurements of abundance, Team A was able to estimate rather closely when the bombs had gone off."

"And?"

"Approximately one year from the twentieth-century base date we are presently using."

"One year . . . from now." Herries stared upward. Blackness met him. He heard the Jurassic rain on the iron roof, like drums.

"Possibly less," Symonds told him. "There is a factor of uncertainty. This project must be completed well within the safety margin before the war comes."

"The war comes," Herries repeated. "Does it have to come? Fixed time line or not, does it have to come? Couldn't the enemy leaders be shown the facts . . . couldn't our side, even, capitulate—"

"Every effort is being made," said Symonds like a machine. "Quite apart from the theory of rigid time, it seems unlikely that they will succeed. The situation is too unstable. One man, losing his head and pressing the wrong button, can write the end; and there are so many buttons. The very revelation of the truth, to a few chosen leaders or to the world public, would make some of them panicky. Who can tell what a man in panic will do? That is what I meant when I said that Senator Wien and his co-workers have not forgotten their oaths of office. They have no thought of taking refuge, they know they are old men. To the end, they will try to save the twentieth century. But they do not expect it; so they are also trying to save the human race."

Herries pushed up from the crate he had been leaning against. "Those five hundred who're coming," he whispered. "Women?"

"Yes. If time remains to rescue a few more, after the ones you are preparing for have gone through, it will be done. But there will be at least a thousand young, healthy adults here, in the Jurassic. You face a difficult time, when the truth must be told them; you can see why the secret must be kept until then. It is quite possible that someone here will lose his head. That is why no heavy weapons have been sent: a single deranged person must not be able to destroy everyone. But you will recover. You must."

Herries jerked the door open and stared out into the roaring darkness. "No traces of us . . . in the future," he said, hearing his voice high and hurt like a child's.

"How much trace do you expect would remain after geological eras?" answered Symonds. He was still the reproving schoolmaster; but he sat on the barrel and faced the great moving shadows in a corner. "It is assumed that you will remain here for several generations, until your numbers and resources have been expanded sufficiently. The Team A I spoke of will join you a century hence. It is also, I might add, composed of young men and women in equal numbers. But this planet in this age is not a good home. We trust that your descendants will perfect the spaceships we know to be possible, and take possession of the stars instead."

Herries leaned in the doorway, sagging with tiredness and the monstrous duty to survive. A gust of wind threw rain into his eyes. He heard dragons calling in the night.

"And you?" he said, for no good reason.

"I shall convey any final messages you may wish to send home," said the dried-out voice.

Neat little footsteps clicked across the floor until the clerk paused beside the engineer. Silence followed, except for the rain.

"Surely I will deserve to go home," said Symonds.

And the breath whistled inward between teeth which had snapped together. He raised his hands, claw-fingered, and screamed aloud: "You can let me go home *then!*"

He began running toward the supervisors' barge. The sound of him was soon lost. Herries stood for a time yet in the door.

OUR LADY OF THE SAUROPODS

Robert Silverberg

*Several years ago in Analog, Robert Olsen published a story
("Paleontology: an Experimental Science") suggesting that
computer synthesis of a dinosaur's DNA structure would give
scientists the ability to bring that species back to life. And while
Robert Silverberg speculates about the decline of dinosaurs in
"Our Lady of the Sauropods," he also is concerned with
expanding Olsen's idea. So inside a giant satellite that is
stabilized in one of the Lagrange slots (points of balance
between competing gravity fields), Bob has reconstituted a
Mesozoic world from surviving flora and "born again" dinosaurs such as Struthiomimus, Stegosaurus, Tyrannosaurus,
Brachiosaurus and Diplodocus (sauropods), Corythosaurus
(a crested duck-bill), Iguanodon (an elephant-sized ornithopod), and a Triceratops. Then into this jumbled Eden, one
bad-apple flings an Eve.*

21 August. 0750 hours. Ten minutes since the module meltdown. I can't see the wreckage from here, but I can smell it,
bitter and sour against the moist tropical air. I've found a cleft
in the rocks, a kind of shallow cavern, where I'll be safe from
the dinosaurs for a while. It's shielded by thick clumps of
cycads, and in any case it's too small for the big predators to
enter. But sooner or later I'm going to need food, and then
what? I have no weapons. How long can one woman last,
stranded and more or less helpless, aboard a habitat unit not
quite five hundred meters in diameter that she's sharing with
a bunch of active, hungry dinosaurs?

I keep telling myself that none of this is really happening.
Only I can't quite convince myself of that.

My escape still has me shaky. I can't get out of my mind the funny little bubbling sound the tiny powerpak made as it began to overheat. In something like fourteen seconds my lovely mobile module became a charred heap of fused-together junk, taking with it my communicator unit, my food supply, my laser gun, and just about everything else. And but for the warning that funny little sound gave me, I'd be so much charred junk now too. Better off that way, most likely.

When I close my eyes I imagine I can see Habitat Vronsky floating serenely in orbit a mere 120 kilometers away. What a beautiful sight! The walls gleaming like platinum, the great mirror collecting sunlight and flashing it into the windows, the agricultural satellites wheeling around it like a dozen tiny moons. I could almost reach out and touch it. Tap on the shielding and murmur, "Help me, come for me, rescue me." But I might just as well be out beyond Neptune as sitting here in the adjoining Lagrange slot. No way I can call for help. The moment I move outside this cleft in the rock I'm at the mercy of my saurians, and their mercy is not likely to be tender.

Now it's beginning to rain—artificial, like practically everything else on Dino Island. But it gets you just as wet as the natural kind. And clammy. Pfaugh.

Jesus, what am I going to do?

0815 hours. The rain is over for now. It'll come again in six hours. Astonishing how muggy, dank, thick the air is. Simply breathing is hard work, and I feel as though mildew is forming on my lungs. I miss Vronsky's clear, crisp, everlasting spring-time air. On previous trips to Dino Island I never cared about the climate. But of course I was snugly englobed in my mobile unit, a world within a world, self-contained, self-sufficient, isolated from all contact with this place and its creatures. Merely a roving eye, traveling as I pleased, invisible, invulnerable.

Can they sniff me in here?

We don't think their sense of smell is very acute. Sharper than a crocodile's not as good as a cat's. And the stink of the burned wreckage dominates the place at the moment. But I must reek with fear-signals. I feel calm now, but it was different as I went desperately scrambling out of the module during the meltdown. Scattering pheromones all over the place, I bet.

Commotion in the cycads. *Something's coming in here!*

Long neck, small birdlike feet, delicate grasping hands. Not to worry. *Struthiomimus*, is all—dainty dino, fragile, birdlike critter barely two meters high. Liquid golden eyes staring solemnly at me. It swivels its head from side to side, ostrichlike, click-click, as if trying to make up its mind about coming closer to me. *Scat!* Go peck a stegosaur. Let me alone.

The *Struthiomimus* withdraws, making little clucking sounds.

Closest I've ever been to a live dinosaur. Glad it was one of the little ones.

0900 hours. Getting hungry. What am I going to eat?

They say roasted cycad cones aren't too bad. How about raw ones? So many plants are edible when cooked and poisonous otherwise. I never studied such things in detail. Living in our antiseptic little L5 habitats we're not required to be outdoors-wise, after all. Anyway, there's a fleshy-looking cone on the cycad just in front of the cleft, and it's got an edible look. Might as well try it raw, because there's no other way. Rubbing sticks together will get me nowhere.

Getting the cone off takes some work. Wiggle, twist, snap, tear—*there*. Not as fleshy as it looks. Chewy, in fact. Like munching on rubber. Decent flavor, though. And maybe some useful carbohydrate.

The shuttle isn't due to pick me up for thirty days. Nobody's apt to come looking for me, or even to think about me, before then. I'm on my own. Nice irony there: I was desperate to get out of Vronsky and escape from all the bickering and maneuvering, the endless meetings and memoranda, the feinting and counterfeinting, all the ugly political crap that scientists indulge in when they turn into administrators. Thirty days of blessed isolation on Dino Island! An end to that constant dull throbbing in my head from the daily infighting with Director Sarber. Pure research again! And then the meltdown, and here I am cowering in the bushes wondering which comes first, starving or getting gobbled.

0930 hours. Funny thought just now. Could it have been sabotage?

Consider. Sarber and I, feuding for weeks over the issue of

opening Dino Island to tourists. Crucial staff vote coming up next month. Sarber says we can raise millions a year for expanded studies with a program of guided tours and perhaps some rental of the Island to film companies. I say that's risky both for the dinos and the tourists, destructive of scientific values, a distraction, a sell-out. Emotionally the staff's with me, but Sarber waves figures around, shows fancy income projections, and generally shouts and blusters. Tempers running high, Sarber in lethal fury at being opposed, barely able to hide his loathing for me. Circulating rumors— designed to get back to me—that if I persist in blocking him he'll abort my career. Which is malarkey, of course. He may outrank me, but he has no real authority over me. And then his politeness yesterday. *(Yesterday? An eon ago.)* Smiling smarmily, telling me he hopes I'll rethink my position during my observation tour on the Island. Wishing me well. Had he gimmicked my powerpak? I guess it isn't hard, if you know a little engineering, and Sarber does. Some kind of timer set to withdraw the insulator rods? Wouldn't be any harm to Dino Island itself, just a quick compact localized disaster that implodes and melts the unit and its passenger, so sorry, terrible scientific tragedy, what a great loss. And even if by some fluke I got out of the unit in time, my chances of surviving here as a pedestrian for thirty days would be pretty skimpy, right? Right.

It makes me boil to think that someone's willing to murder you over a mere policy disagreement. It's barbaric. Worse than that: it's tacky.

1130 hours. I can't stay crouched in this cleft forever. I'm going to explore the Island and see if I can find a better hideout. This one simply isn't adequate for anything more than short-term huddling. Besides, I'm not as spooked as I was right after the meltdown. I realize now that I'm not going to find a tyrannosaur hiding behind every tree. And tyrannosaurs aren't going to be much interested in scrawny stuff like me.

Anyway I'm a quick-witted higher primate. If my humble mammalian ancestors seventy million years ago were able to elude dinosaurs well enough to survive and inherit the earth, I should be able to keep from getting eaten for the next thirty days. And, with or without my cozy little mobile module, I want to get out into this place, whatever the risks. Nobody's ever had a chance to interact this closely with the dinos before.

Good thing I kept this pocket recorder when I jumped from the module. Whether I'm a dino's dinner or not, I ought to be able to set down some useful observations.

Here I go.

1830 hours. Twilight is descending now. I am camped near the equator in a lean-to flung together out of tree-fern fronds—a flimsy shelter, but the huge fronds conceal me and with luck I'll make it through the morning. That cycad cone doesn't seem to have poisoned me yet, and I ate another one just now, along with some tender new fiddleheads uncoiling from the heart of a tree-fern. Spartan fare, but it gives me the illusion of being fed.

In the evening mists I observe a brachiosaur, half grown but already colossal, munching in the treetops. A gloomy-looking *Triceratops* stands nearby, and several of the ostrich-like struthiomimids scamper busily in the underbrush, hunting I know not what. No sign of tyrannosaurs all day. There aren't many of them here, anyway, and I hope they're all sleeping off huge feasts somewhere in the other hemisphere.

What a fantastic place this is!

I don't feel tired. I don't even feel frightened—just a little wary.

I feel exhilarated, as a matter of fact.

Here I sit peering out between fern fronds at a scene out of the dawn of time. All that's missing is a pterosaur or two flapping overhead, but we haven't brought those back yet. The mournful snufflings of the huge brachiosaur carry clearly even in the heavy air. The struthiomimids are making sweet honking sounds. Night is falling swiftly, and the great shapes out there take on dreamlike primordial wonder.

What a brilliant idea it was to put all the Olsen-process dinosaur reconstructs aboard a little L5 habitat of their very own and turn them loose to recreate the Mesozoic! After that unfortunate San Diego event with the tyrannosaur it became politically unfeasible to keep them anywhere on earth, I know, but even so this is a better scheme. In just a little more than seven years, Dino Island has taken on an altogether convincing illusion of reality. Things grow so fast in this lush, steamy, high-CO_2 tropical atmosphere! Of course we haven't been able to duplicate the real Mesozoic flora, but we've done all right using botanical survivors, cycads and tree-ferns and horsetails and palms and gingkos and auracarias, and thick carpets of mosses and selaginellas and liverworts covering the ground. Everything has blended and merged and run amok: it's hard now to recall the bare and unnatural look of the Island when we first laid it out. Now it's a seamless tapestry in green and brown, a dense jungle broken only by streams, lakes, and meadows, encapsulated in spherical metal walls some two kilometers in circumference.

And the animals, the wonderful fantastic grotesque animals!

We don't pretend that the real Mesozoic ever held any such mix of fauna as I've seen today, stegosaurs and corythosaurs side by side, a *Triceratops* sourly glaring at a brachiosaur, *Struthiomimus* contemporary with *Iguanodon*, a wild unscientific jumble of Triassic, Jurassic, and Cretaceous, a hundred million years of the dinosaur reign scrambled together. We take what we can get. Olsen-process reconstructs require sufficient fossil DNA to permit the computer synthesis, and we've been able to find that in only some twenty species so far. The wonder is that we've accomplished even that much: to replicate the complete DNA molecule from battered and sketchy genetic information millions of years old, to carry out the intricate implants in reptilian host ova, to see the embryos through to self-sustaining levels. The only word that applies is *miraculous*. If our dinos come from eras millions of years apart, so be it: we do our best. If we have no pterosaur and no allosaur and no *Archaeopteryx*, so be it: we may have them yet. What we already have is plenty to work with. Some day there may be separate Triassic, Jurassic, and Cretaceous satellite habitats, but none of us will live to see that, I suspect.

Total darkness now. Mysterious screechings and hissings out there. This afternoon, as I moved cautiously but in delight from the wreckage site up near the rotation axis to my present equatorial camp, sometimes coming within fifty or a hundred meters of living dinos, I felt a kind of ecstasy. Now my fears are returning, and my anger at this stupid marooning. I imagine clutching claws reaching for me, terrible jaws yawning above me.

I don't think I'll get much sleep tonight.

22 August. 0600 hours. Rosy-fingered dawn comes to Dino Island, and I'm still alive. Not a great night's sleep, but I must have had some, because I can remember fragments of dreams. About dinosaurs, naturally. Sitting in little groups, some playing pinochle and some knitting sweaters. And choral singing, a dinosaur rendition of *The Messiah* or maybe Beethoven's Ninth.

I feel alert, inquisitive, and hungry. Especially hungry. I know we've stocked this place with frogs and turtles and other small-size anachronisms to provide a balanced diet for the big critters. Today I'll have to snare some for myself, grisly though I find the prospect of eating raw frog's legs.

I don't bother getting dressed. With rainshowers programmed to fall four times a day it's better to go naked anyway. Mother Eve of the Mesozoic, that's me! And without my soggy tunic I find that I don't mind the greenhouse atmosphere half as much.

Out to see what I can find.

The dinosaurs are up and about already, the big herbivores munching away, the carnivores doing their stalking. All of them have such huge appetites that they can't wait for the sun to come up. In the bad old days when the dinos were thought to be reptiles, of course, we'd have expected them to sit there like lumps until daylight got their body temperatures up to functional levels. But one of the great joys of the reconstruct project was the vindication of the notion that dinosaurs were warm-blooded animals, active and quick and pretty damned intelligent. No sluggardly crocodilians these! Would that they were, if only for my survival's sake.

1130 hours. A busy morning. My first encounter with a major predator.

There are nine tyrannosaurs on the Island, including three born in the past eighteen months. (That gives us an optimum predator-to-prey ratio. If the tyrannosaurs keep reproducing and don't start eating each other we'll have to begin thinning them out. One of the problems with a closed ecology: natural checks and balances don't fully apply.) Sooner or later I was bound to encounter one, but I had hoped it would be later.

I was hunting frogs at the edge of Cope Lake. A ticklish business; calls for agility, cunning, quick reflexes. I remember the technique from my girlhood—the cupped hand, the lightning pounce—but somehow it's become a lot harder in the last twenty years. Superior frogs these days, I suppose. There I was kneeling in the mud, swooping, missing, swooping, missing; some vast sauropod snoozing in the lake, probably our *Diplodocus:* a corythosaur browsing in a stand of gingko trees, quite delicately nipping off the foul-smelling yellow fruits. Swoop. Miss. Swoop. Miss. Such intense concentration on my task that old *T. rex* could have tiptoed right up behind me and I'd never have noticed. But then I felt a subtle something, a change in the air, maybe, a barely perceptible shift in dynamics. I glanced up and saw the corythosaur rearing on its hind legs, looking around uneasily, pulling deep sniffs into that fantastically elaborate bony crest that houses its early-warning system. *Carnivore alert!* The corythosaur obviously smelled something wicked this way coming, for it swung around between two big gingkos and started to go galumphing away. Too late. The treetops parted, giant boughs toppled, and out of the forest came our original tyrannosaur, the pigeon-toed one we call Belshazzar, moving in its heavy clumsy waddle, ponderous legs working hard, tail absurdly swinging from side to side. I slithered into the lake and scrunched down as deep as I could go in the warm oozing mud. The corythosaur had no place to slither. Unarmed, unarmored, it could only make great bleating sounds, terror mingled with defiance, as the killer bore down on it.

I had to watch. I had never seen a kill.

In a graceless but wondrously effective way the tyrannosaur dug its hind claws into the ground, pivoted astonishingly, and, using its massive tail as a counterweight, moved in a 90-degree arc to knock the corythosaur down with a stupendous sidewise swat of its huge head. I hadn't been expecting that. The corythosaur dropped and lay on its side, snorting in pain and feebly waving its limbs. Now came the coup-de-grace with hind legs, and then the rending and tearing, the jaws and the tiny arms at last coming into play. Burrowing chin-deep in the mud, I watched in awe and weird fascination. There are those among us who argue that the carnivores ought to be segregated into their own Island, that it is folly to allow reconstructs created with such effort to be casually butchered this way. Perhaps in the beginning that made sense, but not now, not when natural increase is rapidly filling the Island with young dinos. If we are to learn anything about these animals, it will only be by reproducing as closely as possible their original living conditions. Besides, would it not be a cruel mockery to feed our tyrannosaurs on hamburger and herring?

The killer fed for more than an hour. At the end came a scary moment. Belshazzar, blood-smeared and bloated, hauled himself ponderously down to the edge of the lake for a drink. He stood no more than ten meters from me. I did my most convincing imitation of a rotting log; but the tyrannosaur, although it did seem to study me with a beady eye, had no further appetite. For a long while after he departed, I stayed buried in the mud, fearing he might come back for dessert. And eventually there was another crashing and bashing in the forest—not Belshazzar this time, though, but a younger one with a gimpy arm. It uttered a sort of whinnying sound and went to work on the corythosaur carcass. No surprise: we already knew that tyrannosaurs had no prejudices against carrion.

Nor, I found, did I.

When the coast was clear I crept out and saw that the two tyrannosaurs had left hundreds of kilos of meat. Starvation knoweth no pride and also few qualms. Using a clamshell for my blade, I started chopping away.

Corythosaur meat has a curiously sweet flavor—nutmeg and cloves, dash of cinnamon. The first chunk would not go down. You are a pioneer, I told myself, retching. You are the first human ever to eat dinosaur meat. *Yes, but why does it have to be raw?* No choice about that. Be dispassionate, love. Conquer your gag reflex or die trying. I pretended I was eating oysters. This time the meat went down. It didn't stay down. The alternative, I told myself grimly, is a diet of fern fronds and frogs, and you haven't been much good at catching the frogs. I tried again. Success!

I'd have to call corythosaur meat an acquired taste. But the wilderness is no place for picky eaters.

23 August. 1300 hours. At midday I found myself in the southern hemisphere, along the fringes of Marsh Marsh about a hundred meters below the equator. Observing herd behavior in sauropods: five brachiosaurs, two adult and three young, moving in formation, the small ones in the center. By "small" I mean only some ten meters from nose to tail-tip. Sauropod appetites being what they are, we'll have to thin that herd soon too, especially if we want to introduce a female *Diplodocus* into the colony. *Two* species of sauropods breeding and eating like that could devastate the Island in three years. Nobody ever expected dinosaurs to reproduce like rabbits—another dividend of their being warm-blooded, I suppose. We might have guessed it, though, from the vast quantity of fossils. If that many bones survived the catastrophes of a hundred-odd million years, how enormous the living Mesozoic population must have been! An awesome race in more ways than mere physical mass.

I had a chance to do a little herd-thinning myself just now. Mysterious stirring in the spongy soil right at my feet, and I looked down to see *Triceratops* eggs hatching! Seven brave little critters, already horny and beaky, scrabbling out of a nest, staring around defiantly. No bigger than kittens, but active and sturdy from the moment of birth.

The corythosaur meat has probably spoiled by now. A more pragmatic soul very likely would have augmented her diet with one or two little ceratopsians. I couldn't do it.

They scuttled off in seven different directions. I thought briefly of catching one and making a pet out of it. Silly idea.

25 August. 0700 hours. Start of the fifth day. I've done three complete circumambulations of the Island. Slinking around on foot is fifty times as risky as cruising around in a module, and fifty thousand times as rewarding. I make camp in a different place every night. I don't mind the humidity any longer. And despite my skimpy diet I feel pretty healthy. Raw dinosaur, I know now, is a lot tastier than raw frog. I've become an expert scavenger—the sound of a tyrannosaur in the forest now stimulates my salivary glands instead of my adrenals. Going naked is fun, too. And I appreciate my body much more, since the bulges that civilization puts there have begun to melt away.

Nevertheless, I keep trying to figure out some way of signaling Habitat Vronsky for help. Changing the position of the reflecting mirrors, maybe, so I can beam an SOS? Sounds nice, but I don't even know where the Island's controls are located, let alone how to run them. Let's hope my luck holds out another three and a half weeks.

27 August. 1700 hours. The dinosaurs know that I'm here and that I'm some extraordinary kind of animal. Does that sound weird? How can great dumb beasts *know* anything? They have such tiny brains. And my own brain must be softening on this protein-and-cellulose diet. Even so, I'm starting to have peculiar feelings about these animals. I see them *watching* me. An odd knowing look in their eyes, not stupid at all. They stare, and I imagine them nodding, smiling, exchanging glances with each other, discussing me. I'm supposed to be observing them, but I think they're observing me too, somehow.

This is crazy. I'm tempted to erase the entry. But I'll leave it as a record of my changing psychological state, if nothing else.

28 August. 1200 hours. More fantasies about the dinosaurs. I've decided that the big brachiosaur—Bertha—plays a key role here. She doesn't move around much, but there are always lesser dinosaurs in orbit around her. Much eye contact. *Eye contact between dinosaurs?* Let it stand. That's my perception of what they're doing. I get a definite sense that there's communication going on here, modulating over some wave that I'm not capable of detecting. And Bertha seems to be a central nexus, a grand totem of some sort, a—a switchboard? What am I talking about? What's happening to me?

30 August. 0945 hours. What a damned fool I am! Serves me right for being a filthy voyeur. Climbed a tree to watch

Iguanodons mating at the foot of Bakker Falls. At climactic moment the branch broke. I dropped twenty meters. Grabbed a lower limb or I'd be dead now. As it is, pretty badly smashed around. I don't think anything's broken, but my left leg won't support me and my back's in bad shape. Internal injuries too? Not sure. I've crawled into a little rock-shelter near the falls. Exhausted and maybe feverish. Shock, most likely. I suppose I'll starve now. It would have been an honor to be eaten by a tyrannosaur, but to die from falling out of a tree is just plain humiliating.

The mating of *Iguanodons* is a spectacular sight, by the way. But I hurt too much to describe it now.

31 August. 1700 hours. Stiff, sore, hungry, hideously thirsty. Leg still useless, and when I try to crawl even a few meters I feel as if I'm going to crack in half at the waist. High fever.

How long does it take to starve to death?

1 Sep. 0700 hours. Three broken eggs lying near me when I awoke. Embryos still alive—probably stegosaur—but not for long. First food in 48 hours. Did the eggs fall out of a nest somewhere overhead? Do stegosaurs make their nests in trees, dummy?

Fever diminishing. Body aches all over. Crawled to the stream and managed to scoop up a little water.

1330 hours. Dozed off. Awakened to find haunch of fresh meat within crawling distance. *Struthiomimus* drumstick, I think. Nasty sour taste, but it's edible. Nibbled a little, slept again, ate some more. Pair of stegosaurs grazing not far away, tiny eyes fastened on me. Smaller dinosaurs holding a kind of conference by some big cycads. And Bertha Brachiosaur is munching away in Ostrom Meadow, benignly supervising the whole scene.

This is absolutely crazy.

I think the dinosaurs are taking care of me.

2 Sep. 0900 hours. No doubt of it at all. They bring me eggs, meat, even cycad cones and tree-fern fronds. At first they delivered things only when I slept, but now they come hopping right up to me and dump things at my feet. The struthiomimids are the bearers—they're the smallest, most agile, quickest hands. They bring their offerings, stare me right in the eye, pause as if waiting for a tip. Other dinosaurs watching from the distance. This is a coordinated effort. I am the center of all activity on the Island, it seems. I imagine that even the tyrannosaurs are saving choice cuts for me. Hallucination? Fantasy? Delirium of fever? I feel lucid. The fever is abating. I'm still too stiff and weak to move very far, but I think I'm recovering from the effects of my fall. With a little help from my friends.

1000 hours. Played back the last entry. Thinking it over. I don't *think* I've gone insane. If I'm sane enough to be worried about my sanity, how crazy can I be? Or am I just fooling myself? There's a terrible conflict between what I think I perceive going on here and what I know I ought to be perceiving.

1500 hours. A long strange dream this afternoon. I saw all the dinosaurs standing in the meadow, and they were connected to one another by gleaming threads, like the telephone lines of olden times, and all the threads centered on Bertha. As if she's the switchboard, yes. And telepathic messages were traveling. An extrasensory hookup, powerful pulses moving along the lines. I dreamed that a small dinosaur came to me and offered me a line, and in pantomime showed me how to hook it up, and a great flood of delight went through me as I made the connection. And when I plugged it in I could feel the deep and heavy thoughts of the dinosaurs, the slow rapturous philosophical interchanges.

When I woke the dream seemed bizarrely vivid, strangely real, the dream-ideas lingering as they sometimes do. I saw the animals about me in a new way. As if this is not just a zoological research station, but a community, a settlement, the sole outpost of an alien civilization—an alien civilization native to earth.

Come off it. These animals have minute brains. They spend their days chomping on greenery, except for the ones that chomp on other dinosaurs. Compared with dinosaurs, cows and sheep are downright geniuses.

I can hobble a little now.

3 Sep. 0600 hours. The same dream again last night, the universal telepathic linkage. Sense of warmth and love flowing from dinosaurs to me.

Fresh tyrannosaur eggs for breakfast.

5 Sep. 1100 hours. I'm making a fast recovery. Up and about, still creaky but not much pain left. They still feed me. Though the struthiomimids remain the bearers of food the bigger dinosaurs now come close too. A stegosaur nuzzled up to me like some Goliath-sized pony, and I petted its rough scaly flank. The *Diplodocus* stretched out flat and seemed to beg me to stroke its immense neck.

If this is madness, so be it. There's a community here, loving and temperate. Even the predatory carnivores are part of it: eaters and eaten are aspects of the whole, yin and yang. Riding around in our sealed modules, we could never have suspected any of this.

They are gradually drawing me into their communion. I feel the pulses that pass between them. My entire soul throbs with that strange new sensation. My skin tingles.

They bring me food of their own bodies, their flesh and their unborn young, and they watch over me and silently urge me back to health. Why? For sweet charity's sake? I don't think so. I think they want something from me. I think they need something from me.

What could they need from me?

6 Sep. 0600 hours. All this night I have moved slowly through the forest in what I can only term an ecstatic state. Vast shapes, humped monstrous forms barely visible by dim glimmer, came and went about me. Hour after hour I walked unharmed, feeling the communion intensify. Until at last, exhausted, I have come to rest here on this mossy carpet, and in the first light of dawn I see the giant form of the great brachiosaur standing like a mountain on the far side of Owen River.

I am drawn to her. I could worship her. Through her vast body surge powerful currents. She is the amplifier. By her are we all connected. The holy mother of us all. From the enormous mass of her body emanate potent healing impulses.

I'll rest a little while. Then I'll cross the river to her.

0900 hours. We stand face to face. Her head is fifteen meters above mine. Her small eyes are unreadable. I trust her and I love her.

Lesser brachiosaurs have gathered behind her on the riverbank. Farther away are dinosaurs of half a dozen other species, immobile, silent.

I am humble in their presence. They are representatives of a dynamic, superior race, which but for a cruel cosmic accident would rule the earth to this day, and I am coming to revere them.

Consider: they endured for a hundred forty million years in ever-renewing vigor. They met all evolutionary challenges, except the one of sudden and catastrophic climatic change, against which nothing could have protected them. They multiplied and proliferated and adapted, dominating land and sea and air, covering the globe. Our own trifling contemptible ancestors were nothing next to them. Who knows what these dinosaurs might have achieved, if that crashing asteroid had not blotted out their light? What a vast irony: millions of years of supremacy ended in a single generation by a chilling cloud of dust. But until then—the wonder, the grandeur!

Only beasts, you say? How can you be sure? We know just a shred of what the Mesozoic was really like, just a slice, literally the bare bones. The passage of a hundred million years can obliterate all traces of civilization. Suppose they had language, poetry, mythology, philosophy? Love, dreams, aspirations? No, you say, they were beasts, ponderous and stupid, that lived mindless bestial lives. And I reply that we puny hairy ones have no right to impose our own values on them. The only kind of civilization we can understand is the one we have built. We imagine that our own trivial accomplishments are the determining case, that computers and spaceships and broiled sausages are such miracles that they place us at evolution's pinnacle. But now I know otherwise. Humanity has done marvelous things, yes. But we would not have existed at all, had this greatest of races been allowed to live to fulfill its destiny.

I feel the intense love radiating from the titan that looms

above me. I feel the contact between our souls steadily strengthening and deepening.

The last barriers dissolve.

And I understand at last.

I am the chosen one. I am the vehicle. I am the bringer of rebirth, the beloved one, the necessary one. Our Lady of the Sauropods am I, the holy one, the prophetess, the priestess.

Is this madness? Then it is madness.

Why have we small hairy creatures existed at all? I know now. It is so that through our technology we could make possible the return of the great ones. They perished unfairly. Through us, they are resurrected abroad this tiny globe in space.

I tremble in the force of the need that pours from them.

I will not fail you, I tell the great sauropods before me, and the sauropods send my thoughts reverberating to all the others.

20 September. 0600 hours. The thirtieth day. The shuttle comes from Habitat Vronsky today to pick me up and deliver the next researcher.

I wait at the transit lock. Hundreds of dinosaurs wait with me, each close beside the next, both the lions and the lambs, gathered quietly, their attention focused entirely on me.

Now the shuttle arrives, right on time, gliding in for a perfect docking. The airlocks open. A figure appears, Sarber himself! Coming to make sure I didn't survive the meltdown, or else to finish me off.

He stands blinking in the entry passage, gaping at the throngs of placid dinosaurs arrayed in a huge semecircle around the naked woman who stands beside the wreckage of the mobile module. For a moment he is unable to speak.

"Anne?" he says finally. "What in God's name—"

"You'll never understand," I tell him. I give the signal. Belshazzar rumbles forward. Sarber screams and whirls and sprints for the airlock, but a stegosaur blocks the way.

"No!" Sarber cries, as the tyrannosaur's mighty head swoops down. It is all over in a moment.

Revenge! How sweet!

And this is only the beginning. Habitat Vronsky lies just 120 kilometers away. Elsewhere in the Lagrange belt are hundreds of other habitats ripe for conquest. The earth itself is within easy reach. I have no idea yet how it will be accomplished, but I know it will be done and done successfully, and I will be the instrument by which it is done.

I stretch forth my arms to the mighty creatures that surround me. I feel their strength, their power, their harmony. I am one with them, and they with me.

The Great Race has returned, and I am its priestess. Let the hairy ones tremble!

GEOLOGIC TIME SCALE

Era	Period	Epoch	Estimated time span from present	Life forms
Precambrian			4,600,000,000 years ago to 600,000,000 years ago	Beginnings of life. Algae, bacteria, seaweed, and sponges.
Paleozoic	Cambrian	Lower Middle Upper	600,000,000 years ago to 500,000,000 years ago	First marine invertebrates, including widespread trilobites (primitive shellfish) and earliest snails. Lichens appear on land.
	Ordovician	Lower Middle Upper	500,000,000 years ago to 425,000,000 years ago	Most characteristic animals are graptolites (small coelenterates). Beginning of fish and many marine invertebrates.
	Silurian	Lower Middle Upper	425,000,000 years ago to 405,000,000 years ago	Coral reefs become widespread. Lungfishes develop. Animals such as scorpions begin living entire life on land.

Period	Epoch	Time	Description
Devonian	Lower Middle Upper	405,000,000 years ago to 345,000,000 years ago	Beginning of amphibians, insects, land snails, and woody plants.
Carboniferous — Mississippian	Lower Upper	345,000,000 years ago to 310,000,000 years ago	Primitive ammonites. Shell-crushing sharks dominant larger marine animal. Lizardlike amphibian predominant land animal.
Carboniferous — Pennsylvanian	Lower Middle Upper	310,000,000 years ago to 280,000,000 years ago	Scale trees grow as high as 100 feet. Development of primitive conifers. Largest known insect: dragonfly with 30-inch wing-span. Beginning of reptiles.
Permian	Lower Upper	280,000,000 years ago to 230,000,000 years ago	Extinction of trilobites and many other types of marine animals. Predominant vegetation is ferns and conifers. Scale trees decline. Ascendancy of reptiles and development of some modern insects.

GEOLOGIC TIME SCALE (continued)

Era	Period	Epoch	Estimated time span from present	Life forms
Mesozoic (Age of Reptiles)	Triassic	Lower Middle Upper	230,000,000 years ago to 180,000,000 years ago	Dominant land vegetation is evergreens such as ginkgos, conifers, and palms. Evolution of dinosaurs and appearance of bony fishes and first mammals.
	Jurassic	Lower Middle Upper	180,000,000 years ago to 135,000,000 years ago	Climax of ammonites; reptilian diversification; beginning of birds and mammals. First lobsters and shrimp. Cycads dominate flora.
	Cretaceous	Lower Upper	135,000,000 years ago to 64,000,000 years ago	Ascendancy of flowering plants and deciduous woody plants such as fig, poplars, magnolia and then oak, walnut, and maple. First snakes and marsupial mammals. Climax of dinosaurs and last of ammonites.

Era	Period	Epoch	Time	Events
Cenozoic (Age of Mammals)	Tertiary	Paleocene	64,000,000 years ago to 58,000,000 years ago	Development of many modern plants, insects, birds, and mammals such as eagles, pelicans, and rodents.
		Eocene	58,000,000 years ago to 36,000,000 years ago	
		Oligocene	36,000,000 years ago to 25,000,000 years ago	
		Miocene	25,000,000 years ago to 13,000,000 years ago	First appearance of grasses encourages growth and development of grazing animals. Mastodon evolves. Most modern plants and animals in place.
		Pliocene	13,000,000 years ago to 3,000,000 years ago	
	Quaternary	Pleistocene	3,000,000 years ago to 11,000 years ago	Rise of man.
		Recent	11,000 years ago to present	Development of civilization.

GLOSSARY

(Selected Mesozoic Fauna)

allosaur   This is a member of the genus *Allosaurus*. The *Allosaurus* was a 5 ton, 36 foot long bipedal carnosaur with a large, boxlike head and bladelike teeth, which lived in the upper Jurassic.

Alamosaurus   A genus of sauropod, its members lived in the upper Cretaceous.

Anatosaurus   A genus of hadosaurian (or duck-billed) ornithopod, anatosaurs lived in the upper Cretaceous and were approximately 33 feet long.

ankylosaur   This is a popular name for a member of the genus *Euoplocephalus*—a genus previously known as *Ankylosaurus*. An ankylosaur was a low, squat, heavily armored ornithischian dinosaur which lived in the upper Cretaceous. The top of its back was a checkerboard of bony plates and both sides were flanked, from neck to near the tail end, with a row of backward pointing spikes. The tail tip was a large, bony, clublike lump.

Ankylosauria   One of the four suborders of ornithischian dinosaurs, ankylosaurians were low-slung, heavily armored quadrupeds which developed during the upper Jurassic, reaching their climax in the Cretaceous.

Apatosaurus   A genus of giant sauropod dinosaur (about 80 feet long and 30 tons in weight), its members lived in the Jurassic. Once known as *Brontosaurus,* the name of the genus was changed because of historical precedence.

Archaeopteryx   A genus of crow-sized coelurosaur dinosaur, its members had feathers, a long reptilian tail, clawed fingers projecting from wings, and narrow beak-shaped jaws with teeth. *Archaeopteryx* is considered to be the earliest bird, but lacked strong flight muscles and probably was only able to glide down from heights.

Brachiosaurus   This genus of giant sauropod dinosaur (up to 99 feet long and 100 tons in weight) lived in the Jurassic and Cretaceous and was the largest land animal ever. A large nasal bulge on top of the brachiosaur's head and front legs longer than back distinguished it from other sauropods.

brontosaur   Specifically, this is a member of the genus *Brontosaurus*. The *Brontosaurus*, or "Thunder Lizard," is the most famous of the sauropod dinosaurs, and is now known as *Apatosaurus*. Generally, "brontosaur" has come to be used as a popular term of reference substituted for the suborder "Sauropoda."

Carnosauria   One of the two infraorders of theropod dinosaurs, the carnosaurs were large, mostly bipedal, carnivores which developed in the upper Triassic and flourished until the end of the Cretaceous. Most had large heads and daggerlike teeth.

Ceratopsia   Last of the four suborders of ornithischian dinosaurs to develop, these horned and frilled herbivores were mostly large and quadrupedal. After appearing about halfway through the Cretaceous, ceratopsians flourished until the end of that period.

coelacanth   It is a member of the lobe-fin fish which were the commonest of Devonian fishes. Various types ranged in size from 6 inches to 5 feet. Supposedly extinct since the end of the Cretaceous, coelacanths were rediscovered in 1938 and are alive today.

Coelurosauria   One of the two infraorders of theropod dinosaurs, the coelurosaurs were small, lightly built, speedy bipedal carnivores and egg stealers. Developing in the upper Triassic, they expanded, diversified, and flourished until the end of the Cretaceous. One line led to exceptionally intelligent dinosaurs while another eventually led to modern birds.

Corythosaurus   A genus of hadosaurian (or duck-billed) ornithopod, its members lived in the upper Cretaceous and were approximately 30 feet long. Corythosaurs were noted for their front-to-back half-circle head crest.

Crocodilia   Not dinosaurs, but an order of the Diapsida subclass of reptiles, crocodilians developed in the Triassic and continue today with the modern crocodile. Perhaps the most notable member was the 50 foot long *Phobosuchus,* or "horror crocodile," which lived in the upper Cretaceous and possessed a fanged skull larger than the *Tyrannosaurus.*

Deinonychus   The "terrible claw" is a newly discovered genus (1964) of dromaesaurid coelurosaur dinosaur, which developed in the lower Cretaceous. *Deinonychus* is the most formidable carnivore yet found. Standing 3 to 6 feet tall, with a length of about 8 to 10 feet, it would speed to its prey on long, muscular hind legs, then strike vicious blows with each foot's huge sickle-shaped claw.

Diapsida   This is a subclass of reptiles in which the members have two pairs of holes in the head, one on the top and one at the sides. It includes lizards, snakes, crocodiles, pterosaurs, birds, and dinosaurs.

Diplodocus   A genus of giant sauropod dinosaur (about 90 feet long), its members developed during the middle Jurassic and died out in the lower Cretaceous. Though lighter than most sauropods (10 tons), it had an exceptionally long neck (26 feet) and tail (46 feet).

Dromaeosauridae   A family of coelurosaur dinosaurs just recently discovered, its members were bipedal carnivores. Dromaeosaurids developed in Cretaceous times, had large brains, and were the most intelligent dinosaurs yet found.

Dromaeosaurus   A genus of coelurosaur dinosaur discovered in 1914, but not fully described until 1969, its members were descendents of *Deinonychus* and lived in the upper Cretaceous. Somewhat reminiscent of an emu, it is noted for huge eyes and a large cranial cavity (which is presumed to have contained a large brain).

Euryapsida   This is a subclass of reptiles in which the members have one pair of holes on top of the head like the parapsids, but with a different arrangement of skull bones bounding the holes. It includes nothosaurs, plesiosaurus, and placodonts.

Hadrosauridae   A very successful family of bipedal ornithopod dinosaurs, hadrosaurs developed in the lower Cretaceous and were the most populous type of dinosaur by the end of that period. Noted for their ducklike bills, they possessed teeth and a chewing action suitable for the tough new flowering plants; good eyesight, sense of smell, and hearing; large, thick rear legs; and a thick, long, stiff tail used for balance when running. Hadrosaurs averaged around 30 feet in length and 3 tons in weight.

Hypselosaurus   A genus of sauropod, it lived in the Cretaceous.

Ichthyosauria   Not dinosaurs, this order of aquatic creatures, which grew up to 33 feet long, is a part of the Parapsida subclass of reptiles. Resembling dolphins, ichthyosaurs were quick, powerful swimmers, bore their young live, and spanned the Mesozoic from the upper Triassic to the upper Cretaceous.

Iguanodon   A genus of lower Cretaceous ornithopod, its members were primarily bipedal, stood over 16 feet tall, were about 30 feet long, and weighed around 5 tons.

Nothosauria   Not dinosaurs, this suborder of aquatic creatures is a part of the Euryapsida subclass of reptiles. Nothosaurs ranged in length from 1½ to 20 feet and could also travel on land. They had webbed feet, befinned tails flattened sideways for swimming, and were widespread during the Triassic.

Ornithischia   One of the two dinosaur orders, its members were distinguished by a "bird-hipped" pelvic girdle and included ornithopods, stegosaurs, ankylosaurs, and ceratopsians. Ornithischians spanned the entire Mesozoic, were herbivorous, and mostly quadrupedal.

Ornithopodia   One of the four suborders of ornithischian dinosaurs, the ornithopods reached their climax in Cretaceous times. One line was quadrupedal, while the other, which included the highly successful hadosaurs, was largely bipedal.

Parapsida   This is a subclass of reptiles in which the members have one pair of holes on top of the head like the euryapsidas but with a different arrangement of bones bounding the holes. It includes ichthyosaurs.

Placodontia   Not dinosaurs, this order of marine creatures, which averaged about 5 feet in length, is part of the Euryapsida subclass of reptiles. Placodonts were stoutbodied, with blunt heads, strong teeth, short necks, four flippers, and bodies tapering to a pointed tail of short to moderate length. Placodonts lived in the Triassic, functioning much like modern walruses, by feeding on mollusks.

Like pseudo-turtles, some of the later models developed heavy, bony carapaces.

Plesiosauria   Not dinosaurs, this suborder of marine creatures, which reached over 40 feet in length, is part of the Euryapsida subclass of reptiles. Both long-necked and short-necked (plesio) families propelled themselves with four paddle-shaped limbs. The long-necked variety was more successful, eventually becoming the dominant reptile of the sea during the upper Cretaceous.

Prototheria   This is a Mammalia subclass of primitive, oviparous animals. Only the platypus and echidnas survive today.

Pteranodon   A genus of Cretaceous pterosaur, its members had pickaxe-shaped heads, wingspreads of over 24 feet, and bodies no longer than a turkey. These pterodactyls glided over the ocean looking for fish and were probably covered with white fur to reduce heat absorption.

pterodactyl   Specifically, this is a member of the genus *Pterodactylus*. Generally, "pterodactyl" is sometimes popularly used to refer to a member of the order Pterosauria. However, "pterosaur" is the better term since pterodactyls (or, more correctly, pterodactyloids) do not include long-tailed pterosaurs (rhamphorhynchoids).

Pterodactylus   A genus of small, upper Jurassic pterosaur, pterodactyls are the apparent originator of the short-tailed suborder of pterosaurs (pterodactyloids).

Pterosauria   Not dinosaurs, but an order of diapsid reptiles, pterosaurs developed in the upper Triassic and lasted until the end of the Cretaceous. Of the two suborders, the Rhamphorhynchoidea (or long-tailed) was older and more primitive than the Pterodactyloidea (or short-tailed).

Quetzalcoatlus   This is a recently discovered (1975) genus of giant short-tailed pterosaur with a 50 foot wingspan and a shape somewhat resembling an inverted Manta Ray. During the Cretaceous, its members are believed to have flown and fed on carrion in much the same way as do modern vultures.

Rhamphorhynchus   A genus of upper Jurassic pterosaur of long-tailed variety, its members were covered with fur to reduce heat absorption, had huge eye sockets, and a leaf-shaped tail-tip which acted as rudder.

Saurischia   One of the two dinosaur orders, saurischians were distinguished by a "lizard-hipped" pelvic girdle, and included sauropods and theropods.

Sauropoda   One of the two suborders of saurischian dinosaurs, its members—popularly called brontosaurs—were quadrupedal herbivores with long necks and long tails. Having lizard-like (read elephantlike) feet as opposed to theropods' beastlike (read birdlike) feet, sauropods were the largest, longest, and heaviest reptiles which ever lived. Sauropods were previously believed to live in shallow water swamps, but it is now thought they may have grazed in plains and forests much like giraffes. Their climax was in the Jurassic, but some varieties survived until the end of the Cretaceous.

Sauropterygia   One of the two orders of the Euryapsida subclass of reptiles, its two suborders are Nothosauria and Plesiosauria.

Scolosaurus   A genus of the ankylosaurian dinosaurs, scolosaurs were low-slung, heavily armored, quadrupedal herbivores (about 16 feet long and 3½ tons in weight) which lived in the western region of the North American land mass during the upper Cretaceous. Distinguishing features included conical spikes protruding from horizontal bands of armor that ran from neck to the large, two-spiked, tail-end lump.

Stegosauria   One of the four suborders of ornithischian dinosaurs, the stegosaurs were armored, herbivorous, quadrupedal ornithischian dinosaurs. They lived during the Jurassic, had spikes on their bodies and enormous bony plates set along the length of their backs. Besides armor, these vertical plates also created the illusion of greater size and probably released excess body heat.

Stegosaurus   A genus of the stegosaurian dinosaurs which lived in the Jurassic, stegosaurs were the largest of the stegosaurian dinosaurs (about 30 feet long and 2 tons in weight). The *Stegosaurus* had a small head with a walnut-sized brain, two rows of large, bony, spearmint leaf-shaped plates running along its backbone, and two pairs of spikes protruding horizontally from its tail.

Stenonychosaurus   A newly discovered genus (1968) of dromaesaurid theropod dinosaur, stenonychosaurs developed in the upper Cretaceous. Descendants of *Deinon-*

ychus, they were 5 or 6 feet long with sizable heads, very large eyes, binocular vision, and manipulative fingers.

Struthiomimus   A genus of coelurosaur dinosaur, its members averaged a 7 foot height and 12 foot length and are estimated to have run about 50 mph. *Struthiomimus* resembled an ostrich except for its long tail, long arms, and three fingered hands. It lived in the upper Cretaceous, and though a theropod, was at least omnivorous if not herbivorous.

Synopsida   This is a subclass of reptiles in which the members have one pair of holes on the sides of the skull. It includes pelycosaurs and the mammal-like therapsids.

tarsier   This name applies to any of the primates of the genus *Tarsius.* Arboreal animals, they are slightly smaller than rats, with brownish-gray fur, round faces, gogglelike eyes, big rounded ears, and long froglike hind legs for leaping.

Theriodontia   Not dinosaurs, but a therapsid suborder of synapsid reptiles, its members lived in the Permian and Triassic. Theriodonts included carnivores like *Cynognathus* —the size of a small bear, with doglike teeth—and were supplanted by dinosaurs at the beginning of the Jurassic. However, some small therapsids did evolve into, and survive as, mammals.

Theropoda   One of the two suborders of saurischian dinosaurs, its members had beastlike (read birdlike) feet instead of the lizardlike (read elephantlike) feet of their sauropod cousins. Theropods were almost all bipedal carnivores and were divided into two infraorders: Carnosauria and Coelurosauria.

Triceratops   This was the last and largest genus of ceratopsian dinosaur. Somewhat resembling a huge rhinoceros, *Triceratops* was 24 feet long, quadrupedal, and about 8 tons in weight. It had a large frill, a large horn over each eye, a horn on the nose, and a parrotlike beak. It was a herd dweller and one of the upper Cretaceous' most successful dinosaurs.

Tritylodon   This is a genus of extinct vertebrates from the lower Mesozoic. Its members were once classed as primitive mammals, but are now usually categorized as reptiles intermediate in character between therapsids and the most primitive mammals.

Tyrannosaurus   A genus of bipedal theropod dinosaur, it
includes just one species: *Tyrannosaurus rex*. *Tyrannosaurus* appears to have been the world's largest carnosaur
dinosaur (about 50 feet long and 20 feet high), had a huge
head with daggerlike teeth, and lived in the upper Cretaceous.

SELECTED MESOZOIC REPTILES
AND HOW THEY ARE CLASSIFIED

Diapsida
    Crocodilia
        Geosaurus
        Phobosuchus
        Teleosaurus
    Dinosauria
        Ornithischia
            Ankylosauria
                Euoplocephalus (Ankylosaurus)
                Scolosaurus
                Struthiosaurus
            Ceratopsia
                Monoclonius
                Protoceratops
                Triceratops
            Ornithopodia
                Anatosaurus
                Camptosaurus
                Corythosaurus
                Hypsilophodon
                Iguanodon
            Stegosauria
                Scelidosaurus
                Stegosaurus
        Saurischia
            Sauropoda
                Alamosaurus

        Apatosaurus (Brontosaurus)
        Brachiosaurus
        Cetiosaurus
        Diplodocus
        Hyselosaurus
        Melanorosaurus
        Titanosaurus
     Theropoda
       Carnosauria
         Allosaurus
         Gorgosaurus
         Megalosaurus
         Spinosaurus
         Tyrannosaurus
       Coelurosauria
         Archaeopteryx
         Coelophysis
         Deinonychus
         Dromaeosaurus
         Ornitholestes
         Ornithomimus
         Stenonychosaurus
         Struthiomimus
Pterosauria
   Pterodactyloidea
     Pteranodon
     Pterodactylus
     Quetzalcoatlus
   Rhamphorhynchoidea
     Rhamphorhynchus
Euryapsida
  Placodontia
    Henodus
    Placochelys
    Placodus
  Sauropterygia
    Nothosauria
      Lariosaurus
      Nothosaurus
    Plesiosauria
      Hychotherosaurus

    Liopleurodon
    Plesiosaurus
Parapsida
 Ichthyosauria
   Ichthyosaurus
   Mixosaurus
Synapsida
 Pelycosauria
   Dimetrodon
  Therapsida
   Theriodontia
    Cynognathus

FURTHER READING

NOVELS

Arthur Conan Doyle. *The Lost World*. N.Y.: Pyramid Books, 1958.

Geoffrey Household. *The Spanish Cave* (originally entitled *The Terror of the Villadonga*). N.Y.: Berkley Publishing Corporation, 1966.

SHORT STORIES

H. Bedford-Jones. "Wrath of the Thunder-Bird," in *Blue Book*. January, 1939.

Ray Bradbury. "The Foghorn," in *R is For Rocket*. N.Y.: Bantam Books, Inc., 1965.

Ray Bradbury. "A Sound of Thunder." N.Y.: Bantam Books, Inc., 1965.

Fredric Brown. "Paradox Lost," in *Paradox Lost, and 12 Other Great Science Fiction Stories*. N.Y.: Random House, 1973.

Leslie Charteris. "The Convenient Monster," in *The Fantastic Saint* (edited by Martin Harry Greenberg & Charles G. Waugh). N.Y.: Doubleday and Co., 1981.

L. Sprague de Camp: "A Gun for Dinosaur," in *Dawn of Time, Prehistory Through Science Fiction* (edited by Martin Harry Greenberg, Joseph Olander and Robert Silverberg). N.Y.: Elsevier/Nelson, 1979.

Thomas A. Easton. "The Chicago Plan to Save a Species," in *Chicago Magazine*. August, 1976.

P. Schuyler Miller. "The Sands of Time," in *Dawn of Time*,

Prehistory Through Science Fiction (edited by Martin Harry Greenberg, Joseph Olander and Robert Silverberg).

G. L. Knapp. "McKeever's Dinosaur," in *Blue Book*. August, 1943.

Robert Olsen. "Paleontology: An Experimental Science," in *Dawn of Time, Prehistory Through Science Fiction* (edited by Martin Harry Greenberg, Joseph Olander and Robert Silverberg).

Edwin L. Sabin. "The Devil of Picuris," in *Horrors Unknown* (edited by Sam Moskowitz). N.Y.: Walker and Company, 1971.

Clifford Simak. "Small Deer," in *Galaxy*. October, 1965.